BELOW THE CLOCK

'THE DETECTIVE STORY CLUB is a clearing house for the best detective and mystery stories chosen for you by a select committee of experts. Only the most ingenious crime stories will be published under the THE DETECTIVE STORY CLUB imprint. A special distinguishing stamp appears on the wrapper and title page of every THE DETECTIVE STORY CLUB book—the Man with the Gun. Always look for the Man with the Gun when buying a Crime book.'

Wm. Collins Sons & Co. Ltd., 1929

Now the Man with the Gun is back in this series of COLLINS CRIME CLUB reprints, and with him the chance to experience the classic books that influenced the Golden Age of crime fiction.

THE DETECTIVE STORY CLUB

E. C. BENTLEY • TRENT'S LAST CASE
E. C. BENTLEY • TRENT INTERVENES
E. C. BENTLEY & H. WARNER ALLEN • TRENT'S OWN CASE
ANTHONY BERKELEY • THE WYCHFORD POISONING CASE
ANTHONY BERKELEY • THE SILK STOCKING MURDERS
LYNN BROCK • NIGHTMARE
BERNARD CAPES • THE MYSTERY OF THE SKELETON KEY
AGATHA CHRISTIE • THE MURDER OF ROGER ACKROYD
AGATHA CHRISTIE • THE BIG FOUR
WILKIE COLLINS • THE MOONSTONE
HUGH CONWAY • CALLED BACK
HUGH CONWAY • DARK DAYS
EDMUND CRISPIN • THE CASE OF THE GILDED FLY
FREEMAN WILLS CROFTS • THE CASK
FREEMAN WILLS CROFTS • THE PONSON CASE
FREEMAN WILLS CROFTS • THE PIT-PROP SYNDICATE
FREEMAN WILLS CROFTS • THE GROOTE PARK MURDER
MAURICE DRAKE • THE MYSTERY OF THE MUD FLATS
FRANCIS DURBRIDGE • BEWARE OF JOHNNY WASHINGTON
J. JEFFERSON FARJEON • THE HOUSE OPPOSITE
RUDOLPH FISHER • THE CONJURE-MAN DIES
FRANK FROËST • THE GRELL MYSTERY
FRANK FROËST & GEORGE DILNOT • THE CRIME CLUB
FRANK FROËST & GEORGE DILNOT • THE ROGUES' SYNDICATE
ÉMILE GABORIAU • THE BLACKMAILERS
ANNA K. GREEN • THE LEAVENWORTH CASE
DONALD HENDERSON • MR BOWLING BUYS A NEWSPAPER
VERNON LODER • THE MYSTERY AT STOWE
PHILIP MACDONALD • THE RASP
PHILIP MACDONALD • THE NOOSE
PHILIP MACDONALD • THE RYNOX MYSTERY
PHILIP MACDONALD • MURDER GONE MAD
PHILIP MACDONALD • THE MAZE
NGAIO MARSH • THE NURSING HOME MURDER
G. ROY McRAE • THE PASSING OF MR QUINN
R. A. V. MORRIS • THE LYTTLETON CASE
ARTHUR B. REEVE • THE ADVENTURESS
JOHN RHODE • THE PADDINGTON MYSTERY
FRANK RICHARDSON • THE MAYFAIR MYSTERY
R. L. STEVENSON • DR JEKYLL AND MR HYDE
EDGAR WALLACE • THE TERROR
ISRAEL ZANGWILL • THE PERFECT CRIME

FURTHER TITLES IN PREPARATION

BELOW THE CLOCK

A STORY OF CRIME

BY

J. V. TURNER

WITH AN INTRODUCTION BY

DAVID BRAWN

COLLINS
CRIME
CLUB

COLLINS CRIME CLUB
An imprint of HarperCollins*Publishers*
1 London Bridge Street
London SE1 9GF
www.harpercollins.co.uk

This Detective Story Club edition 2018

First published in Great Britain for The Crime Club
by W. Collins Sons & Co. Ltd 1936

A catalogue record for this book is available from the British Library

ISBN 978-0-00-828026-0

Typeset in Bulmer MT Std by
Palimpsest Book Production Ltd, Falkirk, Stirlingshire
Printed and bound in Great Britain
by CPI Group (UK) Ltd, Croydon CR0 4YY

MIX
Paper from
responsible sources
FSC® C007454

This book is produced from independently certified FSC™ paper
to ensure responsible forest management.

For more information visit: www.harpercollins.co.uk/green

INTRODUCTION

THE Elizabeth Tower is purportedly the most photographed building in the UK, and yet most people would not be able to name it. But as the clock tower that dominates the Palace of Westminster and houses the great bell of Big Ben, it is an instantly recognisable global landmark. Completed in 1859 as part of a 30-year rebuild of the Houses of Parliament after the original palace complex was all but destroyed by fire in 1834, the tower and its clock face quickly became the defining symbol both of the mother of parliaments and of London itself, and the hourly chimes of its 14-tonne bell indelibly associated over 157 years with national stability and resilience. When the bell was silenced on 21 August 2017 for an unprecedented four-year programme of essential maintenance, for some it was as though a death had occurred at the heart of Westminster.

In the annals of crime fiction, of course, deaths at Westminster are all too common. But this was not always the case. When Collins' Crime Club published J. V. Turner's *Below the Clock* in May 1936, the idea of a minister being killed in the chamber was rather sensational, not to say disrespectful of the high office. Ngaio Marsh had dispatched the Home Secretary in *The Nursing Home Murder* in 1935, although even she hadn't the audacity to have him drop dead at the Despatch Box. But then Marsh's stories were not as audacious as those of J. V. Turner.

John Victor Turner, known to family and friends as Jack, was the youngest of three boys in a family of six children. His father Alfred was saddle-maker, who married Agnes Hume in Chorlton-cum-Hardy, Manchester, in 1890. Jack was too young to serve in the First World War, but his eldest brother Alfred (after his father) joined up at only 16 and was profoundly affected by shell-shock for the rest of his life. The middle brother, Joseph, moved to London and joined the police, and eventually attained a senior rank at Scotland Yard. Jack himself attended Warwick School and worked on a local newspaper before moving to Fleet Street, where he worked for the Press Association, *Daily Mail, Financial Times* and as a crime reporter on the *Daily Herald*. Turner was seemingly married twice, his first wife having tragically drowned.

At first sight, J. V. Turner was not a prolific author, having written seven detective novels under his own name, all of them featuring the solicitor-detective Amos Petrie, published between 1932 and 1936. However, under the pseudonyms Nicholas Brady and more famously David Hume, Turner wrote almost 50 crime novels in a relatively short writing career. He wrote impressively quickly, publishing up to five books a year, with his obituary in the *New York Times* claiming, 'while still in his early thirties [he] was often called the second Edgar Wallace. At one period he wrote a novel a fortnight.'

Some of David Hume's books bore an author photo and short biography on the back of the dust jacket. Under the heading 'If David Hume can't thrill you no one can', it revealed a little about the author:

> 'David Hume has an inside knowledge of the criminal world such as few crime authors can ever hope to command, for he has had first-hand experience of it for over fourteen years. During his nine years as a crime reporter he spent most of his days at Scotland Yard, waiting for stories to "break". In this way he gained an extraordinarily wide and intimate knowledge of criminals and the methods employed in tracking them down. And his personality is such that he won his way completely into the confidence of the criminals themselves, who revealed to him the precise methods they employ to enter a house or to open a safe. Indeed, no one knows more about the technique of crime or criminal detection: and

> (we should add) David Hume, far from sitting back on his author's chair, is taking care to maintain the contacts from which comes the convincing realism that is the greatest feature of his books!'

Hume's supercharged thrillers, dripping with underworld slang, typically dealt with gangs in Soho and Limehouse and featured Britain's first home-grown 'hardboiled' detective. The Private Eye was an established fixture of the American detective novel by 1932, but when Mick Cardby appeared in the first David Hume novel *Bullets Bite Deep*, he must have been something of a revelation for readers. Hume's version of London was a city of gun-toting gangsters, and the fist-swinging Cardby—a detective who tended to rely on brawn rather than brains—offered a refreshingly exciting alternative to the cerebral whodunits that had grown so incredibly popular over the previous decade. Although they would continue to dominate the genre in the years leading up to the Second World War (and arguably beyond), tastes were beginning to change, and as authors and publishers became more innovative, so came diversity within the genre.

Twenty-seven of Hume's books featured Mick Cardby, two of which were adapted into films: *Crime Unlimited* (1935, remade four years later as *Too Dangerous to Live*) and *They Called Him Death* (1941, entitled *The Patient Vanishes*). Hume also wrote a trilogy of novels about crime reporter Tony Carter, and under his Nicholas Brady pseudonym he created the eccentric amateur sleuth, Reverend Ebenezer Buckle. But it was using his own name that Turner wrote more traditional detective novels of the kind that are now characterised as 'Golden Age', although they had a darker vein running through them than many of their cosier contemporaries. The first, *Death Must Have Laughed* (1932, published in the US as *First Round Murder*), was a classic impossible crime story, and featured an amateur detective, the solicitor Amos Petrie, and his long-suffering Scotland Yard counterpart, Inspector Ripple: *Below the Clock* was their last, and arguably most accomplished, case, and outsold the others—maybe in part thanks to its striking but understated jacket featuring a painting of that famous Westminster clock tower.

As well as writing the hardboiled books (as David Hume) for Collins from 1933 right up to his death in 1945—they were still being published a year after he died—he also participated in the collaborative novel *Double Death* (1939). Often mistaken for a Detection Club book, on account of its principal authors being Dorothy L. Sayers and Freeman Wills Crofts, in fact it was not, and none of the other collaborators were members of that august body. At Turner's suggestion, the writers each included notes in the book about the others' contributions, which although interesting to the fan did rather highlight deficiencies in the novel, which was unfortunate at a time when the 'round-robin' format had begun to drop out of fashion. He also co-wrote the screenplay for the 1941 adaptation of Peter Cheyney's Lemmy Caution novel, *This Man Is Dangerous*.

Sadly, Turner's reign as one of the most reliable crime writers in the UK came to a sudden end. On Saturday, 6 February 1945, he died from tuberculosis at Haywards Heath in West Sussex, aged only 39. His early death and the transitory nature of authors' popularity have sadly resulted in Turner, Brady and even Hume becoming almost entirely forgotten about, and the books very hard to track down. It is to be hoped that the republication of *Below the Clock* will be the first step towards this remarkable and in many ways trailblazing talent being rediscovered by mystery and crime fans.

David Brawn
August 2017

TO MY FRIEND
JOHN MEIKLE

CONTENTS

CHAPTER I

IN THE SPOTLIGHT

THE House of Commons has its moments.

Ascot bends a fashionable knee to hail Gold Cup Day with an elegant genuflection, Henley hesitates between pride and sophistication to welcome the Regatta, Epsom bustles with democratic fervour as Derby day approaches, Cowes bows with dignified grace as curving yachts carve another niche in her temple of fame, Aintree wakens and waves to saints and sinners on Grand National day, and Wimbledon wallows for a week in a racket of rackets.

The House of Commons has its Budget Day . . .

The afternoon sun broke into a smile after an April shower, and beamed through the leaded glass in the western wall, throwing lustre on the dark-panelled woodwork, turning brass into a blaze of gold, brightening the faces of Members of Parliament, revealing dancing specks of dust so that they scintillated with the brilliance of diamonds. One widely elliptical ray wandered from the stream of the beams, and bathed the spot where Edgar Reardon, Chancellor of the Exchequer, was to stand. The ray glistened on the brassbound despatch box at the corner of the table and shimmered beyond to waste its beauty on the floor. Nature, in a generous moment, had provided a theatrical spectacle.

The flood of golden light brought no solace to the men who stared at it from above. For the leaders of finance and industry shuffled their feet on the floor of the gallery, and waited for the worst while hoping for the best. They were not thinking of happy omens, portents, and auguries as they eyed the sun beaming on the despatch box. With the passage of years their hopes had faded until budgets meant burdens. Ladies in the grille abandoned their furtive whispers to advance with muffled tread and peer over the brass-work in front of them, looking first of all for relatives, and later, for celebrities.

Members blinked as the sun winked in their eyes. The lambent glow was even noticed by the Cabinet Ministers, who sat out of the beams, arrayed on the Treasury Bench, endeavouring to look as wise as Pythian oracles. The wandering radiance actually distracted attention from Mr Speaker, resplendent in his robes, although an errant ray stabbed a glimmer on the silver buckle of the shoe which he elevated so carefully in the general direction of Heaven. The sun had fascinated the spectators so effectively that few spared a thought for the lesser glories of the Sergeant-at-Arms, although he wore archaic dress, and exercised his privilege of being the only person in the House to bear a sword.

In the minds of the onlookers the sunbeams had one competitor. They were thinking of the man for whom the vacant place on the Treasury Bench had been reserved—and of his deficit!

A stranger casting a casual glance round the House might well have imagined the Members as wholesale breakers of minor laws. For each one apparently held a police summons in his hand. But they were not summonses—only blue papers giving details of how the deficit was made up, but not a single hint of how it was to be met. The filling of the gap between revenue and expenditure was reserved for a white paper, perhaps so coloured to signify the cleansing power of gold, maybe so blanched to prepare the nervous for the shock, but never issued until industry trembles and the City is at rest.

Joe Manning, the Opposition leader, flung down his blue paper as though the sheet were wasp-ridden and turned to Fred Otwood—a small, beetle-browed man who had been Chancellor in the previous Government, and hoped to repeat the performance in the next.

'Fred,' said Manning aggressively, 'if Reardon runs his household as he does national finance the bailiffs would have called on him long ago. As a Chancellor of the Exchequer he'd make a good confidence man.'

'I said that last year,' remarked Otwood wearily, 'and the tale's getting a bit worn at the corners. No sense in attacking Reardon whatever he says. After all, Joe, somebody has always to pay.'

Manning pulled his whiskers into a new shape and looked at his lieutenant somewhat critically. There were times when Otwood seemed to lack all the requisites for instructing and moulding public opinion. The former Prime Minister glanced away from the sunlight and looked along the line of faces on the Treasury Bench.

'I can't understand it,' he remarked. 'They're all smiling as if they were disposing of a surplus. Anyone would think that Willie Ingram had arrived to give a present to the nation.'

Ingram, the Prime Minister, had a flabby face, a fleshy nose, an outsize in eyebrows, and a polished skull. The eyes redeemed other features. They were brightly keen and puckishly humorous.

'He must think he's backing a winner,' said Otwood.

Joe Manning continued to stare at them until he suddenly gripped Otwood's arm and whispered another pointer for his forthcoming speech:

'Callous indifference, Fred. That's the note to strike.'

'Perhaps it's still a good line, Joe, but doesn't it begin to sound a bit like a cracked gramophone record?'

The conversation was halted by a new arrival. Tranter, a doctor from the north, made his way with difficulty to a place behind them, and sat perched upon the knees of two unwilling supporters. Tranter had one fixed panacea for political ailments, but each time he produced it with the earnestness of an original performer.

'Couldn't we make a stand for inflation?' he whispered. Currency inflation was Tranter's method by which money could be raised without anyone paying for it. As he received no reply he moved away, satisfied that he had struck another blow for national welfare. Fortunately, he did not hear Otwood's comment:

'If that man, Joe, had studied medicine as he's studied economics he wouldn't know enough to bandage a cut finger.'

Manning tugged more viciously at his moustache and peered anxiously at the clock. During all this time the ritual of question time was proceeding, carried on by a scratch crew under the guidance of Mr Speaker. People grew restless, whispers increased, feet shuffled.

There was a crowd at the Bar. Eric Watson, Parliamentary Private Secretary to Mr Chancellor Reardon, sat with his face bathed in the sunlight. He ought not to have been there. On such a day there must have been many other things for him to do. But the occasion was great, and Watson took his share of the limelight, basking with the self-importance of a cock pheasant flaunting before a hen at mating time.

Watson had made a name for himself by a couple of striking speeches. Now he was consolidating his position, pushing steadily towards minor office in the recognised way—by bottle-washing for someone who had already arrived. He was tall and too handsome. The fine features suggested—to those who were unkind—that strength might have been sacrificed in the process of modelling. He looked round the House, and spoke with unnecessary emphasis:

'Wait until Edgar comes. He'll tickle them up more than a bit.'

A Member sitting behind him chuckled softly. It was Dick Curtis, yet another who had joined the long procession and added politics to a legal profession. Curtis imagined that the ranks were full in the present Government. Perhaps that explained why he belonged to the Opposition.

'He may find that he's tickling a pike instead of a trout,' he said. 'Deficits are not like air bubbles. They won't be burst and they refuse to blow away.'

Watson smiled tolerantly. He had faced Curtis in many a wordy war in the Law Courts, knew his gift for banter, his flair for argument. Curtis had a full, round voice, and a tonal range that embraced most varieties of expression. Some air of prosperity was conveyed by the figure which indicated the commencement of a senatorial roundness. His next words showed that his banter covered a judicial brain:

'Reardon's got one great thing in his favour, Watson. The City isn't frightened of him. I know the Account that's closed resembled business in a deserted village, but there was some brisk buying on the Stock Exchange before that. From your pestilential point of view that's not a bad sign.'

'Reardon is pleased about that,' whispered Watson. 'I know he wants to carry the City with him.' He spoke as though he had rendered more than a little assistance to his chief in the bearing of the burden.

'He doesn't seem in any hurry to arrive,' said Curtis. 'Wife with him?'

Watson nodded a wordless affirmative.

'I thought so,' remarked Curtis dryly. 'She'll be keeping him.'

The Parliamentary Private Secretary seemed disinclined to discuss women in general, or his chief's wife in particular. He changed the subject with surprising abruptness:

'Tranter is jumping your seat, Curtis. Turf him out of it.'

Curtis looked lazily. A silk hat threw the light back from his seat like a reflecting glass. His eyes gleamed with humorous brightness.

'Tranter will soon learn wisdom after I've—'

A rising cheer drowned the remainder of the sentence. Mr Chancellor Reardon had arrived in the House.

'I'll have to go,' whispered Watson, hurrying away to return a couple of minutes later with a long glass, filled with claret and seltzer water for Reardon's use during his speech. The Chancellor interrupted his talk with the Prime Minister to place the glass on the table. As he turned Curtis sat on the hat Tranter had left on his seat. There was a muffled sound of constrained mirth, followed by a peal of loud laughter. The noise increased when Curtis withdrew the hat from beneath him, appeared astonished to find it in his hand, and then held it aloft for all to see. He seemed to have some difficulty in recognising it as a hat.

Tranter snatched the ruin from Curtis' hand and ran with it up the steps of the gangway. The overhanging gallery offered shelter from derision. The Speaker had to delay his departure from the Chair to restore a sense of responsibility to the House. Even the removal of the mace was attended with the backwash of earlier laughter.

The speech for which the stage had been set, for which the nation waited with apprehension, started in an atmosphere of levity.

As Edgar Reardon stood in the beam of the sun's spotlight he was revealed to the observant and discerning as a mass of contradictions. The forehead, by its width, depth and sweep, showed intellect, almost patrician nobility; the eyes were vague, flickering and wavering with uncertain darts; his nose was finely chiselled; the mouth was set too low, and the sagging lips might well have fitted a voluptuary; his jaw had the firm, sweeping outline of a determined man; the pale, thin hands moved unceasingly, long fingers wriggling like worms.

The Chancellor had a gift of persuasive speech, and during the customary review of national finance, with which he prefaced the important business, he used the gift to advantage. He reached the end of his preamble at quarter to five. Operators had grown tired of waiting to see the new taxes flashed over the tape machines. But so far Reardon had given no hint of which milch cow he would grasp, of where his money was to come from.

Members leaned forward and there was a perceptible flutter among the financiers and industrialists in the gallery. Relaxed figures became taut.

Mr Chancellor Reardon prolonged the moment of suspense until it became irritating. The way in which the man wasted time was more than exasperating; it was astonishing. He fingered his notes as though he had never seen them before, damping a thin finger on his lips as he turned page after page. He drank from his glass of claret and seltzer, and flicked through his notes again. Perplexity and disquiet increased. Everyone knew that Reardon had worked on the notes for a full week, preparing and arranging them. It seemed that his delay was deliberately insulting, that the Chancellor was verifying unnecessarily that which he must have memorised.

A low murmur rose round the House. The Chancellor was carrying his taunt too far, was playing like a cat with a mouse, refusing to open Pandora's box until nerves were on edge.

The murmurs grew until individual voices were clear. The impatient were begging him to proceed, Opposition members sneeringly suggested that he had every cause to hesitate, and the members of the Cabinet urged him to hurry, admonished him against delay.

At last Edgar Reardon turned away from his notes and resumed his position in the spotlight, leaning his elbow on the Despatch Box. His gaze wandered round the House before settling upon the face of Joe Manning. The leader of the Opposition moved a little uneasily. The Chancellor stared at him as though the first announcement was to be a direct, personal challenge.

But Reardon hesitated unaccountably on the brink of that announcement. Joe Manning's face flushed and he started to rise to his feet. Even as he moved he spoke, his voice burdened with temper:

'Why this farce, Mr Chancellor? Are you so ashamed of the Budget you have to produce that your nerves have failed you?'

The questions provoked cheers from the Opposition members. Ingram, the Prime Minister, rose with a retort, hoping that the Chancellor would save the situation by speaking first.

Reardon frowned. Then his mouth twitched. His left hand groped until it found a corner of the Despatch Box.

For the first time Members began to suspect that something had gone wrong, that all was not well. Within a few seconds suspicion grew to a certainty. Reardon's eyes were strange. They ceased to wander, were fixed in a persistent stare. The pupils shone strangely, and the man's body stiffened until it seemed unnaturally tense.

His appearance changed with each fleeting second. He seemed numbed, almost paralysed. Even the golden light from the sun could not disguise the pallidity of his face. Reardon looked distressingly like a man who stands in a daze after concussion.

A colleague decided that it was time to act. He rose and caught the Chancellor by the tails of his coat from behind.

It seemed that the action was the only thing wanting to upset the Chancellor's balance. He fell headlong to the floor with a crash!

The moment that followed was one of those in which the whole being is concentrated in the eye. The hush that fell over the House was poignantly dramatic. It was an uncomfortable silence.

Tranter broke the spell by claiming right of passage, and dashing forward to the side of the Chancellor. Members who had sat with the muteness and stiffness of statues found their tongues. Ingram cast the secrets of the Budget all over the table in a frenzied search for water. Abruptly he seized the remains of the claret and seltzer, flung it into the face of the Chancellor. Reardon did not move.

Watson, the P.P.S., recovered sufficiently to run for water. As he hurried the Hon. John Ferguson, President of the Board of Trade, worked with trembling fingers and whipped off the man's collar. Sam Morgan, anxious to help, but uncertain of the procedure, stood wishing that he were a doctor instead of a Home Secretary.

In the general confusion everyone succeeded in getting in everyone else's way.

At last Tranter produced some sort of order out of the chaos. As he knelt down by Reardon's side he gave short, sharp directions to those around him. He was definitely a better doctor than he was an economist. The whispering ceased. There was a silence ladened pause. Then Tranter raised his voice again:

'Carry him outside at once.'

The prostrate form was seized by half a dozen willing, but clumsy, hands. Reardon's flaccid muscles writhed under the pull and thrust of the shuffling figures, the trunk bowing as they lifted him. The helpers bustled him into a position they fondly hoped was comfortable. It was a grotesque parody of a chairing. The Chancellor's head wobbled hideously, the body sank into itself telescopically, looking invertebrate and horribly unhuman, swaying and jolting to each step of the bearers as they staggered with their burden out of the House.

The Members watched the procession with bewilderment. This was something that the Chancellor had not budgeted for! They need have felt no sympathy for the sagging figure.

Edgar Reardon was dead!

CHAPTER II

BEHIND THE SPEAKER'S CHAIR

'I SUPPOSE it was apoplexy,' whispered the Prime Minister.

'I can't tell definitely what it was,' said Tranter. His brows were knitted, and there was a tone in his voice that the other misjudged. The group stood in the long hall behind the Speaker's Chair. The body of Edgar Reardon lay on a couch against the wall. The figure was dishevelled, the head was supported on the rolled-up jacket of the dead man, one of the legs had slipped off the side of the couch.

'If there's any room for doubt,' said Ingram after a pause, 'we'd better have him taken across to Westminster Hospital'

The doctor waved his hands impatiently and commented sourly:

'Oh, I know death when I see it. He was dead when we carried him out of the House. I'm not troubled about that. What's worrying me is that I can't figure out how it happened.'

'But, man, you saw it all yourself,' protested the Prime Minister.

Tranter's nerves were ruffled and his temper ebbed. He flung his hands helplessly into the air.

'Of course, I saw all that you saw,' he snapped. 'But I'm a doctor. This, Ingram, is a case for the Coroner of the Household. I don't want to say much more. An autopsy may show that death was due to natural causes. His heart may have given out; a hundred and one things may have happened. But I'm going to say this now: It didn't look to me like natural death at the time when it happened and I don't think it was even now. Just look at him. Does it look right to you?'

The Prime Minister gazed at the corpse and shuddered.

Reardon certainly did not look as though his heart had failed him. There was something odd about the expression of the face, an atmosphere of violence about the distorted limbs. For years Ingram had boasted that he was able to cope with any emergency. That faculty, and his solid sense, had won him the Premiership. But now he felt as though his brain were addled as he groped feebly after an idea.

The Cabinet Ministers who had assisted in carrying the Chancellor out of the House stood in a group like frozen images, staring with awed fascination at the corpse, and not trusting themselves to speak.

A little farther away the widow stood against the wall, her body twitching, her startled eyes, distended but dry, turning from Tranter to Ingram, and from Ingram to the remains of her husband. Her face was tragically pathetic. The skin was marble white and her make-up turned her pallor into a shrieking incongruity. The mascara on her eyelids and lashes showed midnight black against a surround of ghastly white; rouge, high on the cheek-bones, was almost silhouetted against the pale flesh, and the lips swerved in a carmine spread. Her green eyes were overshadowed by grief and mascara. Tufts of golden hair caught the rays of the sun as they waved in curls from the side of a black cloche hat.

Watson flitted in the background like a hovering moth, straying from Tranter's side to whisper condolences to the widow, moving again to stare at the corpse as though he still disbelieved that Reardon was dead. As seconds passed Ingram's brain began to function again.

'Tranter,' he said, 'this is absolutely absurd. I can't understand what on earth you're talking about. Edgar Reardon was a man without a care in the world. Why should a man with position, money, good health, and a devoted wife commit suicide? And you suggest that he didn't die a natural death! The idea is preposterous.'

'You've been thinking instead of listening,' remarked the

doctor caustically. 'I did not say that he committed suicide at the time of his death, and I don't say so now. I haven't mentioned suicide.'

'But . . . but . . .' Ingram paused, bewildered. He did not complete the sentence. Before he could collect his scattered thoughts a shrill laugh interrupted him, a peal that broke abruptly at the end of a high trill. If the roof of the House had fallen through it would not have created a greater sensation than the unexpected sound. On the overwrought nerves of the men in the hall the effect was hair-raising. They wheeled round together.

Mrs Reardon stood with her head tilted back, the face entirely mirthless, the mouth twisting with spasmodic jerks, the eyes wild and distended. Here, at least, was a case which Tranter could treat with confidence. Before he reached her side Mrs Reardon had ceased to laugh and her body was convulsed by sobs. Watson handed the doctor a glass of water. Tranter threw it into the face of the hysterical woman. As she quietened down he tried to speak to her persuasively. The effort was useless. She was quarrelsome and querulous. Watson stood by her side, gripping her trembling hands.

While Tranter was attempting to coerce the woman a newcomer arrived, walked across the hall towards them. He was tall, and a trifle too elegant, his clothes immaculately tailored, his features sharply defined. The grave, dark eyes were luminously brown. He stopped before the widow and bowed. Mrs Reardon moved Tranter to one side and stared at the newcomer ungraciously, almost venemously.

'How on earth do you come to be here, Mr Paling?' she snapped.

The man accepted her insulting tone without change of expression.

'Your husband,' he said, 'was kind enough to procure my admission to the public gallery, and I saw what happened. I have taken the liberty of ordering your car. It is now waiting. That is what I came to tell you.'

'Oh, did you?' Her voice was tart, her manner definitely rude.

'It was my desire to be of assistance,' said the man easily.

'Thanks.' Mrs Reardon sniffed, dabbed at her eyes with a frail lace handkerchief. In an instant her grief changed to anger again. 'I prefer to walk home. Give that message to my chauffeur.'

The men in the hall watched the fast-moving scene with amazement. It seemed odd that a man of such appearance, of such apparent self-confidence, should make no retort. He smiled gently, a chiding smile such as a mother might bestow upon a much loved but unruly child. Then he bowed slightly and retired from the hall.

Tranter led her to a chair, comforted her for a short time and then walked away, leaving Watson by her side. Farther away in the hall an informal meeting of the Cabinet was already in progress. The Prime Minister was urging an immediate adjournment of the House.

'I'm not going to make a Budget speech myself,' he said, 'and I'm not going to listen to one from anyone else. You couldn't expect the House to sit through a speech after what has happened.'

John Ferguson, the President of the Board of Trade, added more weighty reasons to support Ingram's argument:

'Adjourn the House. None of the taxes has been announced so you haven't got to do anything with the Budget resolutions tonight. There isn't any danger of premature disclosure. We're just where we were this morning.'

Ingram nodded. The question was settled. While the Ministers talked Curtis joined Mrs Reardon and Watson in the hall. Between them they persuaded the widow to leave the House, and both gripped her arms as she walked falteringly to the door. Curtis hailed his own chauffeur and they escorted Mrs Reardon to 11 Downing Street.

The Prime Minister said little to the occupants of the House. In two sentences he informed them that Mr Chancellor Reardon had met an unexpectedly sudden death and that the House, as a tribute to the memory of the deceased, would adjourn immediately.

Shortly afterwards the last loiterer departed. The House was empty, except for what had been the Right Honourable Edgar Reardon and the attendants in evening dress, their shirt fronts decorated by the large gilt House of Commons badge. They watched over his bier . . .

For two or three hours Watson and Curtis made inquiries here and there, striving ineffectively to straighten out the mystery for the sake of the distressed widow. They found more difficulties in their way than either had anticipated. A sudden death in the House of Commons, apart from the fact that death has occurred, is unlike that which takes place anywhere else. Rules and laws which have been embedded in the dust for centuries hamper inquiries, tradition erects formidable barriers. The two men were unable to report any progress when they arrived at 11 Downing Street.

They found Mrs Reardon alone in the drawing-room. A black velvet evening gown accentuated her pallor. She swayed to and fro as she spoke to them. Watson avoided her eyes as she looked at him. At other times he looked at nothing else. But once she became conscious of his glance, and searched for it in return, his eyes coasted round the room. It was an uncomfortable and depressing hide-and-seek. Curtis coughed informatively and stroked his hair. Watson blushed. The widow still seemed dazed. An awkward silence arose. The woman broke it:

'But you must have discovered something. What happened? Edgar had never been ill as far as I know. How did he—what killed him?'

'Had he been to see a doctor recently?' asked Curtis.

'No, not since I've known him. Edgar was always terribly fit.'

'Would you mind if I telephoned to his doctor, Mrs Reardon?'

'Of course I wouldn't. I'm only too grateful to you for helping me. It's Dr Cyril Clyde, of Welbeck Street.'

The widow and Watson sat miserably silent while Curtis was out of the room. Fleeting glances passed between them. The woman's fingers were jerking nervously. Again and again a shudder caused her body to move with the agitation of a marionette. They were both relieved when Curtis returned.

'Only makes things worse,' he announced. 'I told him what had happened, and he says that your husband, Mrs Reardon, was a singularly healthy man, that his heart was perfectly sound, that he was not known to suffer from any ailments, and that he was the last man in the world who would die with such suddenness from natural causes.'

'What does he suggest doing, Mr Curtis?'

'He talked about going to the House to take a look at the body. I told him that he could, of course, make an attempt, but I doubted whether he would gain admission. The matter is now in the hands of the Coroner of the Household, and he is not in the position of an ordinary coroner. But he can try.'

The woman was again silent for a time. Suddenly she sat stiffly erect and stared at Curtis.

'Do you mean,' she asked, 'that there is going to be an inquest?'

She was bordering on another lapse into hysteria. The two men glanced at each other. Watson left Curtis to soothe her.

'Just a pure formality,' he said casually. 'Nothing at all for you to trouble about.' From that point Curtis disregarded the curiously embarrassing glances of both Mrs Reardon and Watson as he maintained a thin stream of talk, striving to dim the tragedy in the widow's mind. His idle chatter covered a vast range, skimming here, dipping there, but the light, discursive style had its effect. Ten minutes afterwards neither could have remembered a thing he said. Yet he had fed the woman's mind with a flow of comforting suggestions, sliding away dexterously from any subject which might call for a reply. In that way he broke the silence gently rather than by expressing any views or feelings.

Curtis had just drawn to a conclusion when a knock sounded on the door. A manservant entered.

'Mr Paling would like to see you, madam,' he announced.

The widow closed her top teeth over her lip and tapped her foot irritably. Watson half rose, opened his mouth as though to speak and suddenly sat down again. Curtis looked from one to the other with a puzzled frown on his forehead.

'I do not wish to see the gentleman tonight,' said Mrs Reardon.

The manservant bowed and retired. But he soon returned. This time the widow glared at him angrily.

'Mr Paling says his call is reasonably important, madam, and he thinks it advisable that you should speak to him.'

'Show him in,' she snapped. She moved from her seat and stood at Watson's side. The two men rose. Paling strolled into the room with an easy style and a confident manner. He scarcely looked the part of a man who had been curtly rebuffed.

'What is it?' asked the widow. She might have been speaking to a recalcitrant dog. Paling continued to smile. Small veins were pulsing in Watson's forehead.

'I thought I would call to tell you, Mrs Reardon,' said Paling, 'that a detective—I think his name was Inspector Ripple—has just called on me to ask what I know about the . . . eh . . . the tragedy.'

The widow threw a look at Watson that was at once both startled and apprehensive. The creases on Curtis' brow deepened.

'A detective?' repeated the woman. 'What on earth does that mean?'

'They haven't lost much time in getting to work,' said Curtis.

'Getting to work?' queried Watson. 'What on earth have detectives got to do with Reardon's death?'

'I suppose they're making inquiries instead of the coroner's officer,' said Curtis soothingly. 'You've got to remember that this is not a routine matter. When things happen in the House of Commons the aftermath runs along lines outside the ordinary track.'

'One would have imagined that this man Ripple would have seen me before anyone,' said Watson.

'You've got your turn to come,' remarked Curtis.

'I thought it only right that I should call and give you that information, Mrs Reardon,' said Paling, 'and since I realise the extent of my unpopularity I'll leave. Good-evening.'

The widow did not glance at him as he walked out of the room. She appeared stunned. Watson was in no condition to quieten her nerves. He drummed on the top of a chair with his fingers and licked his dry lips. It seemed that a fresh emotional disturbance had arisen.

'I think,' said Mrs Reardon deliberately, 'that I hate that man Paling more than any person I have ever met. I loathe him.'

'Come now!' pleaded Curtis, 'I don't know him at all but his news wasn't in any way bad, and it was pretty decent of Paling to drift along and tell you. Perhaps he was only trying to be considerate.'

The woman pursed her lips. The men watched her. When she spoke the words poured in a flood, sounded so ladened with venom that hysteria might have explained them:

'That's the trouble. He's always considerate about things that don't matter. For nearly a year I've tried to stop him coming to this house, almost gone on my knees to Edgar to bar the man from here. I couldn't do it, couldn't do it. And I'm supposed to be the mistress of the place! I hate, loathe, and detest the man.'

'He seems a gentleman,' protested Curtis.

'Gentleman? Pshaw! I hate him.'

'Now I should have thought—' The sentence was not completed. A knock sounded and the manservant entered again.

'Chief Inspector Ripple wishes to speak to Mr Watson.'

Mrs Reardon slumped into a chair. Curtis wiped his hand across his forehead. Watson stalked out of the room as though marching to meet a firing squad. The door closed. The widow commenced to sob.

'I think you ought to take a sedative and retire, Mrs Reardon,' said Curtis. 'You are too overwrought, and each minute is making you worse. If you don't get to bed you'll be mentally and physically exhausted.'

'I couldn't sleep, positively couldn't. I just want to be quiet, to be still while I realise that I'll never see Edgar again.'

She pushed a box of cigarettes towards the man. The hint was obvious. He lit a smoke and sat on the arm of a chair, swinging his legs, and trying unsuccessfully to blow rings. Seven or eight minutes dragged by before the door opened again. Watson entered, a little less jaunty, a trifle more pale. She stared at him with wide eyes.

'Has he given you a real third degree interview?' asked Curtis.

'Asked me about two million questions. All of them uselessly mad.'

'Did he happen to worry you at all about the claret and seltzer?'

Watson started. The widow looked at Curtis with the sudden head twist of a frightened bird.

'He seemed to be more interested in that infernal drink than he was in anything. I told him what bit I knew about it.'

'Did he seem satisfied when you'd finished your statement?'

'Those men are never satisfied, Curtis. Why, he even started talking about murder. Either that man is mad or I am.'

Whichever was mad, Mrs Reardon was not conscious. She had fainted.

CHAPTER III

THE START OF THE HUNT

MINUTES passed before Mrs Reardon returned to consciousness. She shuddered, stared round the room with haunted eyes. Watson patted her hands consolingly. Curtis waited for the widow to speak, wondering what her first thoughts would be as full consciousness returned.

'Why didn't Paling die instead of my husband?' she inquired.

The men tried to hide their surprise. Watson slipped another cushion under her head and said nothing.

'Oh! The number of times I told Edgar, grovelled to him, begged him, not to have any more to do with the man. But it made no difference. He was always on the doorstep.'

'Perhaps Edgar was fond of him,' said Curtis.

'Fond of him? I'm sure he wasn't. He got no pleasure out of the man's company. It wasn't that Paling couldn't talk. He certainly could, and he'd been everywhere. But they never had anything to talk about. While they were together it always seemed to me that some sort of a struggle—a silent struggle—was going on. I couldn't understand it. I hated it.' She paused to recover her breath.

Then she rose from the chair. Every sign of her listlessness had gone. The effects of the faint had vanished. Her eyes shone with anger, her breast moved convulsively.

'What was he to your husband?' asked Curtis.

Mrs Reardon flung up her hands and turned to face him.

'What was he? Friend, secretary, factotum . . . anything and everything or nothing. He seemed to do mostly what he liked.'

'He had no fixed appointment with Edgar?'

'I couldn't tell you. I don't think Edgar would have tolerated the man unless he had been useful for something. I only hope that it was nothing disgraceful.'

Curtis elevated his eyebrows, looked keenly at the widow.

'Aren't you being somewhat harsh, Mrs Reardon? Poor Edgar positively basked in affection. Do you think he might have been disturbed by the idea that you and he were drifting a little apart?'

The woman began to tap one foot on the carpet.

'I have often wondered,' she replied softly, 'whether Edgar loved me or whether I loved him.'

Watson interrupted in a voice so strained that Curtis stared.

'Then why did you marry him, Lola?'

She answered and it seemed almost that she was thinking aloud:

'You know that I was very young. And Edgar was Edgar. I think he could have persuaded a nightingale to sing out of his hand. But I doubt whether he would have listened to the song.'

Watson burst into a perspiration. He drew a handkerchief and passed it to and fro across his forehead.

'We'll leave you now,' said Curtis, 'so that you can get to bed.'

The men shook hands with her and left. She was gazing into the fire when the door closed after them.

'I'm sorry for that little lady,' said Curtis as they stood at the corner of Downing Street and Whitehall.

'So am I. It's a rotten shame. Poor little Lola!'

'I hate to think of her being harried by Ripple and it looks as though she's bound to be. Let's hope that it won't be too awkward for her. It certainly will be if she's got a few facts she wants to hide. Those little peccadilloes can be very embarrassing.'

'Don't talk like that, Curtis. It isn't like you to make nasty suggestions. I've known her ever since she was a kid, and there's not one word that can be said against her reputation.'

'Watson, you speak with the confidence of a father confessor, and with rather more than a confessor's warmth. I could understand your tone if she were your own wife. If I were you I wouldn't be so anxious to defend the lady's good name before it is attacked. If the inquiry digs deep the purity of your motives might be suspected. I'll remind you that Inspector Ripple is perhaps a coarse-minded man.'

Colour flooded Watson's face. Even in the blue of the street lamps it was discernible as a widening stain. He looked uncomfortable.

'I . . . I only wanted to make it plain . . .'

Curtis slapped his back and checked the sentence impatiently.

'Man alive, you make it too plain! What you say to me doesn't matter a hoot. What you say to the police might mean everything. They would fasten on your words as eagerly as leeches bite into a piece of bruised flesh. If you're not very, very careful you'll have the coroner asking questions that will write finis to your political career and make Mrs Reardon exceedingly uncomfortable.'

'But there's nothing for us to be uncomfortable about.'

'Quite. You've explained that. So there can't be anything to get excited about. But for the love of crying out loud don't get so pink round the gills each time her name is mentioned. If you act in front of other people as you have tonight everyone will swear that there's something in it. I'm going back to the Temple to work.'

Watson was unwilling to leave things as they stood. He walked with his friend through the quiet streets at the back of Whitehall and along the Embankment. For some time both were silent. Then Watson spoke with startling abruptness:

'Did you know that Edgar cut me out years ago with Lola?'

'No, I didn't. But after tonight, of course, I guessed it.'

'I thought I had given you a false impression.'

Curtis took a cigarette from his case, handed one to Watson and lighted the two, glancing at the miserable face of his friend in the flickering light of the match. He spoke with a tone of smooth toleration:

'Look here, old man, you'd better tell me nothing. You can't prevent me putting two and two together. What does it matter if I think they make five? But you insist on talking, tell me what I am to believe.'

Watson winced and the cigarette glowed and glowed again.

'I don't want there to be an appearance of mystery where there is none. We were boy and girl together. When I came down from the university she floored me. I'd never thought of a woman before. Then Edgar came down for some shooting. After that I never had a chance. It was just as though he'd put a veil on her so that she could only look at him. I was nowhere. The trouble was that even now I fancy Edgar didn't know he was cutting me out. He was infernally friendly.'

'But afterwards? Was he never jealous?'

'He had no cause. I saw her alone very little. Lola encircled her life with her wedding ring. Besides, I came to look on Edgar as a close friend.'

'It was an impression he had a way of creating,' said Curtis, dryly. 'Take my advice, Watson, and tumble into bed. Your nerves are shaken. I'll see you tomorrow. The troubles may have lifted by then.'

A few minutes before Watson and Curtis parted company a conference was in progress in the office of the Commissioner of Police. There were three men in the room. Sir Norris Wheeler, the Commissioner, was fifty, corpulent, bald-headed and irritable. Chief Detective Inspector Ripple was tall, cadaverous and melancholic. Amos Petrie, a solicitor from the Public Prosecutor's Department, was an odd specimen. About five feet four in height, nearer fifty than forty, he had weak eyes that blinked behind rimless spectacles, large ungainly hands, had a nasty habit of staring over a person's shoulder while talking to them and a worse habit of rubbing his hands on a huge coloured handkerchief every two or three minutes.

'I asked you to come round, Petrie,' said Sir Norris, 'because we want some assistance. Ripple suggested to me that I should borrow you, and I think your services might be very helpful.'

Petrie glanced at Ripple with malevolence and coughed nervously.

'I've got plenty of work to do without butting into Yard work,' said the little man. 'Why can't you handle the case here?'

'Because the inquiry is the most difficult we've ever had,' said Ripple, 'and we haven't forgotten what you've done for us in other cases. I don't think this is a job for an official Yard man.'

'Why not? Thought you were paid to investigate sudden deaths.'

'But you must know when such a death takes place in the House of Commons police work is hampered in a hundred and one ways. It looks as though every member of the Cabinet has got to be questioned and some M.P.'s have got to explain things. Add to that the fact that you can't meet them in the House and you'll see the start of the difficulty.' The Commissioner was indignant.

Petrie played with his handkerchief.

'I think you're raising a mare's nest,' he remarked. 'At the moment you don't know what caused Reardon's death. Why not wait?'

'We know enough about the surrounding circumstances to realise that a few preliminary inquiries are justified,' said Wheeler.

'And what part am I supposed to play?' asked the little man. 'Do I sit on the doorstep of 10 Downing Street until I can chat to the members of the Cabinet? Or do I stand back and applaud while Ripple does his stuff?'

Sir Norris opened his mouth to snarl a retort. He hesitated, and changed his mind. Petrie was an odd man. For twenty years he had been known as a person who didn't take kindly to discipline. His usual reply to a rebuke was simple and effective. He pointed out that since his private means were sufficient to sustain him, and since he preferred fishing to hanging around Whitehall it seemed that the time for a quiet removal had arrived. And Petrie was not the type of servant the Department wished to lose.

'I can't give you any details now,' said the Commissioner. 'Ripple can tell you all that there is to be known. You two have worked together many times. I only hope that you will be successful this time. May I take it that you commence to assist us tomorrow?'

Amos pursed his pale lips and played with a thin wisp of hair. The Inspector was gazing at him hopefully.

'I'll make a few inquiries in the morning,' he said eventually, 'and if I then consider that I can help Ripple I'll lend a hand.'

'That's very good of you,' said Sir Norris.

'Actually, it isn't. I don't want to discover how or why Edgar Reardon passed from this world. But I'm glad of the chance to aggravate Ripple somewhat. I'm sure he'll be glad to know that.'

The Inspector sighed heavily. His faith in the powers of Petrie were tremendous; after working with the small man many times he had developed a measure of respect for him. But their association meant the consumption of more beer than Ripple appreciated and the narration of many stories and much advice concerning the art of angling. Amos rose from the chair, looked at his uncreased trousers, picked up a bowler hat that hadn't been dusted for years, pushed a tie that looked like a length of rope a little farther away from his collar, nodded his head to Wheeler, winked at Ripple, and ambled out of the room with the soft tread of an angler and the rolling gait of a sailor. The Inspector hurried after him. Petrie turned to view him disconsolately.

'Sunshine,' he said, wagging a head that was a couple of sizes too large for his thin neck, 'I'm not congratulating you on dragging me into this lot. In other words, damn you! What about some beer?'

'Not yet, not yet. Come into my office and I'll tell you how things stand at the moment. After that we may have a drink.'

'May have?' Petrie sounded aghast. 'I must have misheard you. If I can't have an ale when I want one I'm resigning from this job now.'

'I won't keep you more than ten minutes. Then I'll drink with you.'

'The very soul of consideration, laddie. Lead the way, Sunshine.'

'And don't keep calling me Sunshine!'

'Rather too masculine, you think? I'll try Rainbow if it suits you better. Or shall we call you Epidemic? The words seem to fit.'

Ripple said nothing until they were seated in his office.

'Did I tell you,' commenced Amos, 'about that chub I collected just before the start of the—'

'Forget it,' said Ripple wearily. 'Let's talk about the late Edgar Reardon. Tell me what you know about the affair and that I needn't pass on old information.'

'I don't know much. He was thirty-nine. Graduated into politics after the usual education and a stay of a couple of years in Paris. Tried his hand as a barrister, but had no enthusiasm for it. Turned from the Bar to the City, and built up a name and collected a fair amount of money, as financial adviser to a few trust companies. Married Lola Andrews, only child of Sir Clement Andrews. Elbowed his way into the Cabinet because the other men in the party weren't much good. Slick talker, affected dresser, unusually conceited, fond of company, posed as a friend to everyone, fancied himself as a coming Premier, did a bit of hunting and shooting, played cards a lot and settled down to a life of eminent respectability after he became Chancellor. Rose this afternoon to explain in his Budget how he intended to overcome a serious deficit, collapsed and died during his speech before he indicated the new financial programme. Cause of death at present unknown, but previously regarded as a man in good health. That's all.'

'Seems to be plenty. I've questioned two or three folks, but I can't add much to what you've said. I can't see the point in asking many questions until I know how he died. The whole affair is daft.'

'Then why on earth do you drag me into it, Angel? When do you think you'll have the genuine information about what happened?'

'By lunch-time tomorrow. I've had a word with the Coroner for the House and his officer will pass the information to me as soon as he gets it from the doctor. Perhaps you'd better collect me at the Yard in the morning. Maybe you'll be excused from duty. I hope you are. That'd let me out of it. This death looks everything that's odd.'

'Don't tell me that, Sunshine. Every time they throw you into an inquiry the whole affair bristles with difficulties and trouble.'

'You know perfectly well that I get every rotten job they can find.'

'And you make the best of them, lad! If they delivered the culprit to you with a signed confession in his hand you'd find a catch in it somewhere. Be more like the intelligent carp. They never worry. So long as the *Cyprinus Carpio* can collect an occasional meal it lets the troubles of the world drift by. You, Ripple, never wait for awkward moments. You stay awake at night inventing them. What about this beer you were going to buy for me?'

'The shout is on you. I don't get half your money.'

'Maybe,' said Amos as they walked out of the building towards Whitehall, 'but think of the value I give them for what they pay!'

Ripple grunted, bowed his meagre shoulders in an outsize overcoat. Petrie trotted along by his side, chattering about fish.

The Yard man was not listening. He was thinking about Edgar Reardon, wondering what would happen if he had to arrest a Cabinet Minister. After the second glass of beer he thawed a little. They were alone in a far corner of the bar.

'If Reardon was murdered,' he said, 'he must have been poisoned, and if he was poisoned the stuff must have been given to him in a glass of claret and seltzer. That's all he drank while he made his speech. The drink was given to him by Eric Watson, his Parliamentary Private Secretary. He seemed flustered when I saw him tonight.'

'Might give you a lead. What made you talk to Paling?'

'I was told that he had been seen around a lot with Reardon and was in the House at the time of his death. He's a curious bloke.'

'Aren't they all? Seen the widow yet, Sunshine?'

'I thought I'd leave her until she got over the shock.'

'Did you discover first whether it had been much of a shock?'

Ripple replaced his glass on the table. Frowns ran across his face.

'You're a funny little devil. What do you mean?'

'Nothing. When I see a school of roach swimming like blazes I fancy I can smell a pike behind them. Sometimes when I think of sudden deaths I wonder about women. Perhaps that's why I'm a bachelor.'

'Don't you think we ought to wait a while before we start making guesses? After all, Reardon might have passed away very harmlessly.'

'There is that possibility. If the idea is strong in your mind I can't see why you had to pester me. Have another beer.'

'Not me. I have to keep a clear head. Tomorrow means work.'

'All right. Take some brightness home to your wife. Good-night.'

Petrie strolled out of the public house, whistling cheerfully.

CHAPTER IV

THE MEDICAL REPORT

WORD passed round the House of Commons on the following day that Edgar Reardon had died of heart failure. It was difficult to trace the origin of the information, but members linked it obscurely with the post mortem which had taken place early that morning. The news was received eagerly and immediately accepted. It was satisfactory to all to know that there was no foundation for the vague fears of Tranter.

Curtis first heard the news while waiting in the outer lobby to speak to Fred Otwood. At the time he couldn't find an opportunity. Otwood was talking to a small man with a frightened air and an ill-fitting suit—Amos Petrie.

'I didn't know that Reardon had a heart,' said Curtis. 'In that case Tranter was wrong, almost foolishly wrong.'

'That's old news,' asserted his informant. 'I wouldn't take his word for anything that really mattered.'

Curtis smiled vaguely and was walking away when from the corner of his eye he sighted Fred Otwood. At that instant the former Chancellor of the Exchequer leaped to one side as if he had been stung by a tarantula.

'How dare you, sir?' he cried.

The little man seemed more surprised than any man of his inches had a right to be.

'I'll report you to the House,' shouted another Member. Otwood's trouble seemed to be catching! Petrie blinked his eyes and tugged nervously at his coloured handkerchief. He stared round as though searching for an ally.

With unbelievable suddenness the octagonal space in which members woo constituents and placate troublesome petitioners, was converted into pandemonium. It seemed that before the mind recovered from one surprise the eye was shocked by another. Member after member left those to whom they had been speaking and retreated hastily to the Inner Lobby where the outside world may be defied.

Amos Petrie, his mild face creased in bewilderment, walked over to Curtis.

'Did you see that?' he inquired. 'What's the matter with the man?'

'I was as much surprised as you were.'

A wan smile passed over Petrie's face. He remarked artlessly:

'I only asked him if he could tell me something about the death of the late Edgar Reardon.'

'Well? And what then?'

'He didn't seem to hear me. So I touched his arm to attract his attention. How do you explain it all?'

Curtis laughed and also beat a retreat to the Inner Lobby. Petrie stood with a smile twisting his mouth. Now he realised some of Ripple's difficulties. It may be generally conceded that those seeking news with regard to an occurrence at a particular time and place first ask those who were present. But whenever detectives attempt such a move in the precincts of the House of Commons they raise nice questions about freedom of ingress and egress and the immemorial Privileges of Parliament. It was so now.

The Inner Lobby was seething with discontent and ruffled vanity. The walls were echoing to discordant voices.

'They've no right in here except as servants of the House . . .'

'But if Reardon's death was not heart failure after all . . .'

'Nonsense. Of course it was heart failure.'

'Why this shoulder clapping business anyway . . .'

'A sheer impertinence . . .'

'A gross breach of privilege, too.'

'I've never been so insulted before during my years . . .'

'We must tell the Speaker. We certainly must . . .'

'And discover if he authorised it . . .'

Fred Otwood promised to raise the question and walked into the House. Curtis followed him and immediately walked over to Joe Manning. He told him of the trouble.

Manning was puzzled as well as annoyed.

'You're a lawyer and I'm not, Curtis. What's the constitutional line?'

'That depends,' whispered Curtis. 'I'd advise you to go slow.'

Manning nodded and took no part in the Parliamentary crisis produced by the arrival of Amos Petrie. He did not need to fan the trouble and he couldn't assuage it. The Home Secretary made an attempt to temporise and the House became more and more impatient. Matters were not improved when the Speaker admitted that he knew nothing whatever about the affair. He had been kept in entire ignorance about the inquiries.

That fact disturbed even the Speaker. And if the pale ghost of Charles I had appeared at the Bar of the House the private members could not have been more shocked. The Home Secretary was harried, baited and badgered until anyone but an M.P. would have felt sorry for him. He began to wilt, looked hopefully at the Prime Minister. There was no help coming from that quarter.

Ingram sat on the Treasury Bench, his elbow on his knee, his head supported on his hand, listening to the disheartening exhibition made by his Home Secretary. The Premier decided to close the storm of questions and silenced everyone by stepping to the table.

'I think,' announced Ingram, 'that this House will have to reconcile itself to accepting the aid of the Civil Power. I say that although I should have disapproved of its intrusion without the sanction of the House. To explain why I am of this opinion I must say that I hold in my hand the reports of two eminent medical men who this morning performed a postmortem in connection with the tragic death of the late Edgar Reardon.'

The members moved restlessly. Ingram seemed tiresomely verbose. The forensic mantle dropped from Ingram with cruel abruptness.

'The late Chancellor of the Exchequer died of poison!'

The last word shot through his lips as though it had blistered his tongue. Five hundred breaths were intaken.

'He was poisoned with strophanthin.'

A whisper rose round the startled House. What was strophanthin? To Eric Watson that seemed unimportant. He felt like a fly taken in the web of a spider. He flashed dimmed eyes round the vague sea of faces, half-unconsciously seeking for a friendly glance. Instead he heard five hundred repetitions of the word strophanthin.

Tranter knew what it was. He smacked his thigh to proclaim his knowledge. Those on each side began to question him. The whispers faded away as Ingram opened his mouth to speak again:

'I understand that strophanthin is one of the most dangerous drugs in the pharmacopœia,' he announced.

'How did the deceased Member get it?' The questioner was Manning.

'That is one of the matters demanding inquiry. I am told, though, that in minute pathological doses it is used medicinally.'

'Oh!' Manning sat back and relaxed. 'That explains it, of course.'

'Not quite,' said the Prime Minister unhappily. 'The late Member was not taking such a medicine and more strophanthin was found in the course of the postmortem than could ever have been administered medicinally.'

To Watson that added a further complication to his entanglement. To all others it gave a final element of the fantastic to a situation already incredible. Members rose to insist upon further information being supplied.

'The effect of strophanthin upon the heart is well known,' he said, 'and I am told that it is very peculiar.' He stopped to raise a slip of paper before his eyes. Then he proceeded: 'Even the beat upon which the heart stops tells its tale in corroboration. It stops in systole, and not in diastole, and movement is arrested in a tetanic spasm which the postmortem inevitably reveals. It is somewhat the same condition as that we know as lockjaw.'

Ingram moved back to the Treasury Bench. The Members gaped at him. The facts had now been realised and accepted. The bewilderment grew and grew. Questions were flung with the rapidity of machine-gun fire. Ingram had to return to the table. He shook his head wearily as he listened to the bombardment.

What was the explanation? Why should a man give himself a cramp in the heart that kills? Above all, why should Edgar Reardon have done it? Was it certain that the tragedy was not an entire accident? From whence did the strophanthin come? Was there any connection between the tragedy and the pending Budget?

Those who sought information were disappointed. Ingram replied to all the questions without adding to that which they already knew.

'I share the bewilderment and perplexity of Members,' he said. 'I have been asking myself all these questions since the information was first placed in my hand. I cannot answer them. So far as I know the physicians have no replies to them. It is certain that the late Chancellor of the Exchequer could not have taken the poison outside the House. All who were here yesterday will attest with me that he could not have been poisoned in the House. To all who knew him it is inconceivable that he should have poisoned himself. It seems also impossible that an accident could have happened. Yet our friend is dead. There is nothing further I can say.'

For a space there was a complete silence. Then a voice rose: 'What about the claret and seltzer he drank?'

Watson licked his dry lips, wanted to shriek out that there

was no poison in the glass. He restrained himself with an effort and searched the benches to discover who had asked the question. He could not even find a look of malevolence towards himself. He seemed unnoticed, almost as though he were out of existence. The Members were inhumanly impersonal. The Prime Minister alone deviated from this attitude by a hair's-breadth. He glanced at Watson as he proceeded to answer the question that had been fired:

'I do not know about the claret and soda. But we all know that the greatest part of it was drunk during the course of the speech. That means that if the poison were in that drink the late Chancellor of the Exchequer was slowly absorbing it into his system during a period of approximately an hour. I am told upon the highest possible authority that it would not have been possible for him to do that without experiencing most serious effects. And we all know that he appeared in good health until a minute before he collapsed.'

The Members looked at the Premier and refrained from pressing further questions. They were completely out of their depth. Watson thought that Ingram might generously have used more definite words. A greater emphasis would have been fairer. Still, the underlying truth was one that must be recognised. Watson felt that he was entitled to relax. So he sat back in his chair and sighed with an approach to satisfaction. And in that very instant Ingram robbed his own indefinite words of every semblance of significance.

'Of course, it is not intended to withdraw anything from the police,' he stated. 'All these matters I have mentioned will have to be weighed and considered. I have told you what the medical men have said. I cannot profess, and do not profess, to have any real knowledge upon those points. I have to rely upon the reports of the specialists, and I advise the House, also to be guided by them. I need scarcely tell you that the action taken by the police will depend to a great extent upon the doctor's statements, and that the police have special experience in dealing with such matters. I have myself discussed the matter with Sir Norris Wheeler, the Commissioner of Police, and he assures me that he has taken special steps to ensure that the inquiry which concerns this House so nearly will be under the personal supervision of an investigator well able to discover the truth, and set the mind of this House at peace.'

Watson felt the ground sliding from beneath his feet. The reference to the claret and soda had only emphasised the ambiguity of his position, and the thought of the coming investigation flung his thoughts back in a panic to the position of Lola Reardon. Watson felt sick, wanted to dash from the House and dare not.

Curiously enough, there were those in the House who sat with lips moving in disguised smiles. They could see some element of comedy. A death was shrieking to be investigated, and the only witnesses were objecting to being questioned in a particular place, were arguing about the conditions under which they might give statements.

Joe Manning felt that as Leader of the Opposition it was essential that he should enter the fray. He rose with a cough.

'Everyone knows,' he commenced in sarcastic parody of the Prime Minister, 'that the effects of poison may be long delayed. So why should members be troubled about a matter of which they know nothing when the death may have been the result of something that happened hours before the collapse?'

His supporters cheered feebly but ceased abruptly when Ingram commenced to reply. The Prime Minister spoke slowly, chose his words with scrupulous care:

'I am told that the fatal dose must have been absorbed at some time between a few minutes and a few seconds before death.'

The implication was obvious—and ugly. Eric Watson regarded it almost as an accusing finger. He found himself rising to his feet and stopped when he heard another voice raised. Curtis was up, his hands resting before him, his strong voice strangely strained.

'We naturally accept the statement in good faith as the best that can be afforded at the moment. I think it right to indicate to the Hon. Members, however, that the Prime Minister's final remark definitely implies that every Member is a potential suspect.'

He paused and a rippling whisper wafted round the House.

A Member in a far back bench commenced to giggle. The Speaker intervened with no uncertain tongue:

'If the Honourable Member cannot control his mirth it might be better if he indulged it outside the House. This is a serious matter.'

Ingram looked at Curtis as though grieved. The barrister had said what the Premier had carefully avoided. Curtis sat down.

'In the long history of this House,' said the Premier, 'there has been no such thing as a suicide. It is true that a murder did occur, but that tragical happening took place outside in the Lobby. I mention those two facts for one reason only—so that you will rightly regard the present set of circumstances as entirely without precedent. That being so I feel justified and compelled to ask this House to take exceptional measures to deal with it.'

No arguments were raised. Members were oppressed by the oddities surrounding the death, by the peculiarities of this new type of heart failure. Ingram had certainly suggested that a murder had been committed while they were all looking on!

Watson shivered as though seized with an attack of ague. But the day was warm, and the House overheated. Curtis smiled consolingly. Watson nodded, anxious to get outside the building.

The Prime Minister scribbled a note and had it passed to Watson. Eric read it twice before he grasped the meaning of the contents:

'The small man in the pew under the gallery is in charge of the investigation. Rough hair, untidy clothes, rimless glasses.'

Watson flushed almost guiltily. Why should Ingram pass on

the information to him? Then he pulled himself together, realised that he was solely in charge of Reardon's papers which the police would want to examine. Watson rose and walked to the pew which is reserved for Civil Servants whom Ministers on the Treasury Bench may want to consult at short notice. Watson felt less alarmed when he saw the little man. There was a disarming air of simplicity about him.

'Are you anxious to get rid of me?' he asked Watson.

'I didn't know that you knew me. I only came to say that I'd like to hand over Reardon's papers if you are ready to look them over. The keys have been given to me and I want to go home.'

'I'll be sorry to leave this seat. I found it all most amusing.'

'You're the only person here who could see the joke.'

Watson stopped abruptly and looked at the solicitor. Perhaps, after all, he wasn't as innocent as his appearance advertised. They did not speak as Watson led the way through the door at the back of the pew and entered a lobby, walking from there to the Chancellor of the Exchequer's private room. Amos glanced round the chamber with sudden speed, and sat down on the edge of a table. He seemed quite happy and entirely at ease.

A half empty bottle of claret stood on a side shelf. Petrie eyed it almost casually and passed no comment.

CHAPTER V

WATSON PLAYS FOR SAFETY

'SEEMS impossible that a murder could have taken place in there before hundreds of people until you've seen the place,' said Amos.

'It seems less improbable to you now?'

'Much. I sat in that pew working out a few ways in which it could be done. But most of my schemes lacked finesse.' Petrie wagged his head to indicate that deficiency in finesse was as deplorable as the murder itself. Watson again felt confident. There was nothing to fear about this strange little person. Watson thought it over and decided to take a gambler's throw and clear the atmosphere.

'Among these theories you've been working out, did you find one that fitted me?'

Petrie produced his handkerchief and his voice dropped a tone:

'I've got a separate theory for you—one all for yourself.'

Eric repressed the shiver that coursed down his spine and took another plunge:

'Thinking, of course, of the claret and soda?'

Amos nodded brightly, almost as though seized by sudden delight.

'I don't want to ask you about that now. But I don't mind telling you that one man felt inclined to arrest you last night.'

'Meaning Inspector Ripple?'

'Yes. You know him?'

'His fame reached me last night,' said Watson nastily. 'He was pictured to me as a person lacking in your favourite finesse.'

'Dear me! Poor Ripple would be mortified to hear that. I've

blamed him at times for many things—but never for that. It's too bad.'

'The man deserves all that's coming to him if he thinks I'd poison a friend with six hundred people looking on.'

'It would be gauche,' conceded Amos. 'Very gauche.'

'Why don't you want to question me about the claret and soda?'

'My friend, when I go fishing I study the conditions of the stream before I throw in my line. I don't know enough about this case yet.'

Petrie was staring over Watson's shoulder. The younger man grew restive, turned to discover that the solicitor was looking at a blank wall and bit his lips as he considered the position. Finally, he commenced to speak with a burst of words:

'Look here, I'm in rather a mess. I'm not standing in too good a spot. It might be said that things look suspicious as far as I'm concerned. But I'm prepared to put myself in your hands. You can make any search you like and I'll answer any questions you like. I can't be fairer or more open than that, can I?'

'Perhaps you can't. It might be an advantage.'

'An advantage to me?'

'Possibly. Who can say? Ever do any fishing yourself?'

'Fishing? What on earth has that got to do with it?'

'Nothing at all,' replied the little man easily. 'You've missed a lot, my friend.' He looked round the room as though taking his first glance. Then he pointed to the claret bottle.

'Is that the bottle from which Reardon's last drink was taken?'

'That's the one, and I poured out the drink personally.'

'How interesting. For myself I prefer beer. But it takes all sorts to make a world, and I can't blame anyone for liking claret. I don't think many people would like to drink out of this bottle.'

'Surely you don't think the strophantin was in the claret?'

'I never could guess. Pity I've lost my palate for wine.' Petrie removed the cork and sniffed the contents of the bottle daintily.

He had a wholesome respect for strophantin fumes—if any were present. Watson eyed him suspiciously, waiting for some change of expression on the wrinkled face. The solicitor smiled.

'Can you lend me some sort of a case so that I can take this bottle away? The stuff will have to be analysed.'

Watson produced a small attaché case and the bottle was stowed away.

'Do you live very far from here, Mr Watson? By the way, I didn't mention before that my name is Amos Petrie. Not that the name matters but I suppose there is some sort of etiquette even about murder cases. Now that we know each other—where do you live?'

'I have a flat in St Margaret's Mansions. I live at the top.'

'Like an eagle in his eyrie, eh? Aren't the Mansions in Millbank?'

'That's right. Only round the corner, so to speak.'

'I'd like to amble round and peep about the place for a while.'

'I told you that I am willing for any search to be made.'

'Splendid. We'll start now. I can collect your friend Ripple on the way. Maybe you'll like him more now that the raw edges of a first meeting have worn away. Hand me Reardon's papers and we'll walk.'

Watson felt inclined to protest against the sudden move. Petrie stood near the door, waiting for him. Eric shrugged his shoulders, collected the papers, tucked them into two despatch cases, and handed them over. They met Inspector Ripple in the courtyard. He was talking to a sergeant. Amos handed the case containing the claret bottle to the sergeant, instructing him that the contents were to be sent for immediate analysis. The documents were handed over to be left in Ripple's room. Then the three men walked to Millbank.

They rose in the lift to the fifth floor and were admitted to the flat by a manservant. Ripple took a quick look round, and phoned to the Yard for another man to assist in the search. Amos sat down in a small lounge and waited for the scrutiny of the flat to begin. He was as placid as a removal contractor. Watson found it difficult to settle down and over a whisky and soda he recounted to Amos all that happened on the previous day from the time he entered the House until he left it. He was still adding details to the story when Ripple and his assistant commenced the search. Half an hour later Ripple returned to the lounge, holding in his hand a small bundle of papers.

'These papers and oddments seem to be the only things of any value,' he announced.

'And no trace whatever of any strophantin?' asked Watson.

'None whatever,' replied the Yard man, looking at the speaker curiously. 'Why? Did you think we might find some?'

'I was sure that you wouldn't. I've never heard of the stuff until this morning. Perhaps you're satisfied now?'

'Don't speak before you think,' said Petrie curtly. 'If you gave the strophantin to Reardon it isn't very likely that you'd have kept some of the stuff in your flat. And since you were so certain that there was no poison here why did you ask whether any had been found?' Before Watson could speak Petrie picked up the bundle of papers and commenced to run through them. Eric watched him closely. The search was conducted at lightning speed, paper after paper being dropped on the table as soon as they had been glanced at. Then Amos stopped abruptly. In his hand he held a photograph.

Watson could not see it. He did not need to. He knew it was a woman's. Petrie raised his eyes and Eric reddened under the inspection.

'When you were talking to me you said nothing about the lady. Did you think the matter so unimportant?'

'There's nothing to tell. Otherwise I would have spoken.'

'I see. Well, we'll take a look and see whether the photograph itself can give us any information. I'm sure you don't mind.'

Amos did not wait to discover whether Watson objected or not. He opened the back of the frame and extracted the photo. Watson looked on with dull resentment. His anger rose when the little man turned the photograph over and inspected the face for a full minute. Finally he tapped the frame on the table and examined what fell out, making sure that it was neither makers' shavings nor packer's dust.

'There's no mystery about it,' snapped Watson. 'It's an old photo.'

'I see it is,' said Amos calmly. 'Judging from the last time I saw Mrs Reardon it must have been taken about ten or twelve years ago. You had it in a different frame not long ago. I think the lady was foolishly impetuous when she scribbled on this. Was she a classical student? "Omnia vincit amor. Lola." Very pretty. I suppose that means, "Love conquers all things"? I wonder whether it conquers death—particularly sudden death? Do you think Mrs Reardon imagines that love is quite so potent? Maybe she has changed her mind by now.'

Watson squirmed, wanted to throttle the man. He started to speak and stopped when he saw Petrie take another photograph in his hand.

'Well, well, well, Mr Watson! Now this one does tell a story. I see it's quite new. It's never been framed and there's no dust on it. H'm, rather looks as though the ancient affection has continued to quite recent times. This was taken about a year ago, I imagine. I wonder whether Mrs Reardon ever contemplated inscribing this one as she did the other? I see she hasn't even signed it. I believe I might have suggested something suitable for her to use—although I was never a classical scholar.'

'Oh, yes? And what would you have suggested?' Watson sat forward tensely, wondering whether Petrie would give away a clue to his thoughts. The solicitor scratched his forehead before replying:

'My French is very elementary. Still, I seem to remember someone writing: *Mais on revient toujours a ses premières amour*. Perhaps you'll agree that it would have appeared pleasing on the bottom of this second photograph?'

'I can see no possible reason why Mrs Reardon should write

about one always returning to one's first love. If you think it at all remarkable that I should have been presented with a photograph quite recently may I remind you that I was Parliamentary Private Secretary to the lady's husband? Apart from that your acuteness dazzles me. I don't know how you work these things out.' Watson was too heavily sarcastic and it displeased him to see that Petrie was smiling as though appreciating the rebuff.

'I had recalled, of course,' said Petrie, 'that you were Reardon's P.P.S. But I am incredibly dense. It had not occurred to me that that was why you kept his wife's photograph in your bedroom. I didn't appreciate that it was part of your duties. I will never be able to understand the complexities of politics.' He shook his head almost mournfully and Watson cursed silently. This little man was not quite as harmless as one assumed.

'From the colour of my necktie,' he sneered again, 'I suppose you deduce that I am in love with the lady?'

'Not exactly,' replied Amos casually, 'I imagined that from your former silence and your present anger.'

The calmness of the judgment made it more devastating. It seemed to Watson that those few words encompassed all he dreaded. They stripped him of his anger and his sarcasm. He was unmanned. Now he stared at the curious person whose suspicions he had aroused and whose suspicions had travelled so far.

'Had you forgotten those photographs, Mr Watson, when you asked me to search your flat?'

'Not at all. It never occurred to me that they, or she, had anything to do with the matter. Nor does it now. Even assuming that all your deductions are right I don't see how the photos affect the issue.'

'No? Then you don't recognise that even ladies are at times associated with such crimes as murder?'

'Perhaps, in some cases, they are. But this time you are hopelessly and hideously wrong.'

'I've found myself entirely wrong before today—particularly when fishing. Ripple, you haven't much to say. Are there any questions you'd like to ask Mr Watson before we leave?'

'One or two. You must expect some bluntness from me,' said the Yard man. 'I don't play about with words.'

'My friend does not practise the art of finesse,' remarked Amos.

'I have already been informed about that,' said Eric surlily.

'Did Reardon know that there had been an affectionate association between yourself and his wife before her marriage?' asked Ripple.

'I couldn't tell you. He was not the sort of man to worry about that. In any case, he had every right to trust me and he did trust me.'

'Do you consider that Mrs Reardon is in no way concerned with her husband's death?'

'Good God, man! I am certain upon that point. Don't be ridiculous.'

'Then why have you swerved away from questions, become annoyed over trifles, and acted like a person with a lot to hide?'

'I have acted quite straightforwardly all the way through.'

'Was that bottle of claret unopened when you took the drink out of it for Reardon?'

'Quite untouched. I had to extract the cork myself.'

'You would have noticed if the bottle had been tampered with?'

'Naturally. I can swear that it had not been touched.'

Petrie frowned and rapped on the table.

'Are you trying to make things as awkward as possible for yourself.'

'Certainly not. I am telling you the truth. Don't you believe me?'

'Did Reardon instruct you personally to bring him a claret and soda? I know that he would take a drink, but did he specify what sort of drink he wanted?'

'Certainly. Men don't drink an unusual mixture like that by pure accident. Surely you know that without asking me?'

'Being nothing except a beer drinker I couldn't answer you. I don't think we'll detain you any longer. When you see Mrs Reardon again you might tell her that within the next few hours I'll call upon her. It might save her from a shock when I arrive.'

'Is it necessary, Mr Petrie?' asked Watson anxiously.

'Entirely so—and you haven't helped her position.'

'I haven't?' Watson seemed staggered, quite amazed. 'But I'd never do a thing to make difficulties for her.'

'Perhaps that accounts for most of the trouble. Your object in asking me to come here has failed. Partial revelation is never of any service to a man unless he's fighting for time. Instead of clearing yourself and getting Mrs Reardon out of the line of inquiry, you've merely presented me with a new problem. You have compelled me to ask myself whether you can have any object in gaining time.'

'Mr Petrie, this is outrageous!'

'Believe me, my friend, nothing is further from my immature mind than outrage. I came here thinking that you might assist me and that in return for your help I might give you a few words of fatherly advice. You have not enabled me to do anything of the kind. The only way in which you can help me is by complete frankness. I hope you'll bear that in mind. It might assist you the next time we meet—and that will be before much more water flows under Westminster Bridge.'

'Doesn't sound as though you're satisfied,' said Watson.

'I'm not. Oh! Before I go would you mind telling me what you know about this man Paling?'

'That's quite easy. I only know that he has been associated with Reardon during the last twelve months. I don't know how, why, or where they met, and I don't know what they had in common. It always seemed to me that they were frightened of each other. That's all I know.'

'Doesn't help me. Thanks very much.'

Petrie and Ripple left the building and walked round to the Yard. The miserable Ripple was more melancholic than ever.

'This case will never break in a month of Sundays,' he complained.

'Maybe it won't, Sunshine. You'll find when you do get to the tail end of it that all your trouble has been worthwhile. I can see quite a lot of things that don't fit. It may help us to discover what's happened about the analysis of that claret. At any rate, the report should give us a start. Think it will be ready?'

'I imagine so. I'll give a ring as soon as we reach the office.'

Petrie sat down with a copy of the *Fishing Gazette* while the Inspector got his number. The little man heard Ripple's request for information and then saw the man's jaw sag. The Yard man slapped down the receiver and slumped into a chair.

'Have they got any news for us?' asked Amos.

'They certainly have. There is no trace of strophantin whatever on the bottle, and none in the claret. Just one other thing. I passed along to them the glass that Reardon had used in the House. That shows no trace of any poison whatever. Are we all going mad?'

'Maybe he died through thinking evil thoughts about people.'

CHAPTER VI

A SHOCK FOR AMOS

Petrie spent the remainder of the evening in his flat, gazing lovingly at the cases of stuffed fish, and adding bits and pieces to the mystery of Reardon's death. He arrived at the Yard shortly after ten on the following morning to find a real shock waiting for him. Ripple was the bearer of the news and in his excitement he even forgot to stand like a statue of grief.

'There's been a burglary at Watson's flat,' he announced.

'Eh? What? Are you pulling my leg?'

'I'm not. His place has been burgled during the night.'

'That young man seems to walk from one war into another. Tell me, Sunshine, are my eyes deceiving me or are you smiling?'

'I was just thinking that a couple of things make this the most comical burglary the world has ever known.'

'Lordy, they'll have to be funny if they can make you smile.'

'They are. I've had an inventory taken of all the stolen articles. There is only one item missing from the flat. That's a door key!'

'What a haul for somebody.' Amos looked serious for a second as he added: 'Funny that Watson didn't strike me as a practical joker. He knows that the position is serious.'

'Oh, Watson is serious enough. He's not the joker. It's the burglar who has the sense of humour. He ought to be on the stage.'

'I can't see anything devastatingly funny about stealing a key.'

'Nor can I. But this burglar seems to have taken his pet canary with him, and after giving it a meal in the flat he left some of its food behind! Now work that one out.'

The effect of his joke astonished Ripple. The solicitor was

not amused. For once he was grim, his face set into hard lines. Ripple grew more bewildered when Amos jumped from his chair and stretched out a hand for his battered bowler. The Inspector's smile wore away.

'This is too much of a good thing,' said Amos, 'and I'm going to take a hand in the party. Maybe by the time I've finished the humorist won't enjoy our joke as much as he did his own. I'm going round to that flat immediately. Please yourself whether you come.'

Ripple followed the little man down the staircase and had to lengthen his stride along Whitehall. Petrie was almost trotting. They took the lift to Watson's flat and found Eric talking to his servant. He was not surprised to see them, advanced to shake hands with Amos.

'I thought I'd let you know about this burglary,' he said. 'It might save you the trouble of telling me that I'm not being straight.'

'It doesn't seem to be troubling you very much.'

'Why should it? I reckon it's more a joke than anything.'

'I don't. We left here fairly early last evening. What did you do after we departed? Think hard before you talk.'

Immediately Watson was on the defensive.

'I did not leave this place and nor did John, my servant.'

'Did you have any visitors?'

'None—except the burglar.'

'He didn't happen to tell you that he called to leave a parcel?'

'No,' replied Watson stiffly, 'and I didn't know that the parcel had been left until breakfast time. John had brought in my coffee, and I was sipping it when I saw the parcel on the top of my desk. But . . . er . . . I believe he must have wakened me, or disturbed me. I had been dreaming a bit viciously and woke up. It really was a most odd experience. Shall I tell you about it?'

'In a second,' said Amos. 'Just tell me this first—have you touched or interfered with the contents of that parcel?'

'No, I only showed it to the detective who came round and he told me the burglar had left some canary seed. That's all I know.'

'Right. I'll look at it in a moment. Just tell me what happened.'

Watson reclined in a chair and related a story that lost nothing in the telling. At times Petrie smiled tolerantly. It rather sounded as though Watson had been rehearsing the version of his dream. Most certainly he had dramatised it effectively.

According to him he read for about two hours, had a meal, read a few more pages, and then retired to bed. He was troubled in mind and no sooner did he fall asleep than beings with no existence outside his imagination commenced to pursue him. It seemed to him that they had stepped from a fresco to pace in parade past the foot of the bed. He might have been on the borderline between sleep and waking. Some turned their heads away so that he could not distinguish the faces, others opened their mouths to speak, but said nothing, and when he looked into their faces he could see nothing but a flat and featureless oval. He remembered thinking that they were all women and the thought scattered them.

As soon as they vanished male faces floated through the air. Some were like the angels of Greuze, others like the gargoyles on a Gothic church. All seemed to regard him with peculiar malevolence. It was like facing a regiment of resentful eyes. And the horrible thing about them was that all shared one body—the body of Edgar Reardon! Although dead he was not as he had been after death. Only his body grew, and grew, as if some horrible yeast was working in it. It seemed so huge that it could not be seen in a single glance. It advanced, the floor shaking under its tread. Watson woke.

He found that his pyjamas were saturated in sweat and couldn't realise what had happened to his nerves. It seemed that his ears were playing tricks. He thought he could hear a faint shuffling and called out to know who was there. There was no reply. Some time elapsed before he had recovered sufficiently to appreciate that a nightmare could not shuffle. Then he reached for his dressing-gown and slippers, and walked from room to room, trying the doors and windows. He looked at the time as he left the bedroom. It was one a.m.

Petrie sighed wearily. Ripple was plainly disappointed. As a story it might have been too vivid for broadcasting during the Children's Hour, but it offered very little assistance.

'What length of time elapsed,' asked Amos, 'between you hearing the shuffle of feet and discovering as a result of the search that there was no intruder in the flat?'

'I can't really say. I wasn't properly awake. It may have been about twenty minutes or half an hour.'

'And as you walked through the rooms you heard nothing and saw nothing?' inquired Ripple.

'The only thing I heard was John snoring.'

'Maybe,' remarked Amos, 'he also had seen this man rising as though injected with yeast. Were all the doors and windows secured?'

'Just as they were when I went to bed.'

'A curious sort of burglar. You ask him who he is, and he vanishes, but although he knows that you're awake he stays to lock the door after him with a key that he's stolen. Pretty cool, eh?'

'He must have heard that I did not get out of bed immediately I called to him. That might well have happened.'

'About as likely as a roach attacking a pike. Men usually get out of bed with bare feet and unless the bed creaks they make no sound. You think he might have stopped with his ear against the floorboards making a noise like a mouse to deceive you?'

'I wasn't present at the time so I can't tell you what the man was doing.' Watson was becoming annoyed. 'I didn't attach much importance to it because I thought he'd been disturbed before he could settle down to work. If it hadn't been for the odd business of dumping those seeds on me I wouldn't have reported the matter at all. I remembered what you had told me about revealing everything and that's why I telephoned the Yard.'

'Even my brain can't grasp some of the precise significance of the details,' said Petrie with apparent suavity. 'I want you to let Inspector Ripple have charge of your mysterious parcel while I look round the burgled premises. Do you mind?'

'Not in the least.' He walked over to his desk and returning with a small brown paper parcel, handed it to the Yard man.

'Don't touch that, Sunshine,' said Petrie, 'until I've had a look round. And see that nobody else handles it. I won't be long.'

Amos headed for the kitchen and made an early discovery. Plainly a window had been forced open. There were knife marks on the frame.

'Looks as though your strange caller got in this way,' he said to Watson. 'It would have been easy enough. The door is close to the window and a man putting his arm through could turn the key in the lock. How would he reach that window from the outside?'

'Quite easily—he just walks up the back stairs.'

'I wonder if the doorkeeper below shares your view about the entire ease of the performance?'

'I thought doorkeepers generally slept in the early hours.'

'I'll ask the man about it later.' The little man stood gazing at the two bolts on the door. Then he called the manservant, asking him: 'Were these bolts shot when you came out early this morning?'

'No, sir. I noticed that before I missed the key. I wanted to open the door and couldn't. I think I told the master about it.'

'I see. You're sure that the door was locked and the window was latched when you came into this kitchen?'

'I'm quite certain about that, sir.'

'All right, John. You can go for the time being. Tell me, Mr Watson, how you failed to notice that the back door was unbolted when you made your round? Can you tell me?'

'I thought all the doors were properly fastened. Perhaps I didn't look at the bolts when I found that the door was locked.'

Amos rubbed his hands on his handkerchief. Watson waited nervously.

'The thief,' said the little man, 'may have forced the window and he may even have come in by it. I think he must have done. But if there is one certainty it is that he didn't leave by it—because it was latched. He may have gone out by the door. For though it was locked this morning, the bolts were not drawn and he had the key. I really cannot fathom why you didn't notice that when you made your early morning search of the premises.'

Watson looked at Petrie and stood back a pace. He seemed unwilling to believe the implication and commented falteringly:

'I certainly thought that everything was all right.'

'You might as well have stayed in bed if your inspection was as casual as that. We'll get back to Ripple for a moment and take a look at the present that was left for you.'

The Yard man was sitting at a table, facing the parcel as though guarding a diamond of fabulous wealth. Petrie looked at it for a while before lifting it. The paper was common and the string round it was roughly tied. The latter fact did not concern the solicitor. It had been unfastened since it was discovered. He slipped off the string. The parcel contained a glass bottle. The three men bent down and peered at the contents.

'Melon seeds,' announced Inspector Ripple.

'Melon seeds be damned!' said Petrie. 'Take another look at them.' He held the bottle up to the light.

The seeds inside the container might well have been dyed by a fierce sun filtering through green leaves. They were covered by a fine silky down, and winked back from their satin coats as they glimmered in the light. Amos placed the bottle on the table and looked at the two men.

'Looks more like food for birds of paradise than for canaries,' remarked Watson, still staring at the seeds. Petrie's lips twisted grimly and he nodded without responding. Then he picked up the glass again and moved the stopper about without apparent purpose. A second later he inverted the bottle and shook it. Nothing happened. Patiently he pressed against the stopper, tilted it slightly to one side and shook again. A thin stream of gleaming seeds fell one by one into his open palm. Finally, after examining them, he replaced them in the container, fastened down the stopper and handed the bottle over to Ripple.

'What do you make of that bottle, Sunshine?' he inquired.

'Foreign made. And I know where they're sold and what they cost. Price sixpence. It would be about as easy to trace this bottle as it would to discover the history of an unmarked daily paper.'

'That's not very helpful. Would you mind leaving this room for a short time, Mr Watson?' Eric instantly strolled out. His head was reeling. Immediately Amos touched Ripple's shoulder. 'Is there the slightest possible chance that you could have overlooked this bottle, or these seeds, when you searched this flat yesterday?'

'Absolutely impossible. It's true that I wasn't looking for anything like those seeds, but I could never have missed them. You can rule that chance right out. I didn't leave a corner unsearched.'

'This business gets hotter, and hotter, Sunshine. I'm beginning to feel like a beer. Tell Watson I want to talk to him again, will you?'

The owner of the flat returned somewhat fearfully. After his recent experiences he had lost some degree of confidence when faced by the little solicitor.

'Are you still convinced,' asked Petrie, 'that you can tell me nothing whatever that can help us? Surely there is some small point about this burglary last night—or early this morning—that could give us a lead? Just think, Mr Watson.'

'I am sure that I have said all I can say. Probably I was half asleep at the time when it all happened.'

'You must realise,' said Amos patiently, 'that this is a matter of the greatest importance. I am not concerned because you have had a key stolen. The issue is much more vital than if your flat had been entirely ransacked. It would take some little time, Mr Watson, for your burglar to get off the premises—particularly since he is an obvious amateur. No professional steals a key and leaves a bottle of seeds behind. For all we know he might have been in the building when you were making your rounds. By failing to give the alarm you covered his escape. And if the man who burgled this flat, and then escaped, had not some connection with the murderer of Edgar Reardon he was so close to him that he could have led us along the trail. Now that that's clear to you perhaps you'll see the importance of the questions I've asked you.'

Watson smiled more easily as he replied:

'Clear, yes. But quite mad. Forgive me for saying this, Mr Petrie, but you reason sanely, and finish up with assumptions that sound like complete lunacy. I wish now that I hadn't mentioned this damnation burglary to anyone. After what happened yesterday I was afraid there'd be some misunderstanding about it. But I'd have thought it would have puzzled even you to have connected it with the murder of Edgar Reardon.'

'Is it possible . . .' Amos Petrie commenced and stopped. His eyes blinked as he broke off in the middle of the sentence. He pulled his viciously-coloured handkerchief from his breast-pocket, and waved it in the air. Then he relapsed into his seat with a long sigh, and stared at Watson as though he didn't believe the evidence of his eyes.

'What on earth is the matter?' asked Watson.

The solicitor glanced round the room until he sighted the bookcase. He walked over to it and ran his thumb along the volumes of an encyclopedia. Still sighing he extracted a book from the row, opened it, ran through the pages, and slammed the book on the table.

'Read that, Watson,' he said, pointing with his index finger. Ripple, also, bent over and they read:

'Strophanthus . . . The seeds are about three-fifths of an inch long, one-sixth broad, greenish fawn, covered with flattened silky hairs, and oval acuminate in shape. They are almost odourless, but have an intensely bitter taste.'

'Now take a look at the stuff in that bottle,' snapped Amos.

Watson shot his hands over his eyes and staggered back from the table. He was shaking violently. His face was creamily yellow. Petrie watched him closely.

'Now you know,' he said, 'why I connect your burglary with the death of Edgar Reardon.'

'You mean,' stammered Watson, 'that Reardon was murdered by the use of seeds like these?'

'I mean that he was murdered by the use of poison made from seeds like these, and that by failing to help me you're assisting the person who tried to pin the murder on to you.'

'My God!' said Watson. He didn't speak again for five minutes. The Yard man was more dismal than ever. Petrie was admiring the seeds.

CHAPTER VII

FURTHER CONFUSION

'I'M going to have a few words with your doorman,' said Petrie. He was not away for more than two minutes. Wrinkles corrugated his forehead. 'The fellow in the hall says the outer door is locked at eleven every night and he's sent for the night porter. Things are growing more awkward, Ripple.'

'They couldn't,' said the Yard man. 'What about your burglary now, Mr Watson? There's something very wrong somewhere.'

'I know that. But there are two certain facts. One is that I didn't leave this flat after you left last night. The other is that the seeds were not here when you searched the place. Your business is to discover what happened. I can't help you.'

They waited for twenty minutes before a drowsy night porter arrived. His statement was brief—and disturbing. Only residents entered the building after the front door was locked. In his own ungallant language the first arrival was Mrs 37. She arrived at about quarter to twelve, Mrs 13 and her husband appeared half an hour later. He opened the door to both of them. That was their main protection against burglars. There were no other late comers.

Petrie questioned the man without shaking his statement and then told him he could return to bed. The little man left to meet the occupants of Flats 37 and 13. The first was a widow, inadequate of chest, but with large and prominent eyes, who displayed agitation and false teeth in about equal proportions. Half a dozen questions sufficed to show that she saw nothing and knew very little about anything.

The tenants of Flat 13 presented greater obstacles. The

woman had been a beauty of the small-featured type. The beauty might still have been with her but for the steps she had taken to preserve it. She had replaced the girlish complexion with a flat white and her eyes had the glaze which comes with death or over-brightening. Her mouth was out of curl. Petrie had no other reason for remembering her. In the way ladies have she had sailed up the staircase, leaving her husband to follow and had noted nothing. Her husband, however, had a more curious story to tell. He was short, fat and irascible. But he admitted that someone else entered through the door as he was closing it. He thought that the 'someone' was a resident and took no notice of that fact.

'What makes you think he was a resident?' asked Amos.

'Because he said so. How could I know if he hadn't?'

'Perhaps you might have recognised him?'

'Perhaps I might. But I didn't.'

'Would you know him again if you saw him?'

'How do you think I could tell until I did see him?'

'Are you certain you can't identify him?'

'I might have been able to if I'd kissed the man on both cheeks as they do abroad. I'd even have done that if I'd known that it would save you troubling me. But I had no idea that I'd be pestered by these questions.'

'Was the man in evening dress?'

'Yes . . . no . . . oh, how the devil do I know?'

After another few minutes Amos decided that the stranger might have been tall or short, fat or lean, bearded or clean shaven, and of any complexion between negro and albino. He retired defeated.

Ripple met him on the stairs. The Yard man was plainly excited.

'I took a gamble,' he said, 'and it's come off. They've got the key to Watson's door at Cannon Row Police Station. What do you know about that?'

'Astonishing. How'd it all come about?'

'I just took a blind bet that whoever stole it might have thrown it away. I telephoned asking for a list of all or any keys handed in as found since midnight. Among the half-dozen they've got is the one to this flat. A charwoman walking to the County Hall early this morning picked it up near Westminster Bridge and took it to the station. No doubt about it being the right one. They have given me the number and Watson has identified it as his.'

'Smart work, Sunshine. You do get happy thoughts at times. Now that you've got so far what do you intend to do about it?'

The Inspector's enthusiasm waned and vanished. Melancholia settled on him once again. He shrugged his thin shoulders.

'Never mind,' said the solicitor, 'it might have been worse.'

'But not much. What are you going to do?'

'Just think for a while in case it might save me a lot of unnecessary work. Ever try that way of investigating, Angel?'

'And don't call me Angel. I'm no angel.'

'Leave other folks to admit that. Let's say farewell to Watson for the time being and we'll take a walk.'

'That'll suit me. I'm tired of that man.'

'I'm not. He interests me. But then, so do fish.'

Watson shook hands with them thankfully. The little man had begun to scare him. Amos led the way into Whitehall, recounting angling stories that made Ripple wince. The Yard man was pleased to leave his companion and Petrie headed for the office of the Public Prosecutor, promising to call at the Yard when inspiration of some sort had struck him. Ripple expressed the hope that the idea would strike with sufficient force to render the little man unconscious. On these terms they separated.

Much later in the day many Members of the House of Commons had congregated in the Corridor Bar. To those with extravagant views about the luxurious surroundings afforded politicians in their leisure hours this wood-partitioned structure might come as a surprise. It was like a wayside estaminet in

France, tucked away between the Committee Room Corridor on the first floor, and the staircase leading to the Debating Chamber.

'It really is uncomfortable,' remarked one tactless Member, 'to feel that any man you talk to may be a murderer.'

'There's always a sure way of avoiding the discomfort,' said Dick Curtis.

Members chuckled. A small group sat at each table. Most of them appeared cheerful—including Curtis.

'I feel very inclined to sell my Calicoes . . .'

'Would selling Tin Plates on this rise do me any good . . .'

'I can see five shillings clear on each one and I'm not trying to reach the moon . . .'

'I never expected Great Steels to jump like that . . .'

On all sides conversation turned to stocks and shares. Members abstain from voting when a vote will put money into their pockets. But they would be more than human if they had no interest in windfalls and windfalls were showering on them now. Reardon's Budget was just out and under the exceptional circumstances the news was made public before the Stock Exchange closed its doors. It had certainly 'shaken the trees.' Prices were rising all round. Fred Otwood turned to Curtis:

'Is everyone going into the City?'

'No, they're only trying to sell their Income Tax returns for the benefit of the next Chancellor. That was a damn good Budget.'

Even Otwood had to nod his head. It was an unwilling gesture.

'It was a brilliant arrangement of taxation. I must admit that I had never thought of it. If I had got the idea I'd have been nervous about the way the public would have fallen for it.'

'Lord!' said Manning as he joined them, 'poor Reardon could have made a fortune twice over if he had used the advance information he had a couple of weeks ago.'

'That would have been disgraceful,' snorted Otwood. 'Very, very disgraceful. Thank goodness such things don't happen.'

'Does murder happen?' asked Curtis plaintively. 'I didn't think until now that it was possible in this place. What you were talking about, Otwood, did happen about sixty years ago. The sinner was not a Minister. He was a young fool of an under secretary and got turfed out of politics for ever.'

Curtis noticed Eric Watson enter the bar and stand alone at the far end. He left his own group, strolled over to him. Watson dangled a whisky and soda in his hand. He appeared supremely miserable and Curtis touched his arm consolingly.

'Don't worry yourself, Eric. That won't do you any good. Smile like blazes and damn all of them. Have another drink?'

'I've got one, thanks. It's rotten to be in a position like mine through no fault of my own. I feel as though everybody is staring at me suspiciously.'

'And the more you feel like that the more they'll think that your guilty conscience is showing on your face. Hang it, man, we're all suspected, aren't we? Neither age, respectability, nor adipose tissue has got even me exempt. It seems to me—'

Curtis ceased speaking. A sudden hush had fallen. Watson stared, and his face grew even more pallid. Amos Petrie had entered the bar! Their sacred privacy had been violated. Members stared at the little man as though the devil had arrived—complete with horns. Many of them rose from their seats and moved away. Petrie blinked and rubbed his large hands on his incredibly violent handkerchief. He appeared completely bewildered, looked from man to man like a startled rabbit. The bar emptied rapidly. Only Curtis and Watson remained. He ambled towards them with an embarrassed smile.

'I can't buy myself a drink here, but would one of you take a sympathetic view?' he asked with mock deference.

'But you're only a member of the public,' said Watson, 'and you can't come in here. Please leave immediately.'

'I'm so sorry, Mr Watson, but special arrangements have been made for me. Here is the authority showing that I may enter.'

Curtis and Watson looked at the document. Eric groaned as he returned it. Petrie smiled sympathetically.

'I thought there was one place where we could drink and talk without you butting in?' said Watson. 'Haven't you pestered us enough for the time being?'

Curtis touched his friend's arm and turned to Amos.

'Welcome to the fold, Mr Petrie,' he said. 'What is it?'

'Humble beer, just humble beer. I never impose upon people.'

He fingered his newly filled glass and stared at the empty bar.

'Have you all got guilty consciences?' he inquired.

'You wouldn't have thought so if you'd entered a couple of minutes earlier. They were cheerful enough then.'

'So I noticed as I walked along. My hearing is most remarkable. I developed it listening to the soft breathing of fish. Seems that quite a number have made a killing on the Stock Exchange, eh?'

Both men looked at him suspiciously. Certainly his hearing must have been more than acute.

'They have been taking some of the gifts the gods give them,' said Curtis. Watson did not speak. He looked at the little man as though an ill wind had blown in some unfortunate refuse. Petrie continued to smile.

'Do you think they deserve these gifts?' asked Petrie with doubtful innocence.

There was mockery in Curtis' reply:

'It would be disrespectful to say they didn't. It might be breach of the high privileges of Parliament to say they did.'

On that ambiguous note Curtis smiled and walked away. Watson watched his exit with increased misery. Then he started to follow him. Petrie placed a gentle hand on his wrist.

'Just one moment, Mr Watson. You can tell me a few things I'd like to know. Do you think it improbable that there was any advance buying of shares before the Budget?'

'I do. Astonishing, isn't it?'

Amos smiled tolerantly and rearranged his spectacles.

'Sarcasm, Mr Watson, is a double-edged weapon. I'd advise you not to use it. It may turn out to be a boomerang. I think you're wrong about the advance buying?'

'You have proof of that, of course?' The tone was still scornful.

'I'm seeking information—not giving it.'

'And being in search of information you encourage me by demonstrating that lack of consideration you've given me in the past? Every man here will suspect me further when they know that you've singled me out again for an individual interview.'

'They must have nasty minds. You talked about encouragement. I don't encourage you at all. I make no promises and no bargains. But I do offer you the opportunity of assisting me. I can visualise certain circumstances in which you might be glad of it.'

'I think it might puzzle you to name them.'

'It is at least an alternative to a crime of passion.'

Watson threw back his head as though he'd been stung. His eyes widened as he glared at Petrie. The little man looked at him as though his last comment was endowed with complete innocence.

'You sicken me with your talk about crimes of passion, Petrie.'

'Why? Have you never heard of such a thing?'

'It is pure piffle, absolute rubbish.'

'Quite, quite.' Petrie's manner was entirely unruffled, his tone placid. 'But if you were a policeman . . .'

'Which, thank God, I am not,' snapped Watson, tempestuously.

'. . . you would know that women or money, and sometimes women and money, are at the bottom of ninety-nine murders out of every hundred. Why not help me to show that Reardon's murder was a matter of money? It would suit you better that way.'

The bite in the last sentence was unmistakable. But the little man was still smiling as he toyed with his glass. Then he tilted his head to one side like a bird and peered at Watson.

'I can see through you and your tricks, Petrie.'

'I hope you do, I sincerely hope you do. I've done my best to make my meaning plain. Do you realise that I could have detained you this morning—and would have done so if I had thought that you'd try to get away?'

If Watson's heart did not miss a beat his face belied him. It was purged of anger. Now it reflected doubt, with fear not far away in the background. His ashen cheeks told their own story.

'Isn't this something like gross intimidation?' he asked, trying to bluster and failing hopelessly.

'I hope not. You have only to say that you don't want to speak and that ends the argument.'

'But you had nothing whatever against me on which you could have held me. I am a solicitor myself. You forget that, don't you?'

'I do not. You were nearer to Reardon before his death than any other man. You poured out his drink for him. If the motive was money—well, you could discover the contents of that Budget in time to make a fortune for yourself. If the motive for the murder was passion—well, you loved Mrs Reardon before she was taken from you, and you still love her. The strophanthus seeds were in your flat, and the story of the robbery was not too convincing. You reminded me that you are a solicitor. Work those few odds and ends out for yourself.'

Watson gulped. 'What is it you want to know?' he asked.

'The names of those in this House who might have had advance information about the alteration in taxes.'

'None outside the Cabinet, and the Financial Secretary. I didn't know them myself. Mr Reardon was very, very cautious.'

'Know of anyone outside who would want to delay the Budget?'

'No one knew what was in it. Sometimes trade interests are consulted under pledge of secrecy, but that wasn't necessary.'

'Anyone talking here tonight show special knowledge?'

'No. It was just idle talk—nothing more or less.'

'I think,' said Petrie slowly, 'that I will now see the widow.'

'Have you been playing with me all this time?'

'No. I'm committed to nothing except to finding the murderer. I have a perfectly open mind. But you've added little to what I know.'

'Well, I'll come with you to Downing Street.'

'I won't stop you. I can't very well. But I'll give you a strict warning before we leave this bar. You would be well advised, very well advised, to see that you don't in any way interfere with any inquiries I may make either now, or at any other time. I am ready to see Mrs Reardon immediately. As we walk think over what I have just said. It may save you more than mere trouble.'

Watson turned and breathed a curse into his empty glass.

They left the bar.

CHAPTER VIII

ANOTHER SHOCK FOR PETRIE

THEY walked in silence to Downing Street. Amos was wondering what line of inquiry Inspector Ripple was following. Watson was struggling to assess the amount of the small man's knowledge. The first inkling they had upon their arrival at Number 11 that more trouble had arisen was presented to them with such emphasis that it carried along the passage through two doors. The butler had announced their names.

'Let them come in!' shouted someone. Amos had had a wide and unfortunate experience of frigid welcomes, but never before had he heard an invitation quite so harsh and forbidding. It was with difficulty that he recognised the voice of Mrs Reardon. It was laden with passion, saturated with anger. Before they advanced far along the passage they heard a plaintive remonstrance.

'But my dear . . .'

'Oh, what does it matter?' shouted the widow. 'All London will know by tomorrow. There's nothing else that can happen now.'

Watson almost halted. Petrie wriggled with his handkerchief. As they entered the room their surprise increased. Mrs Reardon was pacing the floor as though anxious to tear some person to pieces, but undecided about the choice of the first victim. Her face was set in grim lines of anger, her hands twitched, her eyes shone with passionate feeling. Her pacing was ceaseless.

Standing near the fireplace was a man in the late sixties, high of colour, white of hair, wearing the resigned expression of one who has been swept away by uncontrollable forces. Occasionally he fidgeted with his tie, glanced at the newcomers without interest. Petrie had seen his photograph many times in the newspapers. It was Sir Clement Andrews, the father of the widow.

Close to him a woman lolled back in an easy-chair. Certainly she was more composed than any other person in the room. Petrie eyed her curiously. Her black gown was a trifle too ornate, her face showed that either she or her maid had abundant patience, her beauty had had its day and passed, but there were traces of a handsomeness in earlier years. She seemed amiably placid, gazed at the newcomers and smiled with an ease born of much use.

Standing by her side was Paling. He, too, seemed unmoved by the widow's anger. There was a trace of amusement playing round his face as he bowed to the two men. Watson walked over to Mrs Reardon; she moved away from him, continued to move to and fro like a caged tigress waiting for a meal. Petrie placed his battered hat under his elbow, coughed gently and waited for an explanation, or a storm. He was not certain which would arrive first.

'This is all very awkward,' said Sir Clement helplessly. Tone had left his voice. He waved his hands as though to indicate that as far as he was concerned conversation had ceased.

'Do you think it wise to speak now, Mrs Reardon?' asked Paling.

'Why should she not speak?' asked the woman in black. Her accent was slow, deliberate, obviously foreign. She chose the words with an effort. The widow wheeled round and glared at her. The stranger met the ferocious stare with a calm smile. Petrie began to feel uncomfortable as he waited for events to happen. He had no intention of starting the ball rolling himself.

'Do you know that woman?' asked the widow, flinging an arm in the direction of the stranger. Watson shook his head, Petrie nodded absent-mindedly, recovered himself, and muttered 'No.'

'Well, that is the former wife of Edgar Reardon,' she said with dramatic emphasis on the word 'that.'

Watson bowed towards the woman, too bewildered to speak. His hands were trembling violently. Amos produced his handkerchief, waved it in the air like a conjurer awaiting applause. For a brief spell the silence was uncomfortable. The little man decided that a short speech might lessen the pressure. He turned to face the strange woman:

'Delighted we should have met, madame. May I be insolent if I ask whether you divorced your husband?'

A laugh, mirthless, harsh and strident, burst from the English Mrs Reardon. Of all those in the room the woman in black seemed alone unmoved. She shrugged her shoulders as she replied:

'No, monsieur. He simply did what you call a bunk.'

Amos felt as though he had been hit in the face with a cold fish. Watson gaped, his mouth opened so wide that one wondered whether it could be closed again. The little man came up for a second breath:

'You don't mean that Mr Reardon abandoned you, madame?'

'Is that the word?' The accent became more definitely Parisian. 'I mean that my Edgar'—the other woman winced and screwed her lips—'just ran away from me. He did a bunk. You understand?'

'Yes,' announced Petrie too confidently. He was trying to cover his bewilderment. Watson's mouth was still open.

The Englishwoman came to the rescue of the party with brutal directness. As a housewife might rip down a curtain and let in the light, so she laid the situation bare:

'She has come to claim her place as my husband's widow.'

Petrie was too surprised to note the Gilbertian humour of the sentence. The Frenchwoman smiled proudly.

'Edgar couldn't have two wives, you know,' remarked Watson profoundly, and no one tittered over the inadequacy. He had expressed a feeling that was running through Petrie's mind. The Englishwoman stared mutely at Watson as though sympathising at his clumsy attempt to console her. Then she placed a hand on her breast and paced the floor once again with the tragic poise of Eleanora Duse. Her father eyed her fretfully.

'Tell me, madame,' said Petrie, 'how you came to know that Edgar Reardon was dead.'

'The newspapers. I read it in them. So I came from Paris.'

'There's a mistake here,' said Watson. No one quite understood what he meant. Probably he didn't know himself. Again there was a silence before he added lamely: 'A mistake, I said.'

'I hope for the sake of everyone that there has been some sort of a mistake,' said Petrie, 'and I'm waiting for one of you to tell me where I can look for it.'

His answer came from an unexpected source—from the English widow. She ceased to stride about the floor and faced Amos.

'There is no mistake about this marriage as far as I can see. How I wish to God there were. This woman seems to be right.' She breathed deeply, rushed into a torrent of words: 'The whole thing is ugly, sordid, revolting, terrible, too shameful to think about. Just think of me and my position. Just for a second—'

Her father tried to dam the flow. He held up a restraining hand and his daughter paused for long enough to give him a start. He spoke directly to Petrie:

'According to our solicitor whom I saw an hour ago there is a very considerable doubt about the validity of this first marriage. There is some issue of law involved. I don't profess to understand it. Apart from this woman's opinion there's no real reason to believe that Edgar committed bigamy. Knowing him as I did I think it will be found that he took advice about it and was informed on high authority that this pretended marriage was not valid in this country.'

His daughter scowled at him and repeated his final words as though they stung her—'in this country.' Again she repeated them. Petrie was expecting another outburst. While he waited he glanced round the room. Paling was smiling sardonically. The whole affair seemed to be amusing him. The Frenchwoman actually winked at the man and they grinned together. The English widow was too enraged to notice the action. She repeated again: 'In this country?'

Sir Clement had obviously tired of the whole affair.

'I said so,' he snapped. 'It's this country we're living in, isn't it? Or have I gone mad with the rest of you and I don't know where I am living? We know that your feelings are wounded, Lola, and that your pride is hurt. But that's no reason why you should get annoyed with me. Damn it, I had nothing to do with the business. You'd better make the best of it until you hear the truth. After all, you can't go back through the years and live your life over again just because something disagreeable has happened. It isn't as though you're not protected by the laws of this country so there's no need to get hysterical. After all, you haven't got to live as his wife. You're his widow.'

The Frenchwoman rose from her chair and stared at Sir Clement as though questioning his sanity.

'His widow? I am his widow. Edgar knew that I was his wife. He has supported me for many years. So I must be his widow. He has sent me money since I found him out about—' she completed the sentence by nodding towards Lola.

'Madame,' said Petrie, 'I think it is better that you should tell me exactly what did occur between yourself and Reardon. Don't hurry, tell me in your own way and be sure that you tell the truth. In this country women who tell lies about such things go to prison. Please start.'

'I was Elaine Peret,' she commenced, 'and was drawing for fashions when I met him.' The story dragged on for five minutes. It was the old, old narrative of young and impetuous people running into matrimony while in the blush of a first love. As Petrie listened the lines on his wizened face became more and more clearly defined. He drew forth his handkerchief and wiped his forehead. As the recital neared its end he slumped into a chair. The woman ceased to speak and everyone in the room looked towards Petrie. He saw that Paling was smiling, that Watson was more bewildered than ever, that Sir Clement looked as though the roof had fallen in on him. Lola was the first to speak:

'And what do you say about it now?' she asked Amos.

'The position is extraordinarily complicated,' replied the little man. 'The marriage was undoubtedly French. But it will take a French lawyer, skilled in the law, to say whether the marriage was valid in France. Then it will require an English lawyer to consider whether, on the view of the French lawyer, the marriage can be recognised in this country. Even then the matter would not be beyond dispute. If the issue was contested it might pass from court to court until it reached the infallible judges. Madame, did you by any chance obtain a divorce in France?'

Elaine had not followed the earlier part of his comments. But she understood the question and shook her head emphatically.

'A lot would depend,' said Petrie, 'upon whether Reardon intended to settle in France when he contracted the marriage.' He waved his hands hopelessly and added: 'But I'm a criminal lawyer and don't profess to know the international laws governing marriage. Paling, you seem to know something about this affair and so far we haven't heard from you. What do you know about this marriage?'

Paling paused before replying. The man was very confident; his hesitation was planned more for effect than reasonable doubt.

'I knew the lady in Paris before her marriage,' he announced, 'and I knew Edgar Reardon. The marriage was valid beyond all question. I can see no cause for argument about it.'

'No?' Petrie's tone changed. 'You have been friendly with the late Edgar Reardon in this country for the past year. You have visited his house, accepted his hospitality and been on terms of some acquaintance with his English wife. Do you mean to tell me that throughout the whole of that time you knew that he was actually a bigamist and that this unfortunate lady was unwittingly living with him in a state of adultery?'

Paling smiled, shrugged his shoulders, and made no reply. His nerves were functioning with uncanny efficiency.

'Tell me,' said Amos, turning to Elaine, 'why did Edgar Reardon make no attempt to divorce you?'

'He said that he would rather pay me than have his name in the newspapers because it would hurt him.'

'I am told,' said Sir Clement, 'that if Edgar did not obtain the consent of his father the marriage may not have been valid even in France, and that's how it looks to me.'

Lola flung her hands in the air and laughed appallingly.

'Thank you for nothing, father. That only makes things worse.'

Watson struggled to throw oil on the seething waters and merely succeeded in making matters worse:

'Was Edgar's father alive at the time of this French marriage?'

'We—eh—we have not been able to discover that in the time at our disposal,' replied Sir Clement. Then he added fuel to the flames in another rescue attempt: 'But either parent might do.'

Amos, without stopping to consider the effect of his words, expressed the thought that had been in his mind for minutes:

'This is going to produce some very unusual evidence at the inquest tomorrow. It will be very remarkable.'

Lola's breast was heaving as she whipped round towards him.

'We've had enough of this humbug. You can't tell how sick I am of the whole affair. I'll tell you all one thing. I will not appear at the inquest tomorrow as Edgar's widow. This woman can give the evidence I should have given. I simply will not do it. If she wants to keep saying that she is the widow she can get along to the inquest and tell them all about it.'

Watson stepped to her side and laid his hand on her arm.

'But, Lola, that will just mean blazing the scandal abroad.'

'The scandal is here,' screamed the woman, flinging an arm out to point to Elaine. 'We cannot stop it now.'

'Rubbish!' said her father. 'You're making a fool of yourself.'

Elaine still twisted her mouth as though slightly amused. So also did Paling. Lola started to shout again. Her father raised a hand and checked her:

'Listen for a moment, my dear, and calm yourself if you can. I've told you already that this trouble can be hushed up. You can't retain the whole thing as a secret if you act like this. Above all we don't want any scenes at the inquest. These things are much better arranged through solicitors and that is what I suggest should be done. We might arrive at some arrangement without wallowing in filthy publicity.'

Petrie was surprised to see that the Frenchwoman nodded her head, and parted her lips to smile more broadly.

'I have come here to get my rights,' she announced.

The little man eyed her closely before firing a bullet:

'But you have no rights, madame, if Edgar Reardon left his money to somebody else.'

Elaine bent back as though she had been struck. It was Paling who spoke for her:

'She has very definite rights if the deceased left his entire estate to his wife. She is his legal wife.'

'I think,' remarked Amos, 'that I can see the position insofar as both of you are concerned. How much would you take to settle the whole matter and retire from the scene?'

'But I want my rights,' insisted Elaine.

'I'm asking you what you want for your rights. How much?'

The woman looked at Paling, and he replied for her:

'Mrs Reardon was being paid twenty thousand francs a year by her husband. If that annual sum were continued I imagine she would make the sacrifice of retiring from the scene.'

'Rather a wholehearted sacrifice,' said Amos. 'What do you say about it, Sir Clement?'

'I am not satisfied about the affair, but I think it is worth the money to avoid the scandal. I advise you to accept the offer, Lola. We don't want our names blasted all over England.'

'All right,' said Lola wearily. 'I hate doing it and I don't think she is entitled to a penny. But I'll agree to save any more unpleasantness. Twenty thousand francs a year it is.'

'C'etait un tricheur, mais il etait adorable,' murmured Elaine, sighing as though it broke her heart to accept the money.

Petrie turned away in order to smile. It seemed a curious epitaph for Edgar Reardon. Watson produced a pen and sketched out a temporary agreement for signature. Amos was amused to note that Paling added his name as a witness.

Elaine left the room like a defeated army. But the smile of a conqueror played round her mouth when she climbed into a taxi.

CHAPTER IX

SUPPER FOR THREE

PETRIE arrived at the corner of Whitehall before the taxi left 11 Downing Street. Luck was with him. A detective was crossing to enter the approach to the Yard. Amos hailed him and gave hurried instructions:

'Man and woman in taxi just leaving 11 Downing Street. Collect a cab, follow them, and let me know all that happens. Don't let them lose you. I'll tell Inspector Ripple what you're doing. If you can get near enough to hear them talking that will suit me.'

The detective nodded, waved for a taxi, and when Paling and Elaine came round the corner the Yard man was tailing them. Petrie watched the two taxis from the far side of Whitehall, breathed relievedly and walked along to the Yard.

The first taxi entered the roundabout at Charing Cross, turned into Cockspur Street, rounded by the National Gallery and travelled up Charing Cross Road. The second cab followed tamely in its wake. Where Charing Cross Road forms one ray of a star-shaped crossing both were halted by automatic signal. The second taxi glided abreast of the other one in the jam. Madame was sitting stiffly in one corner of the taxi, uncomfortably stiff. If she and Paling were old friends it looked as though the friendship needed some refurbishing. The signals flashed, and the first taxi took a sharp turn along Holborn, and both were stopped again where the four roads meet at the top of Kingsway. The Yard man was so near that he could hear the woman shrilling protests. Paling's cab moved down Kingsway, and the Yard man was able to pull abreast. Paling was, by now, a little less deferential. The woman was more strenuously voluble than before, but her words were lost in the roar of London's traffic.

Paling's taxi went westward along the Strand. The Yard man could no longer get alongside. The driver knew his job. One doesn't stand on the nearest rank to Scotland Yard without learning things! It seemed that Paling and Elaine were on their way back to Downing Street, but they swung once more into the eddy that swirls round Trafalgar Square. The Yard man smiled. He had followed people like this before. Again they circled to Holborn and down Kingsway. It was then that Paling noticed the following taxi. His driver twice slowed down to let it pass. Each time the effort was unavailing.

'We're being followed,' said Paling. 'I'll stop this.'

At Wellington Street, Paling was so annoyed that he complained to the point duty policeman. But he obtained no relief. The constable strolled over to the taxi, looked inside, and returned to report to Paling that a driver was entitled to drive an empty taxi anywhere he pleased.

Opposite St Mary le Strand, Paling opened the near side door, handed the driver ten shillings and led Elaine along the pavement. They did not notice the Yard man alight from the taxi on the far side of the road. Had he been nearer to the walkers he would have heard a whispered conversation that would have interested him. There was a briskness, almost amounting to gaiety, in Elaine's step. Paling also seemed pleased with life.

'There is nothing left to negotiate, my friend,' said Elaine, 'so we can enjoy ourselves.' Curiously enough, it seemed that her command of English had strengthened since they had left Downing Street. 'It is quite finished now without your assistance, eh?'

'Is that so?' inquired Paling. 'Another half million or million francs have no interest for you, Elaine? No attractions at all?'

The woman's eyes glistened but her reply was firm:

'I'll not risk what I've got for the sake of what I may not get.'

'You forget, Elaine, that you get only what I choose. I don't want to force you to come in with me. But you've had no reason to complain in the past, have you? You got the allowance I promised you in Paris.'

'But that was from my husband,' she protested.

'Out of his pocket. Got by my hand,' said Paling grimly. 'If it had not been for me you'd have got precious little.'

The suggestion did not suit Elaine. She shook it off as a cat shakes off water.

'Well, if you hadn't got it for me I'd have come over and got it for myself—just as I have now.'

'Yes? If you'd have done, my dear, you'd have been in prison—or dead by now. I fancy you'd have been dead.' She shivered a little. 'Our little Edgar,' he continued, 'could be very, very obstinate. I know he'd got some idea of proving that you ceased to exist.' His tones were low and level, but Elaine could not mistake the menace. She understood the man and pulled her coat closer to her body like someone who has become suddenly susceptible to a draught.

'Listen, my friend,' she replied. 'You went to stay near Edgar so that you could arrange things. You were with him a lot. Poor Edgar died. It was a pity, but it happened so. Now I have no thought or intention of dying. Not me. You understand?'

'Perfectly. What I am proposing is that you should be prosperous as well as long-lived and happy.'

There was a silent pause before the woman commented:

'I know, my friend. But I think that to be all these things I must be a little self-reliant. I must not rely so much upon the kindness of other people—yourself, for instance.'

Paling bit his lip and looked at her. She was smiling, smiling without a trace of amusement in her eyes.

'We stand or fall together, Elaine,' he said. 'I told Edgar that a year ago, and I tell you so today.'

'Let's talk about that over supper,' was the evasive reply. They swung through the doors of a fashionable hotel, the Yard man following four or five yards behind. Elaine immediately walked up to her bedroom. Paling strolled into the dining-room, selected a table for two and beckoned to the waiter. The Yard man chose a seat on the other side of the gangway, not more than five feet away, and ordered a meal. The waiter walked away with a pasteboard in his hand. In the bottom left-hand corner were the words 'New Scotland Yard.' The detective was more than half-way through his meal and Elaine had not appeared. Paling grew more and more restive. He fingered the menu irritably and constantly glanced towards the swing doors at the entrance. Twice the waiter approached to ascertain his order. Each time Paling told him snappily that he was waiting for a companion.

Finally Paling scribbled a note, handed it to the waiter and gave him Elaine's room number. The waiter turned to find the Yard man winking at him. Paling drummed on the table with his fingers. The messenger quickly returned and placed a note before him. The man read it, scowled, and flung it into the fireplace. Then he strode out into the booking office. When he returned it was to inform the waiter that he no longer wanted the table. He ordered food and wine to be taken to him in his bedroom. He retired.

The waiter handed the detective a menu card while he walked over to the fireplace. From there he picked up the piece of crumpled paper. On the back of the menu card was scribbled:

'Please hurry. I am tired of waiting.'

On the paper salved from the grate was pencilled:

'A thousand apologies. I have a headache and have decided to stay in my room.'

The Yard man beckoned to the waiter, handed him a pound.

'Settle my bill for me and find out the number of that man's room. Give me, also, the number of the room to which his note went.'

Within a couple of minutes he had both. Leisurely he ambled into the foyer towards the reception office, informed the clerk that a friend of his was staying in Room 78 and requested Room 79 as a favour. He was compelled to accept room 77. He certainly did not act like one desiring sleep when he reached the bedroom. He spent some time balancing the advantages of the hinges and the keyhole for purposes of observation. By comparison there was little to be said in favour of the keyhole. So he set the door at a convenient angle, turned out the bedroom light, selected a chair and sat down by his observation point.

Two hours passed and the noises of the hotel died down into the stillness of the night. It was tedious waiting. The Yard man rubbed his legs to prevent stiffness. At last he heard a creak of boards on the corridor floor and peered through the door hinge. Paling stood outside the woman's room.

Softly the man tried the door handle. The detective heard him mutter. The door was locked. Paling beat lightly on the panel. No sound came from Elaine's bedroom. He repeated the signal and again there was no answer. This time he knocked more insistently.

'Who is there?' called Elaine.

'Paling,' whispered the man. The detective could hear both of them. There was a pause before the woman called angrily:

'If you don't go away I'll raise the hotel.'

'You little fool,' muttered Paling savagely. Then he dropped his voice to a pleading tone: 'It is me, Elaine. I want to speak to you.'

'Oh, it is you,' called the girl in a full, round voice. She spoke almost as though she thought Paling was deaf. He glanced with apprehension along the corridor. So far there was nothing to disturb him. He sent a penetrating 'shish' through the door to warn her. Apparently she did not hear him. Her tones were more penetrating as she called:

'I thought it was a thief. What a pity that I can't open the door. I'm in bed. You'll have to wait until the morning.'

'What I want to say can't wait,' he insisted.

'It must,' shouted the girl, speaking as though stifling a yawn.

'Just listen to me, Elaine. If you—'

He ceased suddenly. The tinkle of an electric bell sounded in a distant part of the hotel. After a moment of silence a door banged. Voices were heard and the approach of footsteps. Paling swore again, this time in a louder voice. But he returned hastily to his own room.

Elaine had summoned help! A night floor waiter appeared and knocked on her door.

'Yes, madame? You rang?'

'I thought some man was knocking at my door.'

'There is no one here, madame.'

'Thanks. Sorry to have caused this trouble.'

The waiter retired. So did the Yard man. In a couple of minutes he was heading towards Whitehall. The hour was late, but he found Petrie and Ripple waiting for him. The Inspector was yawning and miserable. Petrie was immersed in a copy of the *Fishing Gazette*. They listened for ten minutes to the story told by the detective. Amos appeared intensely interested.

'Congratulations,' he said. 'You've done a very fine job of work. Now you'd better get along to bed. See you tomorrow.'

As the door closed Ripple yawned again.

'And what exactly has that taught you?' he inquired.

'You'd be surprised, Sunshine. Human nature is very funny.'

'I think that every time I meet you. Joking apart, what sort of headway have we made? None. You've miked around with the whole affair ever since it started. Every time I suggest that we do things you tell me that you're waiting for the inquest. Why? Do you think that it's going to present you with a solved murder?'

'Not a bit, Angel. But I fancy it will tell me where to start, and that's something to be going on with. I know plenty even now, but if I make a rush I'll probably spoil the whole shoot. Be patient, little one, and see what the inquest brings forth.'

'You can afford to talk like that, but I can't. If anyone has to take a fall it'll be me—not you. Had you thought of that?'

'I had. Tell me, Sunshine, have I stopped you making any inquiries? Have I fastened you down in your chair, and told you to be a good boy and stay in the nursery?'

'Damn it all, though, this isn't an ordinary murder. They haven't found a servant girl battered to death in Battersea, or a tramp throttled in Tooting. The dead man was the Chancellor of the Exchequer and the murder was in the House of Commons.'

'You surprise me. Who told you all this? Better have a sleep and see what tomorrow brings forth. That's what I'm going to do. And, little one, next time you want to find a man for promotion you might remember the lad who did that job tonight. It was smart.'

'Quite good. I'll see you here in the morning—unless I've been sacked in the meantime for doing nothing.'

'No, I won't come here. I'll see you at the inquest, but don't sit with me. I'd rather find my own place.'

'Getting rather fastidious, aren't you?'

'Always was. We fishermen were born that way. It's an old angling custom. Watch the folks carefully at that inquest, Ripple. You might see more than you'll hear. Adios. I'm on my way.'

Petrie walked to his bachelor flat whistling cheerfully, but most catastrophically out of tune. He had no head for music.

CHAPTER X

THE INQUEST

LOLA REARDON imagined that inquests were unpleasant, but she never anticipated that the discomfort could be so considerable. Her seat was greased and blackened by the clothes of those who had occupied the benches before her and the air was tainted with the smell of carbolic, dirt and perspiration. Beyond all that, however, the Frenchwoman was sitting not more than three yards away. Watson, her father, and her solicitor tried in vain to assure her that all was well, that everything would soon come to an end.

Ripple sat facing the Coroner's table, immediately in front of Lola and her party. To his right were Curtis, John Ferguson, Sam Morgan, the Home Secretary, and Tranter. To his left were Elaine, Paling, Petrie, and Sir Norris Wheeler. It was most assuredly a distinguished inquest. That was one of Lola's main objections. She had attended with the deluded idea that inquests were matters for the police and members of the deceased's family. Watson, out of sympathy for Lola, was staring indignantly at Elaine, but she didn't wilt for a second under his glance. Still, there were shadows under her eyes. It seemed that there had been some inroad made on her self-control.

The Coroner's Officer bent over the English widow:

'Excuse me, madame, have you seen the body?'

The solicitor protested without success and she was led downstairs and across a yard to a wooden shed in the rear where she viewed her husband's remains through an imperfectly-cleaned window. The Coroner's Officer raised the draperies so that she might have a better view. Watson tried to smooth the way for her. While this gruesome ceremony was proceeding

Amos Petrie was trying to make things awkward. He was with the deputy for the Coroner of the Household, priming him with information, offering confidences about the difficulties connected with the inquiry, insisting upon points that required elucidation.

Mrs Lola Reardon was the first witness and it was not long before she discovered that it was easier to get on the witness stand than it was to leave it. Even over the matter of simple identification there was a difficulty. Whether her nerves were shaken or whether her conscience troubled her she alone knew. But she baulked over saying that she was the deceased's widow, and had been his wife. The hesitation irritated the Court.

Mr Deputy Coroner Leyland had a complexion not unlike that of the corpse. His mouth was closed in a thin, impatient line, and his cheeks twitched reproachfully—like a pair of ears that move. To close the matter Lola produced her marriage certificate from her vanity bag. She was less difficult when asked about the last occasion when she saw her husband. Before he entered the Chamber she was with him in his private room.

'And did he seem happy when he was with you, or did it seem to you that he was worried about something?'

'He seemed quite happy as he talked to Mr Ferguson and myself.'

'So the President of the Board of Trade was with you both?'

'That is so. I remember that Mr Ferguson offered to show me the Budget before the speech was delivered.'

'Mr Ferguson did? Sure you're making no mistake?'

'I'm quite certain that I'm not.'

'How did Mr Ferguson come to be in possession of it?' Leyland seemed astonished. A murmur of whispering passed round. Ferguson raised a hand and loosened his collar.

'I don't know that he was in possession of it,' replied Lola. 'I suppose he could have got it from somewhere if I wanted to see it. He certainly didn't have it in his hand if that's what you mean. He may just have been joking with me.'

John Ferguson rose to his feet somewhat haughtily:

'Perhaps I may assist the Court? As a member of the Cabinet I would naturally know the contents of the Budget. At most, had I spoken, it would have meant a disclosure to a Minister's wife. No such disclosure was made. Insofar as the witness is concerned the papers remained locked in the morocco case.'

'Thank you,' said Leyland.

The Deputy Coroner put his finger on the vital point: 'You are sure, Mrs Reardon, that the case containing the papers was locked?'

'Oh, no. I'm not. I can't swear to that. I assumed that it was, but I don't know. My husband would have had the key in any case.'

Her reply caused some uneasiness in Court. The witness was making heavy weather.

'Did you see the speech, or hear what was in it, until your husband commenced to deliver it?'

'No. I was in France when my husband was preparing it.'

Amos had not prepared Leyland for any answer like that. It was news to him. Leyland blundered in:

'Was it your husband's wish that you should be away during that period, Mrs Reardon?'

Petrie waited anxiously. Leyland saw the apprehensive expression on the little man's face and his cheeks twitched.

'He didn't exactly tell me to go away. But he did not want to go to Paris himself so I went alone.'

Elaine sat back on the bench and smiled. Petrie did not.

'Were you in the private room all the time Mr Ferguson was?'

'No, but he was present the whole time I was there. I actually left the room with Mr Ferguson.'

'Did either Mr Ferguson or your husband drink wine while you were in the room?'

'No. I didn't see any wine at all. I don't know how many people saw my husband in that room before he entered the

Chamber but there were others. Mr Watson must have been one of them and I heard—'

'No, no, no!' said Leyland raising his hand. 'Don't tell me what you heard. We must get that in direct evidence from another source. Only tell me what you know. Did you see Mr Watson in the room?'

'No. But he was my husband's Parliamentary Private Secretary. They hadn't met for a week. Mr Watson had been in Paris.'

A whisper ebbed round the room.

'Was Mr Watson with you in Paris?' asked Leyland tonelessly.

'Most certainly not!' snapped the witness indignantly. 'I was with my father.'

Mrs Reardon spoke:

'Of course, I met Mr Watson in Paris. He happened to be staying in the same hotel as my father and myself.'

'Then he was with you?'

'Only in that sense.' She reached for her smelling bottle. Watson was becoming hot round the neck. Amos glanced quickly round the Court as each question was asked and answered.

'You must forgive me for asking these questions,' apologised the Deputy Coroner. 'I don't know the facts and it is my duty to ascertain such facts as I can. May I take it shortly that you did not go to Paris to meet Mr Watson, or because he was there?'

'Certainly not. I went with my father as I have told you.'

'You probably did not know that Mr Watson was going to stay at this hotel at all?'

'It wouldn't have made any difference if I had. The hotel is much used by English people and I was with my father.'

Leyland frowned. There was a little too much insistence on the presence of the father. He recalled someone saying that a chaperon could cover a multitude of sins. Mrs Reardon seemed determined to talk herself into trouble. Before Leyland could ask another question she added:

'Mr Watson has been a friend of mine for years.'

'Did you meet Mr Watson at all last night?'

Petrie bent forward with a hand cupped over his ear.

'Yes. He called to see whether there was anything he could do for me in my trouble.'

'Did you meet Mr Watson by any chance the night before?'

Both Ripple and Amos waited eagerly for the answer. Leyland had reached the night of the robbery at Watson's flat.

'No, I did not. I was too upset to meet anyone. I wanted to be alone with my troubles. I was heart-broken. I remember that I was getting into a terrible state of nerves and went for a walk towards the lake in St James's Park. I was beside myself.'

'I well understand that. What time would it be when you took this short walk, Mrs Reardon?'

'Dreadfully late. It must have been almost midnight.'

'Of course you would not be out for long?'

'Certainly not more than half an hour.'

Petrie was working things out. So was Ripple. They glanced at each other significantly.

'Do you know of anything which would make a person wish to cause your husband's death?' The Coroner had got back to the questions which might be recognised as part of his routine.

'On the contrary, he was always on the best of terms with everyone. I don't think he had an enemy in the world.'

'Had he any living relatives except yourself, Mrs Reardon?'

'None that I know of.'

'That is not true!' shouted Elaine, springing to her feet and moving towards Lola. 'You know that is a lie!'

'Silence!' roared the Coroner's Officer. Elaine refused to leave the centre of the stage.

'Do you know that woman?' the Coroner asked Lola. The solicitor jumped up to speak. He was too late to prevent his client.

'I saw her for the first time yesterday,' said Lola slowly.

'Who is she?' inquired the Coroner.

The solicitor raised a restraining hand. Mrs Reardon refused to be curbed. She eyed Elaine, twisted her lips scornfully.

'I don't know very much about her. She puts forward some absurd claim to be my husband's wife. I believe she was his mistress in Paris many years ago. Because of that I have agreed to make her a compassionate allowance.'

Elaine's face blanched; her body shook. Paling shifted nervously on his seat, waited for the outburst.

'That is a deliberate lie, a most foul lie,' shouted Elaine. Then she added, as though further emphasis might be effective: 'It is a damn lie and she knows it is.'

The Coroner's officer bellowed a demand for silence. His chief flung down his pencil, cheeks twitching in agitation. But there were other and more active spirits in the room. A shuffling broke out near the door. The Coroner's officer put his mouth into shape for another shout. But before he could call, silence had been restored, unexpectedly restored.

Paling had bundled Elaine out of the room.

Amos admired the piece of stage management. He succeeded in attracting the attention of the Coroner, nodded to him. The old man looked towards Ripple and the Yard man also bent his head.

'It seems unproductive to proceed further with this inquiry until further evidence has been secured,' said the Coroner. 'I will adjourn the inquest for seven days.'

There was no opposition.

CHAPTER XI

AMOS PROBES DEEPER

On returning to Scotland Yard Petrie settled down beside the telephone. First he rang up Reardon's solicitors. His reception was coldly cautious.

'I am anxious to obtain some information about your client's financial dealings with the man Paling,' he said after introducing himself. 'Would you mind assisting me?'

'We don't know very much about the affair.'

'But you know enough to give me a little help.'

'I don't see that we can offer any assistance.'

'You must have papers, documents of some sort.'

'We have not got such documents as would enable us to supply the necessary information.'

'Really, I don't want to press you unduly, but it seems impossible that, as the deceased's legal advisers, you cannot assist me.'

'Apart from any other consideration, Mr Petrie, we are entitled, as you know, to reply that we are protected from inquiry.'

The little man was startled. He frowned and paused for a second.

'Do I understand,' he inquired unbelievingly, 'that you are claiming privilege?'

'You are a solicitor yourself, Mr Petrie.'

'And you realise that I am investigating a murder?'

'Quite. But that doesn't affect us, you know.'

Petrie pursed his lips. Veins throbbed at the sides of his brow.

'And you know that I can make you produce every paper you have?'

'By use of the proper machinery, no doubt,' was the smooth reply. 'Employ that machinery and you'll have no difficulty with us.'

Amos swallowed hard. This was a check he had not anticipated.

'Thank you. Before I ring off would you mind telling me the names of Reardon's executors?'

'Certainly. There were three, but one of them, William Ingram, has refused to act. The effective executors are John Ferguson and Richard Curtis. Perhaps they can assist you. Good morning.'

The little man telephoned Curtis at his chambers. He was not to be found. A call to the House of Commons was no more successful. At long last he managed to run Ferguson to earth. But the President of the Board of Trade was uncommunicative. Amos plied him with queries without success until he became exasperated.

'Mr Ferguson,' he said, 'I hope you'll do me the credit of assuming that I'm not asking these questions out of idle curiosity.'

'Yes, I quite appreciate that, Mr Petrie; but I'm afraid I haven't enough knowledge of the details to help you.'

'Broad facts will do at present. Can you tell me whether Paling received much money from the dead man?'

'I believe he received some.'

'About how much?'

'I'm afraid I can't help you there, Mr Petrie.'

'But, good gracious, Mr Ferguson! Don't you know whether it was a matter of hundreds, thousands, or tens of thousands?'

'My ideas about it are very vague. I believe it was a reasonably substantial sum. But you'll have to ask Mr Curtis about that.'

'I've tried to get in touch with him and can't.'

'I'm sorry that I can't assist you any further.'

It was hopeless. He telephoned Mrs Reardon at Downing

Street. Amos would not have been surprised to hear that she had flown to Paris, retired to bed, gone hunting, or was patrolling the bargain basements. He was surprised, however, when informed that she had gone out with her father, Watson and Curtis to take tea on the Terrace. He looked oddly at Ripple as he replaced the receiver and passed on the news.

'That little lady, Sunshine,' he remarked, 'seems to possess great powers of recuperation, but she hasn't much idea about what folks consider decent and fitting.'

'I've had doubts about her ever since I heard about that trip to Paris. I don't think she's exactly mother's blue-eyed angel.'

'Maybe not. Telephone Paris, grab anybody there who can make a tactful inquiry for us and ask them to find out whether she smells at all earthy in the place. When you've done that get in touch with Curtis at the House of Commons. Don't interrupt him at his tea, or they'll throw you into prison in the Clock Tower. Just lie in wait for him and after he's abandoned Watson and the widow ask him a few questions about Reardon and Paling. Don't say anything to Mrs Reardon. You can leave me to look after her.'

Petrie spent the next hour drawing cubist cows and wondering in which direction to make the next move. He telephoned Mrs Reardon and arranged to visit her immediately. She seemed excited when he arrived, more flustered than the little man had anticipated. Her father seemed to feel that there was a need for explanation.

'My daughter allowed herself to be persuaded by Mr Watson and Mr Curtis to go out for tea. I confess I didn't altogether approve at first of her visiting such a public place as the Terrace. But I am glad now that she went. The change has done her good.'

'The Terrace,' agreed Petrie politely, 'is very beautiful.'

Lola certainly did not appear improved by the change. Amos was regarding her steadily. She did not seem anxious to speak.

'And,' said her father, 'she has been much upset by what happened at the inquest and afterwards.'

'Afterwards?' Petrie's surprise vanished as speedily as it came. 'Ah, yes. You'll have received a letter from the Frenchwoman, I suppose?'

Both father and daughter stared at him.

'From her solicitors,' said the father eventually. 'That woman has been got at, definitely got at.'

'By Paling,' said Amos cheerfully.

'Eh? What's that? I knew she'd been got at by somebody. Lola, didn't I tell you that this afternoon?' He turned to her for confirmation.

She disregarded the appeal, herself putting a question to Petrie: 'How did you know?'

'Inference, Mrs Reardon, pure inference. At the inquest it was most obvious that they wouldn't stick at trifles to embarrass you, to make you thoroughly uncomfortable. But they did it in a way that preserves the value of what they have for sale. People like that never destroy their stock-in-trade. By now the Frenchwoman is well on her way back to Paris—if she has not already arrived. A man from the Yard saw her off. Still, there is something funny about this morning's affair.'

'I don't know what you mean.'

'I never imagined that she made today's demonstration for the joy of sneering about that allowance. It is equally clear that Paling does not intend to shout about what happened, because that would spoil his market. He relies with confidence on you saying nothing.'

'I certainly don't intend saying anything,' said Lola, shivering.

Petrie sympathised. 'Of course not. It was an outrage on your feelings. They were only able to do it with impunity because the inquest was private. If the Press had been present it would never have happened. Still, having made the threat the next step was plainly to make some claim against you in proper legal form.'

'That's precisely what the scoundrels have done,' said the father.

'Mr Curtis thinks we have no right to complain about the letter from the solicitors,' said Mrs Reardon. 'He says it is just the ordinary introduction to an action at law.'

'Mr Curtis ought to know,' assented Petrie. 'Of course, that's just what I would expect. They'll get all they can out of you without breaking the law. It is possible that that may content them. But it wouldn't surprise me if Paling wanted another bite at the cherry. I don't want to depress you, but your troubles may not be over when you've settled the action these solicitors are about to start.'

The father shifted uncomfortably in his chair.

'You mean that we'll have to fight it?' he asked anxiously.

'Or maybe separate the Frenchwoman from Paling.'

'How on earth do you suppose we can do that?' inquired Lola.

'That remains with you. Perhaps, Mrs Reardon, you wouldn't mind giving me Paling's address since you must know it. After that I would like you to invite him here for dinner. Would you mind?'

'Invite him here for dinner?' repeated the woman. Her tone might have suggested that Petrie had invited the bailiffs to distrain on her furniture.

'That's right. You do that and I may be able to help you. When he arrives you can talk to him about anything you like so long as you keep him here for an hour. Telephone him now, will you? Please give him the impression that the appointment is important.'

Lola hesitated for a while. Her father came to Petrie's rescue:

'The gentleman wouldn't suggest it, Lola, unless he had some very good reason. I would do as he wishes.'

She shrugged her shoulders hopelessly and grabbed the telephone. A couple of minutes later Petrie crossed Whitehall to the Yard. He found the lugubrious Ripple munching a ham sandwich.

'Hallo, lad. What has Curtis got to say for himself—if any?'

'This business is sending me mad. Everybody has gone dumb. I saw him after waiting for years and all I got then was that he was not in a position to discuss the matter until he had inquired further into Reardon's affairs. I tried to start him talking. Hopeless!'

'Too bad, Sunshine. I'm going to do something very illegal. Paling has accepted an invitation from Mrs Reardon to dine with her. While he's there I'm going to take a look over his rooms. Let me have a man to take with me.'

'But you can't do that without a warrant!'

'I'll chance that. Something tells me that if I wait for a warrant I might as well forget Paling altogether. After all, laddie, the risk is mine. Let me have a man and while I'm breaking the law you can scout round and nose along the same trail—what exactly was the scope and nature of the financial dealings between Paling and Reardon? That'll keep you away from the beer bars for a while.'

'Keep me away? Hell, man, all the King's horses and the King's men couldn't do that for you. I'll collect this man for you, but I know nothing about what you intend doing. Is that quite plain?'

'All right, Catastrophe. Find a man for me who can open locks.'

Ripple grimaced unpleasantly and hurried from the office. Five minutes later Petrie and a detective were on their way to Paling's. Once inside the flat they settled down to a systematic search. They groped inside the wardrobe, extracted everything from the desk drawers, looked into the bed, tested the floor-boards and Petrie even peered up the chimney. Eventually he settled down to search the man's clothing, turning every pocket inside out, examining the seams and peering inside the sleeves. Even each crumb of wool was scrutinised, shredded over a piece of paper and examined under a magnifying glass. As he worked the detective combed through the desk. He interrupted Amos to hand him a small cardboard box. The man made no comment. Petrie opened it, stirred the contents, looked at the inscription inside, stirred the contents again, made a note on the box, slipped it into an envelope and put it into his pocket.

'I wonder whether Paling ever took medicine for his complexion?' he asked. 'I knew he was fairly particular about his appearance, but I don't imagine he went as far as that.'

The Yard man shook his head. He did not know Paling; neither did he know what Petrie was talking about.

'I don't suppose he would,' said Amos apparently talking to the ceiling. 'But it's a great beautifier. At one time quite a lot of women took it for their complexions. They may still take it as far as I know. Course, you can make it into a medicine of various sorts. What they're all for—'

He suddenly ceased talking. There was every reason why he should stop. The angry voice of Paling cut through the air!

The man's tone was metallic and his eyes glittered. His appearance was as effectively dramatic as if it had been arranged with cue and prompter. The Yard man opened his mouth as though to speak, decided otherwise and remained silent. Petrie greeted him with a sunny smile.

'Well, well, if it isn't Mr Paling. Come right inside. You're very unexpected, but frightfully welcome all the same. You turn up just like fish, Mr Paling—when you least expect them.'

'What is the meaning of all this?' Paling pointed to the articles strewn over the floor.

Amos produced his handkerchief and continued to smile.

'Looks something like the aftermath of a jumble sale, eh? Come in and take a seat. I was beginning to feel the need of your assistance. May I congratulate you on the lightness of your step? Really, you should be decorating a ballet, Mr Paling.'

The man drew himself to his full height. He was four or five inches taller than Petrie.

'There was no special lightness of step required. Does one have to tread cautiously when entering one's own flat? But I am still waiting for your explanation.'

'Please don't grow impatient. Sit down and we'll have a brief and friendly talk.' Petrie did not apparently appreciate that he was inviting the man into his own home!

Paling scowled, walked over to the mantelpiece and stood with his elbow resting on it. The little man straddled on a chair with his arms leaning over the back of it. The Yard man, without waiting for instructions, stood between Paling and the door. Paling gave no indication that he had observed the move.

'Show me your search warrant,' he snapped.

'You travel far too fast,' said Petrie easily. 'I am here partly on Mrs Reardon's account, partly for other reasons.'

'Did she expect that you'd find some of her spoons here?'

'No, not spoons,' replied the little man placidly, 'but your acuteness has already recognised one set of circumstances which might have justified us being here.'

'But not without a search warrant. This is a most unpardonable outrage. You can't come into a man's flat like this and turn all his stuff upside down. I mean to see your search warrant. You hear me? I insist upon seeing that warrant.'

'I'm afraid you're going to be terribly disappointed.'

'What on earth do you mean? Haven't you got one?'

'If you make so much noise you won't even be able to hear why you're to be disappointed. That would be just too sad. I came here on an inquiry of some importance and I want to ask you a few odd questions about what we've discovered.'

'Naturally I shall refuse to answer any of your questions. Get out of my flat. Then I'll lodge my complaint in the proper quarter.'

'In that case I must take the responsibility of acting on the information I possess. But I must remind you that it is your duty to assist me if you can do so without incriminating yourself.'

'There is no question of incriminating myself. If you had come to me in an ordinary and decent way I would have been only too pleased to give you all the help possible. But after breaking into my flat and ransacking the place without a search warrant you can't expect me to say anything at all. Leave this place at once.'

'Well,' remarked Petrie calmly, 'let's see just how far you are prepared to go. It might be very interesting and very instructive.'

Amos paused deliberately, and commenced to play with his handkerchief. The Yard man and Paling stared at him as he continued to finger the silk square. The delay was producing a feeling of almost intolerable tension. Paling moved his feet restlessly, and slid his elbow along the mantelpiece. They could hear the clock ticking out the seconds. It seemed that Petrie had no intention of speaking. But at last he swung round a little on his chair, smiled at Paling disarmingly, and asked his first question:

'May I ask, Mr Paling, how it comes about that you have in your possession, or, at least, in this flat had in your possession, enough arsenic to kill at least ten men?'

The tick of the clock seemed to increase in volume until it filled the room.

CHAPTER XII

MR PALING'S METABOLISM

Petrie pursed his lips, and continued to fondle the handkerchief. The man near the fireplace coughed nervously. Then he straightened his shoulders as though the action gave him confidence. He sneered.

'My metabolism needs help from time to time, as you yourself might have acutely deduced.'

Petrie spread his hands in a gesture that might have meant much or nothing. He was still smiling.

'I see,' he said. 'Of course, that explains everything, doesn't it? Funny, I thought you resented it when I mentioned the arsenic.'

'Not at all. I resented your impertinence in coming here without my permission, and without a warrant.'

'Well, well. We've got beyond that stage now.' He produced the envelope from his pocket, and extracted the cardboard box, looking intently at the lid. 'Would you object to telling me when you purchased this aid to your metabolism?'

'I don't see why I should tell you, but the matter is of no importance. I bought it in Paris last January.'

'First week, second week, third week—or when?'

'I think it was on January 28th.'

'What a memory! How do you manage to arrive at the date?'

Paling checked himself when about to reply. The check was obvious, but not the reason. He broke forth impatiently:

'That wouldn't interest you in the slightest, Mr Petrie, and you can't possibly have any right to know what I was doing in Paris four months ago. I refuse to reply.'

'Can't you tell me why you went to Paris?' asked Amos artlessly.

'Why does anyone go to Paris?'

'Depends upon the individual disposition. I go there to get bored. Others go to make themselves ill. I don't know you well enough to take a guess. What had you been doing before you visited Paris?'

'Oh, if it'll save trouble and time I'll tell you. I'd been in Spain on holiday. I stopped in Paris on my way back.'

Petrie stirred his finger among the contents of the box.

'And in spite of your holiday in Spain you had to purchase this as an aid to your metabolism?'

'Yes, if you like to put it that way.'

'I can see no other way of putting it. And I see that your worst forebodings were realised. You have used the arsenic.'

'Some of it.' The air of outraged dignity was fast slipping from Paling, and he eyed Petrie narrowly. The little man slipped the box back into his pocket and changed the subject abruptly.

'Did you see much of Edgar Reardon during the week prior to his death?'

There was a momentary hesitation before the reply came:

'We were together throughout the whole week.'

Petrie elevated his eyebrows, and moved his fingers faster through the crumpled handkerchief. Paling licked his dry lips.

'You surprise me. Were you and your disturbed metabolism alone with Edgar Reardon?'

The Yard man smiled. Paling snapped his fingers irritably.

'We were no more alone than one generally is when staying in an hotel. You've found another mare's nest, Mr Petrie.'

'That's a habit of mine. I really am a most unfortunate man. You didn't mention this matter of the hotel to Inspector Ripple after the murder. Why not?'

'He didn't ask me, and I didn't think that it was important.'

'Really, really, really! You astonish me. What hotel was it?'

'A little place at Milford. We arrived on the Saturday, and returned to London a week on the following Monday. Anything criminal about it?'

'Not yet, Mr Paling.' Amos was too deferential. Paling paled again. The little man passed on artlessly: 'And at the hotel you either met people you knew, or you had visitors?'

'We had visitors. Mr Curtis and Mr Ferguson used to come over every night for dinner.'

'Every night—to Milford? Where on earth were they staying?'

'They were at Brockenhurst—staying for the golf, I think. They may have missed a night or two at the start, but I'm sure they were with us for dinner every day after the first Tuesday.'

'But whether they were there or not you were always with Reardon, and you stayed in the same hotel at night?'

'Of course. I'd hardly stay with him all day, and then sleep on the beach at night.'

'I expect that would have played the deuce with your metabolism. Was there any sort of quarrel or difference between you that week?'

'Not the least. He was one of the most intimate friends I had, and I'm certain that nobody enjoyed his confidence more than I did.'

'Had you any other position with him than that of friend?'

Paling looked a polite inquiry. Petrie put the question bluntly: 'You were not paid any sort of a salary by him?'

Paling laughed scornfully: 'I should say not.'

'Thanks. May I take your presence at Milford as a guarantee that nothing untoward happened, or could have happened, to him there?'

'Undoubtedly.'

'And that he met no one there who even threatened him?'

'Yes. I think I may say that positively.'

'Good. And you returned from Milford with him?'

'Yes, we returned together by car.'

'Arriving at?'

'Ten o'clock on the morning of his death. Mr Reardon had a lot to do that morning.'

'And you, Mr Paling?'

'I had plenty to occupy me, Mr Petrie.'

'Something absorbing but vague, perhaps?'

'Pardon me, you are wrong. Something definite, but private.'

'Very well. I won't press you. When did you see Reardon next?'

'After lunch. It would be about half-past two, I think, but maybe a little later. It would certainly be well before three o'clock.'

Paling drew out his watch and looked at it wistfully. He repressed an inclination to yawn. Petrie slid his handkerchief into his breast pocket and interlocked his fingers.

'Sorry to trouble you with all these details,' he apologised, 'but they're important. Let me make sure that I've got them accurately. Ten days at Milford with you during which time he saw no one but the hotel people, and Messrs. Ferguson and Curtis—one a member of the Cabinet, and both Members of Parliament. Then a gap of about four-and-a-half hours, which I can fill up if necessary. After that an hour in his private room at the House of Commons seeing you, his wife, Watson, and Ferguson. After that—'

'Just one second, Mr Petrie. Not forgetting that the folks you've named saw him after me.'

'I am not forgetting that. After that he spent one hour in the House of Commons in full view of everyone. And after that—death.'

'From a poison that acted on him within a minute or two of absorption,' added Paling.

Amos looked at him curiously, pulled out his handkerchief again.

'I had not forgotten that either,' he said quietly.

'I thought you had when you were questioning me about the arsenic. It certainly seemed as though you had.'

'Then you were wrong, Mr Paling. Your metabolism is not without interest for me. But I have not forgotten for a second that I am looking for a murderer who used quite a different poison.'

Paling moved away from the fireplace and smiled, showing two even rows of white teeth.

'Then let me advise you to look for your murderer among those who were on the floor of the House rather than among those who were in the galleries. I imagine you'll find it more productive.'

'Thank you for the advice. I will remember that.'

Paling commenced to move towards the door. Without moving, without change of expression on his face, Petrie's voice rose peremptorily:

'DON'T GO!'

Paling halted in the middle of his stride, stood uncertainly. His eyes distended a little, and his lips had parted. Then he looked from Petrie to the man between himself and the door.

'Sit down,' said Amos. 'You are being most helpful, and I'm sure you can tell me a lot more if you will.'

'Don't try ordering me about, please. It isn't the will that's lacking on my part. It is lack of knowledge and shortage of time.'

'We all have to manufacture time when assisting justice forward.'

Without further argument, Paling slumped into a chair and pulled out a cigarette-case. Petrie's next remark startled him.

'What you have said to me convinces me that you've formed a theory to account for the murder.'

'Not me! I leave that job to you experts. I have no business with it.'

'Surely your interest can't be so casual when the murdered man is your great and intimate friend? You were in the House of Commons and saw it all. You must have formed some impressions. Tell them to me. I'm a good listener, and they may be helpful. Fire away.'

Paling pulled at his cigarette. He spoke reluctantly:

'I would rather say nothing. If I express an opinion I may well be doing a grave injustice to somebody.'

'On the other hand, you might do a damnable injustice by remaining silent. I'll do my best not to be prejudiced by what you say. Come now, confess that you're thinking of that claret and soda.'

'It was a thing I noticed,' said Paling cautiously.

'When did you first think of that as a means of administering the poison?'

'When I was trying to work things out in my mind, piece things together, after the tragedy.'

'It never occurred to you as a possible danger beforehand?'

'Of course not. The idea never entered my head, and I can see no reason whatever why it should.'

'From your knowledge of Reardon, you wouldn't have dreamed that he could be hocussed into drinking poisoned wine that way?'

Paling blew smoke into the air and shook his head.

'Ah, that I cannot say. There may be so many factors. He might have drunk absent-mindedly, or he may have been thinking deeply.'

'Let me remind you, Mr Paling, that the dead man drank some of the claret and soda before he became really engrossed in his Budget speech. Have you tried to piece that into your scheme of things?'

'Yes, I remember . . . I'd rather not express an opinion.'

'I want you to help me about this if you will, because you knew Reardon's habits and faults—' Petrie hesitated, and added slowly: 'And you knew his tastes.'

Paling nodded and waited for the inevitable question.

'The dead man had a cultivated palate so far as wines went?'

'So, so. I wouldn't praise it too highly. He didn't help it by the spirits he drank. But it was pretty fair.'

'He would know a well-matured wine from one that was rough?'

'Oh, yes. I should say so. Certainly.'

'And claret and soda has a much less well-defined taste than pure claret. It's rather insipid, isn't it?'

Paling stifled a yawn and laughed.

'That depends upon the amount of claret and the amount of soda. You are asking me an impossible question, Mr Petrie. I don't drink claret and soda, and I have never tasted strophanthin.'

'I believe you! Let me make one further attempt. After all, I'm only asking for your opinion, based on your knowledge of the dead man. We will assume that claret and soda has as full a taste as pure claret, and I'll try to give you a means of assessing the taste of strophanthin.'

Paling waved the suggestion away with both hands

'Let me try,' persisted Petrie. Paling conceded with a weary bow.

'You know the taste of arsenic?'

Paling replied with a nod that was almost a start. His eyes were turned towards Petrie with a fascinated stare.

'Well,' said the little man, 'in the Seddon case, and again in the Vaquier case, arsenic was administered in medicine—if you call salts a medicine. But in both cases the victims detected the taste of the arsenic. In the Armstrong murder the stuff used was very much the same as that in this box. And there we had complaints of the taste, though the poison was given in wine. Now arsenic is not regarded as possessing a pungent taste. Generally it is spoken of as comparatively tasteless. On the other hand, strophanthin is referred to as bitter, extremely bitter. Does that help you to judge whether Reardon would be likely to accept doctored claret and soda as a sound drink?'

Paling pulled out his handkerchief and wiped his forehead.

'I don't see why I should be asked to make any guess of the sort,' he said. 'You have got the wineglass in which the drink was given. It seems to me that you're taking an unfair advantage of me by playing on my feelings for my dead friend.'

'Indeed I am not. I'm simply disregarding your feelings for the sake of obtaining your opinion. The wineglass you mention was washed long before I had a chance of laying my hands on it. Otherwise I wouldn't have been seeking indirect evidence. And you know Watson claims that the murderer is trying to saddle him with the guilt. I don't say the claim is justified, but I have to take account of it.'

'Well,' said Paling gloomily, 'you seem to be in a better position to judge than I am.'

'You don't know the drug strophanthin?'

'No, not at all.'

'Been to Tropical Africa?'

'Travelled there quite a lot.'

'And during those travels you have never even met it in its crudest form?'

'When I travelled in Africa I was there for the shooting. I did not go there to study native poisons.'

'So you can't be of any assistance to me?'

'I've helped you all I can.' An uncomfortable silence followed.

'I don't think so, Mr Paling,' said Petrie mildly. 'No, I certainly do not think so. I'm going to ask you to step across to Scotland Yard with me so that you can give the matter further consideration.'

'And if I refuse?' Paling showed some of his former spirit. He rose from his chair. The detective moved nearer to him. Petrie watched the scene, and wagged his head almost mournfully.

'With even your small experience of the ways of Scotland Yard,' he said, 'you must know that such invitations are never refused.'

'Do you mean—do you mean that I'm under arrest?'

'Dear me, no. But, if you insist upon some element of coercion, you may say quite accurately that you are detained.'

'Shall I take him, sir?' asked the detective.

'Thanks,' replied Amos. Paling offered no further arguments. He had arrived at the door when Petrie stopped them.

'Mr Paling, there is just one thing I want to say to you.'

'Then say it as quickly as you can.'

'Right. I want you to consider whether your own interests do not require you to make a statement in writing of all that happened at Milford, and up to the time you left Reardon in his private room at the House of Commons. What I have said to you tonight should clearly show you the need for it. If the theory of the poisoned wine has to be rejected, this murder cannot be dismissed as a haphazard affair conceived and carried out on the spur of the moment. There is a real possibility that something you might tell us would lead directly to the discovery of the murderer. Of course, you have to decide for yourself whether your own interests permit you to make such a statement. It is also my duty to remind you that such a statement might be used in evidence. Think it over. And please remember if you do make a statement that it will be of no use to make one which contains only that which you want me to believe. If you can't tell the whole truth it would be better to say nothing.'

Paling nodded his head, and walked from the room as though he carried a burden of great weight. Amos Petrie continued to sit in his chair, staring with vacant eyes at the open door.

When he finally moved he ambled over to the telephone, and rang Mrs Reardon. The woman's voice was agitated.

'How did it come about that Paling did not dine with you after he had made the arrangement?' asked the little man.

'I couldn't really tell you, Mr Petrie,' replied Lola. 'He seemed very nervous when he arrived, and suddenly said that he'd remembered another appointment. That's all I know about it. Why?'

'It doesn't matter. Tell me, how did your husband spend the New Year? Was he at home?'

'No, he was not. Why do you ask?'

'I'd just like to know where he went. Surely it's no secret?'

'No, it isn't. He went to Kenya. I remember it only too well, because I was nervous about him. And in Kenya it was difficult to keep in touch with him as he darted all over the place with his plane.'

'And what was he doing by the end of January—say the 28th?'

'He would be returning. He had to be back at the Treasury by the end of the month. Oh, I remember. He had met Mr Paling in Paris, and they returned together by plane. Was that what you wanted to know?'

'Thank you very much indeed. Good night.'

When Amos replaced the receiver he was smiling. He was still smiling when he continued to search the flat. Apparently it was the appointment to meet Reardon in Paris that reminded Paling of the needs of his metabolism!

The telephone bell jangled. Petrie walked over to the instrument. Ripple's startled voice, came over the wire:

'For the love of Mike come back to the Yard immediately!'

CHAPTER XIII

A CABINET MEETING

AMOS found Ripple pacing his office ceaselessly. The cadaverous face was more miserable than ever.

'Cabinet Ministers have been telephoning you here for the last few minutes,' said the Inspector. 'I managed to put them off until Sammy Morgan, the Home Secretary, rang up himself. I'm scared stiff. I dare not tell them you were out rifling Paling's place without a warrant.'

'What the devil do they all want me for?'

'It's a helluva mess all the way round. They got to know somehow what you were doing, and they want you to hold your hand against Paling until they've seen you.'

Petrie burst out laughing. Ripple became more worried.

'I'll be damned if I can see anything to laugh about,' he said.

'I can, Sunshine. I'm glad you didn't tell me that before. I might not have done what I have done. I've sent Paling round here—had him detained. I thought you'd have heard about it by now.'

'Oh, my God!' moaned Ripple, sinking into a chair, his face cupped in his hands. 'I should think you're sorry now that you did it.'

'Not I. What exactly do the lads of the Cabinet want me to do?'

'They want to see you. You know when we've worked together before you've left me a nervous wreck, but this time I feel as though the roof has fallen in on me. Try and not drag me into it. It doesn't matter if you get the sack because you've got enough money to fish for the rest of your life—and that won't last long. But I'm only a poor split. Gosh, I'm scared stiff. Damn Reardon! What did he want to go and get murdered for?'

'Maybe he enjoyed it. Listen for a moment, Dynamite. I've got a job for you, and it's important. Telephone Milford, or, better still, Lymington, and get the local police to discover all they can about what happened at the Milford Hotel. I want—'

What he wanted was postponed by the strident call of the phone. Petrie lifted the receiver. The Home Secretary was on the line.

'Yes, Petrie here,' said the little man. 'Sorry I was out when you rang before. I am just coming over. Right.'

'Morgan again?' asked Ripple as one might ask whether the mourners have yet passed through.

'Right first guess. I've got to go over to the House right away. Do what you can about Milford. I want to know what happened at that hotel during the week before the Budget. Get them to send some sort of a report in the morning. Oh, and get into touch with Paris, and see whether they know anything about Paling.'

Amos was still giving instructions as he hurried from the room. At the House of Commons he found the Rt. Hon. Samuel Morgan in a curious mood. The Home Secretary seemed nervous and vague.

'There is trouble of some kind,' he said. 'I don't exactly know what it's all about. But I can tell you, Petrie, that I don't like it. Ferguson is kicking up the bother. I know that strictly speaking it is none of his affair, none of his business at all, but he's got some sort of an interest in it. Ferguson is an awkward fellow to run up against, and I want to quieten things down. They're all in the Prime Minister's room now, and I told them that I'd take you along. I can't give you any details about the trouble, because I know nothing myself.'

Morgan seemed so apprehensive that he led Petrie to the P.M.'s as he might have led him to the stake. But in spite of his marked uneasiness he gave the impression that he was prepared to go to the stake himself if the work of the police and Amos was to be thrust under fire. They found five Ministers of the Crown waiting for them. One sat on the corner of the table, swinging his legs, Ingram sat in his chair, the others stood near the fire, watching Ferguson. The President of the Board of Trade was striding up and down the carpet as though on a quarter-deck. He stopped in full stride as Petrie and Morgan entered the room, looking at Morgan with a mute question. The Home Secretary shook his head, and Ferguson commenced to walk to and fro again.

'I thought so,' he muttered. 'I thought so. Upon my soul, if it isn't enough to make a dog sick.'

'Let's return thanks,' said Ingram, 'that there isn't a dog here.' He ceased bantering, and turned to Petrie seriously. 'Petrie, you've been worrying us to death. Partly that's the result of some of the questions you yourself asked Ferguson. Can you tell us what you have been doing since? We are most anxious to know.'

'Certainly I'll tell you,' said Petrie, calmly, looking closely at the men as he spoke. 'I have had Paling detained at the Yard.'

'Whew!' whistled Ingram. 'That's caused it.'

Ferguson ceased parading. The muscles of his face were twitching.

'What have you against the man, Petrie?' The smooth question came from the fireplace—from the Attorney General. Even those who did not recognise the mellow voice would have picked him out at a glance as a lawyer. The wig-polished scalp betrayed him. He was small featured, like a woman, with deep-set eyes, dark and glowing, and a mouth that closed as though operated with a zip fastener.

Amos wiped his hands on his handkerchief, his eyes blinked behind the thick-lensed spectacles. The Ministers waited eagerly.

'He had more opportunity of committing the murder than any other living being. Motive? I can't say yet. But I've found something which suggests intention. I don't say it isn't capable of explanation. I know quite well it is. But his explanations so far have not been very satisfactory. If he didn't commit the murder himself he's taking great risks to shelter somebody or to hide something.'

'Hide something,' snorted Ferguson. 'He may be trying to hide something that we all want hidden. What is this something?'

Petrie replaced his handkerchief, turned to face Ferguson.

'If Paling will give me an explanation which is more than a mixture of spoof, chaff and downright lying I may know. Failing that I thought it best to detain him until Inspector Ripple and myself discovered what that something was for ourselves.'

'Seems rather rough on Paling,' said Ingram, 'that you should lock him up on such slender grounds. I take it that you haven't made up your mind on the question of guilt?'

'Far from it.'

'But you've got far enough to dismiss Watson from your mind?'

'No.' The reply was emphatic.

'I thought you'd let him out when you detained Paling.'

'What have you got against Watson?' inquired the Attorney General.

'Opportunity, possession of the poison on the day after the murder, a possible motive in passion, and a great deal of foolishness.'

'You have not, however, thought it necessary to detain him?'

Petrie's mouth twisted oddly as he smiled.

'Not yet. But I wouldn't be surprised if he tried to leave the country without taking the formality of telling me first.'

For a space there was a heavy silence. The Attorney General was the first to speak:

'Do you mean that you've warned him?'

'I indicated to him that such a move on his part might create an unfortunate position.'

He saw the quick look flash between the Attorney General and the Prime Minister. Willie Ingram nodded.

'I think we can rely upon Mr Petrie's discretion,' he said.

Ferguson nodded glumly. The man appeared crestfallen.

'Well,' he remarked sullenly, 'you all know what my position is.'

The door opened. An M.P. hurried into the room.

'Joe Manning is up,' he shouted.

Ingram turned instantly to Ferguson:

'And you have to reply for the Government.'

'Oh, damn!'

'You'd better go,' said Ingram. 'They'll think it looks bad if you're not there to hear Manning. I don't expect I'll be long before I join you. While you're away I'll explain the position to Mr Petrie.'

'Don't worry,' said the Attorney General. 'I'll put in a word for you as well to see that you're treated as well as Watson.'

Ferguson nodded miserably and hurried through the doorway. Ingram clasped his hands together, and motioned Amos to a chair. The little man was smiling cryptically.

'I'll explain matters to you, Petrie. Ferguson is worried because he agreed to act as executor under Reardon's will. I would not have advised it myself. In fact, I don't know that I'd have permitted it had I known at the time that Ferguson contemplated taking such a step. In his own interests he'd have been better to have kept clear of the whole thing. But the other executor—Curtis—would not act without him, and there might have been a dreadful scandal. I am sure that Ferguson was inspired by the best of motives.'

The Attorney General cut in quietly:

'I don't think you need beat about the bush. We know Petrie of old. He's no fool, so I expect he knows what's coming.'

'I have people in the City making inquiries,' said Amos helpfully.

'What have they discovered?' asked Ingram, almost breathlessly.

'They have discovered,' replied Petrie deliberately, 'that there was a good deal of buying in industrials between three weeks and a fortnight before the Budget. I am now waiting'—he paused and slowed down to emphasise his words—'to obtain the names of the principal buyers.'

The Ministers looked at each other hopelessly. The Attorney General cleared his throat and settled the issue with dramatic suddenness.

'At the end of your inquiries, Petrie, you will find that under one name and another the biggest buyer of all was Reardon!'

There was an embarrassing silence. Petrie looked from one to the other at the men in the room. Ingram looked worried and ashamed. The Home Secretary was wiping beads of perspiration from his forehead.

'Let me understand exactly where I stand,' said Amos slowly. 'I don't want any unequivocal answer. Do you want this thing covered up at *all* costs?'

The Prime Minister looked towards the Attorney General for some guiding lead. Petrie stared at the ceiling and waited. The little man was no longer smiling. His lips had straightened into a thin line.

'It is not quite as bad as that,' said the Attorney General. He paused while weighing his words, and then added: 'We want you to use tact, Petrie, and avoid a scandal if you can.'

Amos shook his head and rapped on the table with his fingers.

'But the cause of the scandal may be the cause of the crime.'

'In that case the murderer will hang, and the scandal will have to be made public,' said Willie Ingram. 'If Ferguson gets mixed up in the scandal that'll be his funeral. He can't blame us.'

'I take it that our inquiries are to proceed as we think fit?'

'Don't misunderstand me, Petrie. We don't want to shield anyone from any punishment that ought to be coming to him under the ordinary law. If Reardon were alive himself I would conceive it my duty, and make it my business, to see that he not only retired from office, but was booted out of politics altogether, and for ever. But the man is dead. We can't punish him. The only question is this: Can the demands of justice be met without washing a very great deal of dirty linen in public?'

'In other words,' interposed the Attorney General, 'can you continue to treat the case with the judgment and discretion you've already exercised in regard to Watson?'

'I can certainly do that,' replied Amos. 'That's easy.'

'It is all we want,' said Ingram, sighing relievedly.

'There is one assurance I want,' remarked Amos. 'Can I take it beyond all question that once the murderer is found—if he is ever found—there need be, and will not be, any respecting of persons?'

The Prime Minister was so comforted that he lapsed into familiarity:

'My dear fellow, you can have me arrested if you get any evidence to justify it. We do not bind your hands in any way.'

'I am content,' said Petrie.

'Thank God that's settled,' commented Sam Morgan fervently.

'Not quite settled,' remarked the little man. 'Do you know what I'm wondering? What has all this got to do with any question I asked Mr Ferguson?'

The Attorney General clapped his hands and laughed.

'I've been waiting for you to get to that point, Petrie. It's been puzzling me all evening, but I left the job of discovery to you.'

The Prime Minister frowned, and looked round the room.

'I am afraid,' he said, 'that I have no very precise information about your question. Ferguson didn't make it quite clear to me.'

'It might be very helpful to know,' remarked Petrie.

'Well, I can't very well drag him out of the House while Joe Manning is on his feet. Besides the effect of the interview on Ferguson might be upsetting, and he's speaking for the Government in a few minutes.'

The Attorney General had a suggestion to make:

'Suppose I draft a questionnaire, and send it to Ferguson?'

'What sort of a questionnaire?' asked Amos.

'One to which he could give a simple answer.'

'I'm sorry, but I'll have to refuse your offer. I cannot put all I want into a questionnaire susceptible of simple answer.'

Again the Attorney General came to the rescue:

'What about Curtis, Ferguson's co-executor? Couldn't he supply all the information you want? We could send for him if you like.'

'Yes,' said Amos, after a pause. 'Curtis might do—so long as you made it plain to him that there is no longer any need to keep me in the dark, and fence with my questions.'

'I can arrange that without any trouble,' said the Attorney General. 'He is in the same boat as Ferguson, and he's no better pleased with it. It's rough on them both, of course. They are only doing their best—doing their duty by the House of Commons—in trying to hush up the scandal.'

'You can see him here if you like,' assisted Ingram. 'He's in the House tonight, and I expect he'll want to hear Ferguson. But we'll have him thrown out to you. You'll have the room quite to yourselves. We've all got to go into the House.'

Ingram swept his papers into an attaché-case. Amos smiled again when the Prime Minister slid a bottle of whisky, siphon, and a couple of glasses on the table. As the men were preparing to leave the Attorney General walked over to Petrie.

'By the way, Petrie, how did our lamented, but rather disreputable, colleague meet his end?'

'I won't know until tomorrow,' replied Amos hesitantly. Then he added: 'My people haven't found what I expected, and so it—'

'I suppose you hope that you won't have to trouble much about it after tonight? Isn't that what you're trying to indicate to me? Well, I hope you're successful, Petrie. Don't be too hard on the men who have been uncommunicative in the past. They didn't really mean to obstruct you. They were simply squirming away from the truth because they didn't want to take the lid off the story.'

'I'll try to bear no malice. We anglers have ample patience. There are times—' He stopped and turned suddenly to the Prime Minister: 'I've just remembered that I can't get along without a copy of the Official Debates for Budget Day. Do you think I could have one sent to me immediately? I can pass my time away reading that while I'm waiting for you to throw Curtis into the lion's den.'

The men grinned. This small, partly wizened, apparently nervous, and soft-spoken man didn't look much like a lion!

'Get it without going out of this room,' said Ingram. He walked over to a pile near the window, picked up his own copy, and handed it to Amos.

'Do you really think you'll find out how the murder was done by reading that?' asked the Attorney General.

'I hope so,' replied Amos modestly. The men stared at each other and strolled out of the room. Petrie was ploughing steadily towards a realisation of that hope when Dick Curtis found him later. Reading had thrown three vertical ridges on the little man's brow. But he was smiling happily as he turned down the page he had reached. Then he closed the volume.

CHAPTER XIV

PETRIE PLODS ON

'Ah, Mr Curtis,' he said 'I'm glad you've come at last. I have been deputed to offer you some of the Prime Minister's whisky.'

'To make me "talking drunk" I suppose?' Curtis smiled expansively as he walked to the table, and poured out a drink. They toasted each other, and Curtis turned his eyes back to the glass. 'Coming on top of the lecture I've just been listening to,' he said, 'this really does taste like an attack on the strings that tie the tongue.'

'Good barristers should never be tongue-tied. After our last conversation I thought it necessary to ask for some stimulants.'

The corners of Curtis' mouth twitched as he grinned.

'Perhaps I did err on the side of discretion. I am afraid your man Ripple must think the same too. But you understand the position now, don't you?'

'The Attorney General explained some of the difficulties.'

'I don't suppose he's left anything for me to add. What exactly do you want to know? I'll be a willing victim this time.'

'I want to know everything. But tell me this first. Why do the words "Paling" and "money" start everyone thinking of scandal?'

Dick Curtis sipped his second drink before replying:

'Because there is scandal, and because Paling is the original and true begetter of it.'

The little man shook his head with emphasis.

'Won't do, won't do at all. You'll have to be more explicit, much more explicit, if you're going to be of any help.'

Curtis slapped his glass on the table with a gesture of anger.

'Then I will be explicit, most explicit. Paling screwed about thirty thousand pounds out of Edgar Reardon in just over two years. That was roughly half the Reardon fortune. But Paling even then was not satisfied. He wanted more. Fifty-fifty did not satisfy him. That was what drove Reardon to the courses you've been exposing sedulously while we've been trying to cover them up.'

'Do you mean to tell me that it did not occur to you—you, a barrister—that these things might have a definite connection with the murder?'

Dick Curtis laughed softly while Petrie waited for the reply.

'It did not, my friend. Murder of Paling by Reardon—perhaps. But it certainly did not occur to me that Paling would want to murder his own milch cow. Work that out for yourself, Petrie.'

'Did Edgar Reardon ever threaten to murder Paling?'

'Oh, no. Edgar would never have dreamed of such a thing. I merely meant that he was driven half-frantic by his troubles. What he did was inexcusable, I know. But if you knew as much about the circumstances as I do you wouldn't be surprised that an honourable and public spirited man like John Ferguson is willing to take risks in order to protect his memory.'

'Then I'd like to put myself in Ferguson's position by knowing all about these circumstances. Before we come to that can you tell me when you first thought of Paling as a potential murderer?'

'After they told me that you had detained him.'

Petrie's eyes blinked as he looked inquiringly.

Curtis amplified: 'The human mind is a funny thing, Petrie. At tea time I would have laughed at anyone who suggested Paling as the murderer. Now I accept him as a possibility, and I look round for ways in which he might have hoped to make the murder profitable to himself. Yet the only thing that has happened in the last few hours is that you've locked him up. Have you ever tried to work out why a man's mind should jump in that way?'

'No. I only try to take advantage of the jump. I'd really like your assistance on the question of motive.'

'Oh, be fair, Petrie. I've only been guessing. I've nothing to go on.'

'Never mind. You can't commit criminal libel in here. We'll call the occasion privileged. Let's have the guess.'

'I'll do my best. There was a lawsuit being threatened. I needn't go into all the details, but there was a question of proceedings being taken to have Reardon's marriage declared a nullity. You are a solicitor so I need hardly remind you that if a marriage is void, and not merely voidable, a second marriage is not necessarily bigamous. Paling, of course, knew about that threat of a legal action, and in that fact you might find a motive.'

'But you didn't take that view of it when you were talking to Mrs Reardon. Why the sudden idea?'

'I've got no excuse. I never dreamed of it when I was talking to Mrs Reardon. It is one of the ideas at which I would have laughed.'

'Is that so? And what makes you dream of it now?'

'A sort of Hobson's Choice. If Paling did commit the murder that's the only way I can see in which he could have expected to make money by it. Of course, it simply begs the whole question: Did Paling commit the murder?'

'And it raises the question of whether it was more profitable to kill than to continue the extortions you've been talking about.'

'Quite. It assumes that Reardon grew tired of paying out. But these are questions for you, Petrie. Not for me.'

'Puzzling questions too,' admitted Amos, 'and I can't hope to solve them without assistance about the facts. Help me with those. Have you any reason to suppose that Reardon had made a stand and refused to be blackmailed further about this French marriage?'

Curtis sipped his whisky, smiled, and shook his head.

'I have and I haven't,' he answered.

'Let me judge,' suggested Petrie.

'Certainly. That's what I'm here for. But the facts seem to me to cut two ways. Payments made to Paling must have made it obvious to Reardon that a final breach was inevitable. Without full knowledge of the facts I told Edgar myself that he'd have to call a halt, and make a fight of it. He said he would. But he always wanted to put off the fight. So far as I could make out at the time he never took the step to bring it to a head. He didn't want to fight Paling, because the contest would have put him on the political shelf for two or three years, if not for ever. On the other hand he risked political damnation to retrieve his financial position. And he must have known that it would be impossible to keep Paling satisfied without running over the same course again. The man was a sink for money. Am I plain?'

'Admirably so. Did you know Paling's capacity for money?'

'Not a fraction of it. I only knew his type. Edgar used to come to me with his troubles from time to time—not as a lawyer, but as a friend; and he told me of some of the payments he had made. That's what made me advise him to fight Paling. But I hadn't the ghost of an idea that he'd parted with half his fortune until I began to look into his affairs as executor.'

'You knew enough to know that he couldn't keep pace with Paling?'

'I knew that Paling was a blackmailer, and that it's the hallmark of the type to double the demands, and then redouble them.'

'Have it so. And even if I am to assume that Ferguson is a fool—'

Curtis interrupted with an unusual brusqueness:

'You are to assume nothing of the kind. It is unfair to say that, or anything like it, about Ferguson.' He flung his cigarette into the fireplace, and poured out another drink.

'Oh, I'm not trying to be offensive,' said Amos. 'Still, my point is not unimportant. I've drawn my own deductions about the lawsuit, even though I know next to nothing about it. You carry your deductions further than I dared go, and your addition is one that I can't under any circumstance disregard. Let me present you with a personal problem. How is it that a man who can make such a helpful suggestion failed to see the relevance of the information you've been giving?'

'A searching question, Petrie.' There was something like approval in the nod with which Curtis accompanied the concession. He was no longer irritated. Neither was he embarrassed, nor apologetic for not having seen the point. 'I think your question disregards the vital importance of what I did *not* know.'

'Meaning that you were viewing the whole problem from an angle distorted by partial possession of the facts?'

'Precisely. But your question has set me delving into my mental processes in a way I find interesting. As the thoughts were mostly unconscious—sub-conscious, if you like—it isn't altogether easy to reconstruct them now. But let me try.'

Petrie poured some whisky into his glass, and squirted soda to the top. Curtis watched him suspiciously.

'Trying to drink plain soda water while I take whisky, Petrie?'

'Not at all. I'm a beer drinker pure and simple. Don't like short drinks. Now what about this reconstruction?'

'Here we go. Start with this. During Edgar Reardon's life I could see that my advice about making a fight of it with Paling was not being taken. Add that when I came to look into his affairs everything suggested that he had yielded to Paling right up to the end. There were quite recent payments, and the aggregate was staggering. Now in the ordinary way I don't expect a blackmailer to turn murderer. It is against his interest and against his nature. Generally speaking the blackmailing mind does not run to violence. Therefore, the extortion and the murder remain distinct in my mind. There are other things, vague things, in my mind, but those two stand out distinct. The murder and the blackmail are things apart, like this cigarette and this glass of whisky. Am I clear so far?'

'Definitely. Your legal brain is working well.'

'Right. Then I hear of the threatened lawsuit. Now that to

me does not stand out as a thing apart. Just as the blackmail might be represented by this cigarette, and the murder by the whisky so, to me, does the lawsuit compare with the soda in the whisky. Take the soda. Its neutral tint, its flatness of taste, and, above all, its stillness, make it sufficiently difficult to recognise as the ingredient that gives pungency to this drink. So I associate the lawsuit with the murder.

'Very well. Next thing I hear is that Paling has been detained on suspicion. That's a new idea, and it sets things moving inside my head. From the clouds in my brain a streak of lightning leaps, linking things that had previously been separate and distinct. I can't tell you how that flash started unless it sprang from something I had unconsciously observed. As I look back it occurs to me that I've often noticed peculiarities in the people who submit to blackmail. Why they don't go the sensible way about it and inform the police I don't know. But they don't. Generally they stand a terrible lot, and then do something utterly surprising. Mostly they go to the police when they're utterly ruined, and have nothing else to lose. Reardon, of course, did not do that. I said they act surprisingly. His surprise lay in the recoupment of his losses by an abuse of his position. When he had done that I can imagine him saying to himself, "Now I've thrown everything overboard. But I'm going to get away with it. Have I done it for Paling's benefit, or my own?"'

'That's not improbable,' granted Petrie. He was sitting tensely, following the theory with concentrated attention.

'It is not improbable. It is just possible that it may be right. But is it obvious? That is what I will ask you, Petrie.'

Curtis smoked while Petrie played with his glass. He seemed disappointed to discover that Amos had no intention of answering the question. The little man started on a new tack.

'You've spoken a good deal about blackmail.'

'I think that's the right description although I wouldn't use it to anyone else. In other circumstances I would not have used it now except that I was instructed—even ordered—before I came in here that I had to speak plainly, that it was an essential condition of our interview.'

'I appreciate the way in which you've opened your mind to me. I am grateful. There is something puzzling me very considerably. I have heard about Reardon's stay down at Milford. I understand you took dinner with him most nights. Tell me, wasn't there any sign of this trouble between the pair of them at Milford?'

'I knew of the trouble, of course. But unless I'm an awful duffer there was nothing special to be seen.' He paused, stared at his glass, and added: 'No, I can't recollect anything.'

'That rather tells against your theory, doesn't it?'

Dick Curtis waved his hand as an amused protest.

'Oh, have a heart, Petrie. I never put it forward as more than a guess. Don't saddle me with all your difficulties. I'm not the leading counsel for the prosecution. You're giving me his work without fees!'

'I want to make the most of you while I've got you in here.'

Curtis shot another tot of whisky into his glass, and raised it aloft with a smile. Petrie bowed towards him.

'Since I'm feeling both thirsty, and charitable,' announced Curtis, 'I'll give you until the end of the Prime Minister's whisky. If you don't regard that as a gesture of marked generosity I shall regard you as a dissatisfied man.'

CHAPTER XV

A MISSING DOCUMENT

PETRIE looked at his whisky as though calculating how long it would last. His own toll on the bottle had been light. But Curtis had helped himself with a heavier hand, and blood was beginning to suffuse his cheeks.

'If Paling murdered Reardon,' said Amos slowly, 'it seems to me most extraordinary that there should be no row, no noticeable friction even, in those eventful days at Milford.'

'It would be,' agreed Dick Curtis, 'and I don't say nothing happened. All I can say is that neither Ferguson nor myself noticed any sign of it. Paling dined with us each night, and, so far as we could see, everything was as it had always been. Paling wasn't exactly the best company in the world. But judging from his attitude while at Milford you wouldn't suspect him of having anything on his mind.'

'Would you say the same about Reardon?'

'He seemed apparently untroubled, and quite cheerful.'

'To you—with your inside knowledge—they must have seemed an amazingly odd pair.'

'They did,' replied Curtis emphatically. 'I looked and wondered.'

'What made you wonder?'

'That there was nothing more to wonder about.' Curtis' eyes twinkled as he raised his glass.

'If you carry on like this much longer,' said the little man, 'I'll be feeling like a white mouse in a revolving cage. My dear Curtis, it is information I want—not mental exercise.'

'So be it. I can condense what you want to know into a sentence. There was so little restraint between the two that Edgar had the bad taste to get drunk one night at Milford.'

'That's better. At least you've opened the door of my cage. That certainly doesn't sound like the action of a man living in fear.'

'No, Petrie. It did not. I thought that at the time.' Amos fastened on the change of tense.

'You think now it might be reconciled with what happened afterwards?'

'If I guessed hard, I think it might. But you'll want more than my guesses if ever you go before a jury.'

'I know, I know,' sighed Petrie; 'but we're not in Court. Fire away.'

For a moment Curtis eyed his companion curiously.

'You seem to have an unnatural passion for guesses, Petrie. Do you plaster conundrums over everyone you talk to about murder?'

'To all who might assist me. It helps to straighten out my ideas.'

'Well, I'll humour your appetite for guesses. Let me offer three possibilities. Guess One: Edgar Reardon was really frightened, and he drank either to hide or drown his fright. In either case he overstepped the mark. But his condition was exceptional. It wasn't that he ordinarily drank much, but he usually carried it well. Guess Two: There hadn't been any breach between them right up to the time they left Milford, and it only occurred in the car on the way home—'

'Wait one second. Reardon saw Paling in his private room here later on the same day. Work that into your theory.'

Dick Curtis threw his hands in the air.

'My dear Petrie, it's for you to judge whether there's anything or nothing in my guesses. I'm only playing a parlour game because you asked me to. As they say abroad, I overrule your objection as incompetent, irrelevant, and a breach of the rules of the game. But I offer you a third possibility. I suggest that the breach may have occurred, but that for different reasons both Reardon and Paling were both anxious to conceal it. And now, if you're not satisfied with anyone of my three guesses the Lord help you for I can't!'

'Do you think the third guess likely?'

'I certainly consider it possible.'

'Why?'

'Remember the conditions on which these two people had lived for a considerable time—Paling quietly bleeding his victim, and Reardon fighting a losing battle to avert ruin, and save his political position. The one thing on which they were united all that time was to cover everything under a mask of friendship until the time came for the final break. I was told enough to qualify me to give advice. But Mrs Reardon, constantly with her husband, frequently meeting Paling, never knew definitely that there was anything wrong. She's told me since that she suspected it. But she didn't know. All she did was to sense it. No outsider could even have done that. Why, when I gave a hint of it to Ferguson he wouldn't believe me.'

'I was going to ask you about that. It seems to me extraordinary, almost unbelievable, that you should leave a man like Paling—since you knew his character—in a position in which he could acquaint himself with the contents of the Budget papers. Explanation?'

'I dare not have done anything, Petrie. It was a terrible position for me. That was why in Reardon's own interests I was bound to throw a hint to Ferguson. Besides, it wouldn't have been fair to Ferguson to keep him entirely in the dark. We had been dining with Paling on the night when I dropped the hint—and that was the occasion when Reardon took too much to drink. Everyone knew that we had been in Edgar's company during the week. If anything had happened as a result of that night we would both have been in the soup. That's why I had to warn Ferguson.'

'I can see that quite clearly. I agree with you. But what I want to know is the effect of your warning on Ferguson. After you had convinced him that your statement was true how did he respond?'

'Very effectively—by rushing back to the hotel and grabbing all the papers he could lay his hands on. He took care of them that night. Precious good care too!' Curtis smiled reminiscently.

'You seem to have created quite a commotion in this little hotel.'

'Not more than we could help.'

'But because you couldn't help yourself you told Ferguson that Paling was a blackmailer?'

Curtis made a gesture of deprecation, raised his glass, and smiled broadly as he looked at Amos over the top of it.

'I see that even now,' he said, 'you do not realise the damnable awkwardness of my position. I was Reardon's confidant—or thought I was. I had to keep the balance fair. It wouldn't have done to give him away completely. That would have been doing exactly what Edgar feared Paling might do. It would have ruined him. Besides, it wasn't necessary to use such a word as blackmailer.'

'You just dropped a broad hint, and Ferguson's fears did the rest?'

'That's just about the size of it. I tried to use tact.'

'I must be dense. To me it all seems a most curious mix up. Still, I think I've got the position more clearly in my head than I ever had before. I suppose I'm right in thinking that Paling's power to blackmail arose solely out of the existence of the French wife?'

'That—and the attitude the English wife might take up if she knew. You must take the two together. They're inseparable.'

'Mrs Lola Reardon never knew about that first marriage?'

'I think not. It wasn't only the fear of a bigamy charge that scared Edgar. He had a vision of being hauled through the Divorce Courts. That would have been as bad for him as anything. In any case, no Cabinet could work with a man under suspicion of bigamy.'

'I have heard very strong doubts expressed about the validity of that French marriage.'

'No doubt you have. For what it's worth to you that was the view taken by Edgar Reardon himself.'

'Had he anything on which to base that view?'

'Counsel's opinion.'

'I take it that you didn't think much of that opinion?'

'Oh, I don't say that. I'm not a divorce lawyer. Also, I thought the point worth trying in a court of law. An opinion, after all, is only an opinion, and however good it might be Reardon couldn't take advantage of it without facing a scandal.'

'He might have used it as a weapon to keep Paling at bay.'

'He might.' Curtis threw back his head and laughed heartily.

'Apparently you don't think that Paling would have been impressed?'

'Only with the need for haste. Why, man, he got eight thousand out of Reardon in the first three months of this year!'

The size of the figure, and the short space of time during which it was paid, made Amos blink.

'That's good going, Curtis. By itself it seems to indicate that a crisis was approaching. Don't you think so?'

'I've no doubt about it at all. In fact, you know, and I know, that it did cause a crisis of one kind. The question is. Did it also produce a determination to revolt? On that point I've helped you all I can. As I've told you before, it's your pigeon after all.'

'You think there is nothing to be deduced from his attitude towards the validity of the French marriage?' persevered Petrie.

Curtis shook his head, and lit a cigarette.

'No. I'm afraid not. What I saw was equally consistent with a determination to stave off the fight until his party went out of office. As a matter of fact, I sometimes thought that was his game.'

'You mean he'd lost interest in the point of law?'

'Not at all. Quite the contrary He spoke to me about it on the day of his death, and if he hadn't died we'd have had another meeting to discuss the whole affair more fully. What I meant was that there was nothing more in existence at the time of his death than there had been before to suggest that he meant to make immediate use of it. Rather complicated, but that's the best I can do.'

'Then why did he want to see you that day?'

'Oh, he was always preparing for the fight, or persuading himself that he was. He said he had just received an opinion for which he had been waiting.'

Amos bent forward more eagerly, and fingered his handkerchief.

'A favourable opinion?' he asked.

'So I understood. But you'll have found it somewhere while the Yard men were searching his stuff. I hadn't time to read it then, and I've never had an opportunity since.'

'Sure it wasn't at Milford he spoke to you about this opinion?'

'Quite certain. He hadn't got it then.'

'And you are equally certain that he had it with him when you saw him on Budget Day?'

'Absolutely, Petrie. I had the thing in my own hands, and I handed it back to him when we parted at the end of the Ministers' Corridor.'

'Do you happen to know who gave that opinion?'

'Yes. Quiller.' He stopped while Amos made a note of the name.

'Carry on,' said the little man. 'That's just the sort of thing I want to know. Tell me more.'

Curtis revolted at last. 'Not me,' he exclaimed. 'I've talked myself dry because I thought you'd practically finished. But if you're off on a new tack—' He reached over for the whisky, poured a strong tot out for Petrie, another for himself, and lit another cigarette. Then he lolled back in his chair, tried to blow a smoke ring, and turned tolerantly to Petrie.

'From your interest in the devastating Quiller I assume that his opinion has vanished?'

'Right first guess. That's why I want to know all about it.'

'You're in luck's way. I'm not likely to forget it. My meeting with Edgar spoiled my lunch.'

'That would naturally impress the fact on anyone. Tell me the details. How did it affect your appetite?'

'It wasn't the appetite that failed, Petrie. It was the food. The fact is that I ordered a steak in the dining-room, and had gone back to the library while it was cooking. It was when I was returning to the dining-room that I met Reardon.'

'How did he happen to be there?'

'What a man for details! It was an accident, and, for me, a most unfortunate accident. Reardon had been feeding in the Ministers' dining-room. Being full of steak himself, he forgot all about my meal, and dragged me off to hear about Quiller's opinion.'

'Yes. Carry on. This is most interesting.'

'I'm not exactly thrilled about it. He gave the opinion to me to read as we were walking along. Of course, that was impossible. I can't concentrate on law when my stomach is crying for steak. Neither is it helpful to try it while you're perambulating corridors. I just glanced at the thing, and saw what it was. But by then we'd walked the length of the Library Corridor, and down the Ministers' Corridor before I could get rid of him.'

'You didn't get the impression that he had just received it, and was looking for you?'

'No, I can't say that I did. I don't know that I had any definite impression at all, except a feeling of irritation. But if you want my opinion you can have it. I think it was the sight of me that reminded him of the opinion.'

'He must have attached a lot of importance to it if he managed to keep you with him against your own marked inclination.'

'Undoubtedly he did. But it doesn't at all follow that he wasn't thinking of something else until he saw me. Edgar was like that. He could always put things out of his mind, and produce something new.'

'You can tell me nothing whatever about when he received it?'

'Oh, yes. I've said so. It must have been some time that day.'

'I mean at what time? And where? Was it at his house when he got back from Milford, or did he find it waiting for him here?'

'Now you're taxing me too high, Petrie. I might guess that it was waiting for him here since I don't expect he'd like such a letter sent to his home. But I might be wrong. I really don't know. I don't think he said anything about that. If he did I've forgotten it.'

'Was there an envelope on it when it was handed to you?'

'I think there was. I have no recollection, however, of reading any address in it. It didn't hold my attention. I'm sorry that I can't help you about this. You have to remember that I didn't know he was going to be murdered that afternoon. You are asking me about details which no man would ordinarily notice.'

'At any rate, you're certain that document was not left with you so that you could consider it at your leisure?'

'Not the slightest doubt about that.' His eyes twinkled. 'You have forgotten, Petrie, that there was only one thing I was prepared to consider at that time—and that was the steak ruining in the dining-room. Hungry men recall such details.'

'It certainly seems to have impressed itself on your memory. Tell me, was this matter of the waiting steak the only reason for postponing the discussion about the opinion, or were there stronger, and additional reasons for postponing the discussion?'

'That was my only reason. I'd better explain, though, that Reardon might well have had other reasons. It would never have done for me to be found in his room discussing whether he had, or had not, committed bigamy. The matter goes farther than that. If we had been successful in concealing the object of the discussion any really bright lad might well grow suspicious to find me in the Chancellor's room before he introduced the Budget. I need hardly remind you, Petrie, that I am a member of the Opposition. It is all right to be seen talking in corridors, or even in his own room under normal circumstances since everyone in the House knew us as friends. But a Budget Day is somewhat different. If I had gone to his room someone might have begun to smell a rat. And Edgar was in a position in which he could not afford to have folks smelling even the wrong rat. From his point of view delay was wise,'

'No doubt you're right. Yes, you're probably right. Now tell me this, and I'll pester you no more. At exactly what time did you meet?'

'As nearly as possible, I should say it was half-past two.'

'And about how long were you with him?'

'It seemed a long time. That may have been because I was hungry. Allowing for that, I'd say I was with him for five minutes.'

'Thank you very much indeed. I'll release you from further service for the time being. Any time you get any bright ideas perhaps you'll give me a ring. I can do with them.'

'You've worn out my supply of ideas for months to come.'

Petrie returned to his flat, read a new fishing book, and retired cheerfully to bed.

CHAPTER XVI

CONSULTATION AT THE YARD

On the following morning it was established beyond doubt that Quiller's opinion was waiting at the House of Commons when Reardon returned from Milford. His solicitors unbent condescendingly enough to admit that the document they had dispatched to their late client had not been returned to them. But it was impossible to estimate the time of its disappearance. There had been an interval between the murder and the police search of the dead man's room. That made the chance of abstracting the paper as good after death as it had been before. Petrie asked for the attaché-case containing the original Budget speech to be brought to him from the safe at the Yard. With that under his arm he walked along to the Home Office, leaving the case, the key, and the contents, with Sir Ralph Wade, the analyst.

From there he telephoned Ripple, informing him that he would be in his own office at the Public Prosecutor's Department throughout the morning, and did not wish to be disturbed unless the matter was of vital importance. In his own room Amos sank into a chair, and remained for half an hour without a move. Whichever view he took it seemed to him equally important to observe the exact sequence of events. For three hours he sat with a paper, and pen, collating the evidence, and throwing it into the form of a timetable. Thus:

A.M.	
10	Reardon returned to Downing Street by car in company with Paling.
10.5	Reardon went to Treasury. Sees Permanent Secretary, and other officials. Arranges for speech to be typed.

10.50	Reardon went to 10 Downing Street, taking typescript with him. N.B—This typing was not whole of speech. See Prime Minister.
11.0	Attends Cabinet meeting until
P.M.	
1.0	Cabinet breaks up. Reardon returns to Treasury. Interviews as before.
1.15	Reardon walks alone to House of Commons, and finds Quiller's opinion awaiting him.
1.30	Lunch at House of Commons with Ferguson, Morgan and the Attorney General.
2.30	Lunch over. Reardon meets Curtis while going to private room. Reardon then has Quiller's opinion with him. They walk together until
2.35	Reardon and Curtis separate near private room.
2.40	Treasury Messenger delivers Budget papers in locked attaché-case to Reardon, who is alone in room. He opens case, inspects papers. Sees messenger to door, tips him, and looks along corridor as though searching for someone. Reardon not seen again outside room, and nobody seen to enter until
2.55	Paling calls, finds Reardon alone. Attaché-case is on table.
3.5	Watson sees Reardon for first time in ten days. Paling left before Watson arrived. Reardon is alone. Watson does not know whether case locked or not.
3.15	Ferguson arrives. Watson leaves immediately.
3.25	Lola Reardon joins husband and Ferguson. Ferguson offers to show her Budget speech. She refuses. Does not know if case is locked.
3.35	Ferguson and Mrs R. leave together. Reardon left alone.
3.40	Reardon enters House of Commons.

3.55 Reardon begins Budget speech.
4.50 Reardon dies.
5.20 Budget papers collected from House of Commons table by Financial Secretary to Treasury, replaced in case, the case locked and key handed to Prime Minister.
5.30 Attaché-case received back at Treasury and locked in safe.

Tuesday

P.M.
2.0 Key of attaché-case given by Prime Minister to Watson.
3.0 Prime Minister speaks from duplicate copy of speech.
7.0 Original speech in locked case handed to me together with key by Watson.

Amos had drawn the horizontal lines through his timetable before he discovered that his lunch hour had passed. He slipped the table in his pocket, hurried out for a quick snack, consumed a pint of beer, and strolled along to the Home Office. There Sir Ralph's secretary handed him the locked attaché-case, the key, and a letter from the analyst. Petrie read the note as he walked along Whitehall. He was humming brightly when he entered the Yard. Inspector Ripple seemed to have aged. His shoulders were more bowed, the face was seamed with even more lines than usual, his eyes lacked lustre. He looked up at Petrie and nodded dismally.

'Well, Angel, what's the big news from the front line?'

'I'm going mad. This case has given me concussion. I've tried some tough stuff at odd times, but preserve me from anything like this. It seems to me that everything that happened didn't happen, and what didn't happen did happen. The whole affair ain't human.'

'What've you been doing this morning?'

'Trying to find out who really did visit Watson's flat the other night, and the only thing I can't prove is that he was visited by nobody. One damned drunk beat me there. But I can't show that those seeds came to him by the delivery van, by an angel, or by a miracle. I've spent hours tramping streets looking for traces of folks who have never been in the streets, of climbing stairs to check facts that make no difference when you've got 'em, of asking taxi drivers about fares they've never had. Strewth! I think I'll resign.'

'Before you resign I want you to take a look at this.' Amos threw his timetable on the desk. Ripple sighed heavily as he picked it up and glanced at it. 'I don't guarantee that you'll be able to spot the murderer by running your eye over the entries,' said Petrie, 'but he's there somewhere.'

'You know him?' Ripple looked up, startled.

'I haven't got quite as far as that, Sunshine.'

'I see you've put Paling and Watson down. Here, wait a minute! Why, you've got Ferguson down on your list! Are you mad, too?'

'I'm leaving nobody out. The Prime Minister told me last night that I could arrest him if I wanted to. I don't think it's very likely, but I'm overlooking nothing. He promised not to interfere, and that gives us a free hand.'

'Seriously, though, you're not thinking of Ferguson?'

'Seriously, Brighteyes, I'm thinking of everybody. At present I may be fancying some folks more than others, but I don't know how long they'll hold that exalted position. Everything is still too indefinite. I'll tell you something that will interest you, Angel. If the murder was done as I am sure it was we can't be certain yet that it wasn't committed in full Cabinet, in the presence of all the Ministers. What d'you know about that one?'

Ripple answered with a heavy groan, sank his head into his hands. He looked up to gape at Amos and groan again. It seemed to him that the little man was throwing bombshells with an air of unnecessary calm. Amos was whistling and looking at the attaché-case.

'Of course,' he said, 'I don't think it is the least likely that it was done in the Cabinet room, since there were so many people there. But with the knowledge we have at present the possibility can't be excluded. It would be nice for you, Earthquake, to have the chance of arresting a Cabinet Minister, wouldn't it?'

'Yes. And get the sack without a pension for doing it. Still, why talk this rubbish when we know that the murder was committed in the House of Commons?'

'Be more accurate, laddie. The death occurred in the House of Commons. That's a very different thing. I'm talking about the cause of death. The murder wasn't arranged in the House of Commons. That happened before Reardon rose on his feet. If I'm right it could have happened at any time between eleven in the morning and twenty minutes to four in the afternoon.'

Ripple seized the timetable and studied it for a while. Those names and figures said so little and meant so much! He read them, and re-read them, checking item by item. At the end of a third perusal Ripple slapped the paper down on the desk and blew out his cheeks.

'I'm no good at these games,' he announced despondently. 'I like something easy. Hand me a tram ticket, and ask me the surname of the man who bought it, how many more instalments he's got to pay on his house, which is his lucky colour, and whether he strikes his wife, and I might manage it. But this small Bradshaw is too good for me.'

'Don't be fretful, little one. Things are moving. By the way, have you still got a man tailing Watson?'

'Yes, but what the hell he's doing it for I don't know. I wish you'd find somebody to tail that man who bust into Watson's flat. Gosh! It's like trying to find the Invisible Man!'

'Soon, Sunshine, we'll try to clear up a few odds and ends. There are about half a dozen things I am anxious to find out. At the moment of going to press I can't make up my mind at which end to start. Almost like standing at the side of a lake, knowing that the pike are there, and being uncertain whether to spin for them or whether to use live bait. Of course, at that game you can try both of them. But with this case if we try the wrong ones first we might bring the whole structure—such as it is—round our heads. Then we'd have to start rebuilding.'

'Structure? If the structure I've built fell down on top of a gnat it'd only think that a fresh breeze was blowing. I haven't got any structure. I suppose you're playing round with ideas that look like skyscrapers to you?'

'Not exactly. Still, I've built about three walls. Now I'm waiting for the last wall and the roof.'

'Does one of these walls happen to tell you how Reardon was murdered? That part of my structure seems to be missing!'

'Oh, I've got that bit all right, I think. Why it took me so long to work it out I don't know. I deserve to have a bad day's fishing for being so dumb. Trouble is with me, Sunshine, that I will insist on looking at what should be the obvious until I can't see anything else. It was the claret and soda that led me adrift. Even when I knew that there was no trace of strophanthin in the stuff I couldn't get the idea of it out of my mind.'

'You don't really mean you know how it was done?'

'Pass me over that attaché-case and I'll show you.'

Ripple hastened to lodge a protest.

'I've looked over them, and there's nothing there at all.'

'When you were looking them over did you notice any heavy thumb marks, or weren't you looking for them?'

'I didn't take much notice, because I knew the papers had been handled before they got here. I wouldn't notice a little dirt.'

'Did you read the speech from the point at which Reardon stopped?'

'I can't say I read it. I just flicked over the pages.'

'That's exactly where I made my mistake. I ought to have found out immediately what had happened to Reardon. But I only glanced over his speech. Once I took the trouble to start reading it I could see a mile away what had happened. I am a very lucky man, and you're most unlucky, Sunshine. If it hadn't been that I am lacking only one habit you wouldn't have had me to pester you any more.'

'You're talking in riddles, and I hate the damned things. I've got a head like a piece of soddened earth now. If I hear any more about these mysteries I'll go stark raving mad. That's not a joke.'

'I'm hoping it's a promise. Hand me that attaché-case.'

CHAPTER XVII

MURDERER'S BOOBY TRAP

AMOS unlocked the case, and produced the fatal Budget speech whilst Ripple bent over the desk, staring with fascinated eyes. The little man laid the volume of papers on the table, and then halted.

'Take a good look at this speech, Ripple. I know you've seen it before, but you were probably as careless as I was myself. First of all you'll see that the speech is divided into seven sections, and that each section is fastened with a paper clip.'

'Nothing very remarkable about that. I expect most Chancellors arrange it that way.'

'I expect they do. Now follow this carefully. Look at the first four sections. They consist of a review of national finance. Take a careful look at the bottom corners of the pages. They're very, very slightly crumpled, but perfectly unmarked by any stain. See that? Right. Now bend over and take a look at the bottom right-hand corner on the first page of the fifth section. See anything?'

'Only faintly. Looks something like a faint smudge, just a small discoloured smear. That's all I can see.'

'That's all I expected you to see, Sunshine. Look at the next page and tell me what you see.'

'The same sort of dim mark. What's the point about all this?'

'I'll turn over the next few sheets so that you can take a look at them. Follow them closely.'

Ripple stared while the little man slipped back the pages. The Yard man stopped him abruptly.

'That smear has vanished. I can't see it any more.'

'I know you can't. I went through them all carefully myself, and could only find that mark on the first seven pages of this section.'

'Yes. And the answer to it all is what?'

'That,' announced Petrie, 'is how Edgar Reardon was murdered.'

Inspector Ripple continued to gaze at the speech.

'I'll tell you how it was done. First let me say this: If Edgar Reardon had not licked his finger and thumb when he tried to turn these pages he would have been alive today. You see—'

'I'm not falling for that theory. Not by a mile. I know some folks have got the nasty habit of wetting their finger and thumb as they turn pages, but only one person in ten would ever do it. If I am right the odds would be ten to one against Reardon doing it. And men planning murder don't gamble as wildly as that. No, no, no, it won't do at all. I see what you're getting at—that the corners of the pages are coated with strophantin, but no man in his senses would expect to be successful with a trap like that. We know enough about the murderer to know that he was a cunning devil.'

'He certainly was. So far, Ripple, you've only got half the story. The corners were coated with strophantin. But that was not all. I'll tell you exactly how it was done. Then you'll see that there was no ten-to-one shot about it. First of all, let us bear two things in mind. One, Reardon was nervous on Budget Day, as the murderer knew only too well. He had gambled on the Stock Exchange, abused his position, risked everything for money, and wouldn't be feeling too happy when he started his address. That is not a theory. No man with the load he had on his mind could have faced that House without feeling shaky, nervous and apprehensive. About that you must agree.'

'Nobody could argue about that, knowing what we know now. He must have been in a pretty bad state.'

'And the murderer knew it. Right. That's the first step. Now we move to the second. The first hour of a Budget Speech is of relatively little importance. The Chancellor makes his annual review during that time, and the interest is small. All the Members and the general public know roughly how the national finances have fared during the year. What they all want to know, what industry is standing still for, what the Stock Exchange is waiting for, what Mr Everyman is worried about, what politicians want to make capital from, is the Government's plan of taxation for the coming year. Once again, Ripple, you'll admit that that is the vital portion of the speech?'

'Can't be any doubt about that. Go ahead.'

'Very well. Edgar Reardon progressed splendidly through his review of past events. I listened to him, as you know. He was nervous, and seemed to become a little more apprehensive as he approached the scheme for new taxation. At last he finished his review, and the House waited more or less breathlessly. They knew he had arrived at the kernel of the address. Now, for a second, I am going back to point something out to you. Watch me turn the pages of the earlier sections of this speech.'

Petrie flicked them over rapidly with finger and thumb. There was no hesitating pause, no fumbling, no difficulty. At last he arrived at the fourth section. Then he stopped.

'This is where we make a little experiment, Ripple. Stand up for a minute as though you are making the Budget speech. Here is the fourth section. I will take the fifth chapter. Wait one moment now.'

The little man placed the fatal section on the desk, pressed on the bottom right-hand corner of it with the palm of his hand. Then he pushed it across the desk, placing it underneath the fourth section. Ripple watched the moves with wrinkles corrugating his brow.

'Now make a start. Turn those pages just as you would if you were making the speech. But for the love of God stop for a moment when you've come to the end of that section.'

Ripple turned them without difficulty, each page rising between his finger and thumb smoothly. At last he reached the end of the section and laid it on one side to leave the next chapter on top. He turned to Petrie and waited.

'Just place yourself now in the position of a Chancellor of the Exchequer. You have arrived at the vital part of your speech. The whole House is waiting. So far I haven't told you the important part of this murder, the almost uncanny cunning of the man who arranged it. That can wait for a minute while you make this small experiment first. I want you to turn those pages as you did the others. But don't wet your fingers. If you do you'll die.'

Ripple nodded and placed a thumb and finger on the first sheet. He frowned. It would not move. He couldn't separate it. His hand rose towards his mouth. Petrie jumped from his chair.

'Wait, man, you're doing just what Reardon did! Try the pages all you like, but keep your fingers away from your mouth.'

Ripple shivered. A chill mounted from his jaws to the roots of his hair. Petrie wiped his face with his handkerchief. After another attempt Ripple managed to turn the first sheet over. But the next page gave him more trouble and it was half a minute before he could separate it.

'That will do,' said Amos. 'Sit down now while I explain things to you. The murderer knew that Reardon under normal circumstances would not wet his fingers. So he devised a plan, a double plan, to ensure that he would lick that strophanthin into his mouth. He painted the corners of the pages with a substratum of gum and mixed the strophantin in the gum. When Reardon reached that portion of his speech he found that the pages were sticking together slightly. Of course they were. The murderer had fastened them just as easily as I did a moment ago. That is one half of the trap by which Reardon was caught. Clever, eh?'

'Phew! it makes me sweat to think about it. Who the hell would think out anything like that? And you say that's only one half of the arrangements for the murder? If that is only part of it I'm glad the man wasn't trying to see me off the globe!'

'The other part, I think, is even more ingenious than the actual murder itself. Before I explain it to you I want you to bear in mind all the time that the murderer knew precisely what mental troubles were afflicting Reardon, knew that his heart would be bumping, his nerves gnawing him, his conscience worrying him, all through the speech. He would be wondering if he was going to get away with his deceit, with his gross treachery, whether he would be unmasked, whether any eleventh hour episode would occur that might blow his life, his hopes, everything, sky high. Just bear that in mind and then you'll appreciate the skill, the brilliance, the forethought with which the whole thing was arranged.

'Reardon completes his reading of section four. He turns his attention to the section on which he has gambled his all. Suddenly he stops. To say that he was staggered would be gross understatement. The man's world must have slipped from under his feet. *The first page he had never seen before. The taxes referred to he had never heard of!* Let your mind rest on that for a minute.'

Ripple was too stunned to speak. His mouth opened and closed like a distressed goldfish. He stared at the page before him until his eyes protruded. He pulled himself together when he heard Amos:

'Let me put the thoughts of that man before you. I think I can guess them fairly well. A Chancellor in normal circumstances would instantly have halted his speech, wouldn't he? Immediately he saw that the material had been tampered with the House would have been adjourned while the essential inquiries were made. That is obvious. Ripple, the murderer was no mean student of human nature. Long before Budget Day he had envisaged the track along which Reardon's mind would travel. That is the track along which I am going to take you now. I'm sure it is more fact than guesswork.

'Reardon knew that he had sold the Budget secrets for a mess of pottage. He knew that he had betrayed the nation for money. He was a political Judas. His nerves were racked before he reached that fatal section. When his eyes told his brain that a fraudulent series of taxes had been transposed for his own, what would be the first thought to flood his mind? Just this: "I have been betrayed!"

'Probably a dozen wild ideas swamped his brain. If he revealed the fraud would everything be disclosed? Could he remember the new taxes with sufficient confidence to abandon the speech and announce them from memory? Was the criminal supposing that the fraudulent taxes would be announced as a price for his silence? Was it a cruel hoax? Had some financial interests in the City bribed someone to break him as a result of his pre-Budget gamble? The more he stared at the page, the more restless the House became. The more restless the Members grew, the more panic-stricken Edgar Reardon became. You don't need much imagination to draw aside the curtains from his mind.

'Suddenly he saw one ray of hope, a ray dim and distant. Perhaps the page had been inserted by some unfortunate accident, or some unfeeling joke. There was one way in which he could discover the truth. He could look at the following sheets. Perhaps below he might find his original manuscript. His nervous fingers clutched the page. He could not raise it. The House became more restless, impatience was turning to anger. Frantic, almost demented, Reardon licked his fingers and flicked over the page with an effort. His hopes fell. The second page, also, was bogus. It contained material he had never seen before. Voices of protest rose round him. Nervously he licked his fingers, clutched the next page, stared at it with anxiety stabbing at his senses. Again the sheet was false. His panic grew, his brain was failing to act.

'The noise of rising voices buzzed in his ears and he licked his fingers again and groped for the next page. By now the typescript was swaying in drunken lines before his glazing eyes. He groped for another sheet. Pain seized his heart, a wall of blackness was mounting before his sight, the mutter of voices now meant nothing to him, the Budget was something without meaning, the world and all it meant was passing from him. Then—Edgar Reardon was dead!'

Petrie stopped abruptly. Ripple wiped globules of sweat from his face. His hands felt cold and clammy. The Yard man was not squeamish, but before his eyes was a picture of the frantic Reardon, blundering in panic towards death. He could see the increasing redness in the Chancellor's face, the fixed brightness of his eyes, almost hear the increasing heaviness of breath, as the man plunged to his end in a frenzy of bewilderment.

'And that,' remarked the little man, 'is all that can be said about the way in which he was murdered. Horribly ingenious, eh?'

Ripple shivered, looked again at the speech, quite fascinated. 'When did you first find this out?' he asked.

'In the early hours of this morning. I knew that Reardon had not been murdered by a miracle. I knew that the claret and soda had not been tampered with and that he touched nothing else—other than the speech—within an hour of his death. I had looked at the speech, but had not read it. The error on my part is beyond excuse. So I rectified it by reading the stuff. You remember I'd taken it home with me. I was brought up with a jerk when I reached the start of that fifth section. I had read in the newspapers the Budget speech made by the Prime Minister. It was made from a carbon copy of the original speech. It was then I noticed that the new taxes were not those typed on the speech Reardon took into the House.

'After that I started to examine the pages. Like you, I saw those slight smears. I took a look at them under a magnifying glass and came to the conclusion that gum had been painted on the corners. The rest was simple. I took the speech along to the Home Office this morning and after lunch I got the report I expected. The gum was heavily impregnated with strophanthin. There ends that part of the story. It all seems so simple now we know the truth.'

'Damnable! But it seems to land us more into the mire than ever. We know how the murder was done. But that's all we do know. How on earth do we reckon to make any headway now?'

'You're wrong, Sunshine. We know a lot more than that. There are one or two important points that you've overlooked. We know that this fraudulent section did not in any way resemble the original manuscript in material, that the words and figures were all wrong. In fact the section was wrong in everything except one thing—it was not wrong *in appearance*. Follow me?'

'I think I do. That thought had occurred to me.'

'Very, very important, Ripple. But for that the murderer might just as well have used a selection from the Bab Ballads. Let me see if I can lighten the clouds for you, Angel. For the time being don't bother about what the murderer didn't know, or pretended not to know. Instead, let us look carefully at the precise information he had got, let us examine what he did know. Obviously this imitation section was prepared some time before it was inserted in the speech. That means this: He must have known how the Budget speech was to be prepared and assembled. Think that over.

'I'm willing to assume, Ripple, that any Member of the House of Commons might have guessed that the notes of Reardon's speech would be typed on notepaper taken from the House of Commons. It is certainly less likely any Member would have guessed that the speech would be typed on paper of this particular size. The murderer knew it, though.

'And that isn't the extent of his knowledge. He knew that the speech would be divided into sections, and that each section would be clipped separately. You have to remember that the whole scheme of substituting one section for another rested on that knowledge. Without this particular information the substitution could not have been made in the time available to any of the potential murderers. I am reducing to an impossibility the idea that it might have been done at the Cabinet meeting.'

'I don't see why you should, but I'm glad to hear you say so.'

'I wipe that out because Reardon would have been poring over that one section at the meeting. It would have been impossible for him to work with them and hide the fact that he wasn't looking at his own notes. And if he had discovered the fraud he would never have taken them into the House. We can wipe that out entirely.'

'Thank the Lord there is something we don't have to worry about.'

'We've got more than enough to keep us awake. It seems to me—'

Petrie stopped. Ripple picked up the little man's timetable and waved it excitedly in the air. Then he crashed a fist down on the desk. Amos smiled. The Yard man rarely showed any emotion other than permanent depression and misery.

'My oath!' he exclaimed. 'Ferguson! That man is everything that opens and shuts. He fills the whole bill. Just think. He had the draft of Reardon's speech in his possession for a whole night. He was at the Cabinet meeting. He was in Reardon's private room at the House. He even offered to show the speech to Mrs Reardon so he had access to it. And he was the last person to be alone with Reardon.'

'I know all about it, little one. And you didn't even add then that he knew quite a lot about Reardon's private affairs. But I'm not so certain. I'd feel much more excited about him if there were not others who could have done it equally well. Think of Paling. He was with Reardon all the time the speech was being prepared. He motored up with him on Budget Day. He was with him in his room shortly before the speech was made. You could build a monumental case against him. Then there's Watson. He was Parliamentary Private Secretary to the dead man and shows very clearly that he's most hopelessly in love with the widow. There are other considerations.'

'If he had anything to do with it Ferguson must have given him an almighty shock when he offered to show the speech to Mrs Reardon.'

Petrie seized the telephone and dialled for Ferguson. A minute later he jumped from his seat and grabbed his hat.

'What on earth is the matter?' asked the startled Yard man.

'Hold the fort here until I come back. Ferguson is out of town. He has gone to Brockenhurst. And Watson has gone with him! I'm going down to join the party. I'll slip over to Milford while I'm there. Try to get Paling to talk while I've gone.'

The door slammed. Amos Petrie was on his way.

CHAPTER XVIII

THE ODD AFFAIR AT MILFORD

PETRIE'S chauffeur piloted him down to Brockenhurst, but the little man met with an early disappointment. At the hotel he was informed that Ferguson, Watson, 'and the rest of the party,' had gone out for the day, leaving behind a message stating that they would not be back until late in the evening. Surprised, Amos inquired the names of the remaining members of the party. He was shown the register, and his surprise increased. Watson and Ferguson were with Lola Reardon and her father!

Amos left his case at the hotel, ate a hurried snack, and ordered the chauffeur to drive him into Milford. It was dark when he arrived at the hotel in which Reardon and Paling had stayed. At first Petrie found the proprietress somewhat difficult. After ten minutes' conversation the little man found her more amenable. She led the way into a private sitting-room and he ordered drinks for both. It seemed that the prospect of refreshment removed the last barrier of the woman's reserve. Amos decided that nothing could be gained by beating about the bush. He told her bluntly who he was and why he'd called. The woman was startled, but a double whisky seemed to soothe her nerves.

'Did you notice anything odd about them while you were keeping your eye on the hotel?' he asked.

The woman's massive bosom heaved and she nodded her head.

'I've never had folks like them staying here before and I never want anything like them again. They might call themselves gentlemen but that they could never be? Disgraceful, it was.'

Amos inclined his head appreciatively and sipped his beer.

'I am sorry to hear that. What was the trouble?'

'Trouble? Enough to send any poor woman stark, raving mad. How would you like to be told that your wine was pig swill?'

'A most ungracious thing to say. Who told you that, madame?'

'Mr Reardon said it was and Mr Paling said it was worse.'

'Most distressing, I'm sure. Would you mind telling me all about it?'

'But that's not all, sir. Somebody had put poison in it!'

Amos sat bolt upright and almost dropped his tankard.

'They did what?' he asked incredulously.

'They put poison in it,' she asserted. Petrie pulled out his handkerchief of many colours and rubbed his hands. Then he dived for his tankard before speaking again.

'Start from the very beginning and let me know all about it.'

The woman gulped down some whisky, straightened her frock.

'It was the night after they got here, sir. They had their meals in my private dining-room. We'd served them with dinner and about ten minutes afterwards there was such a noise going on in their room that I thought the place was on fire. I've never heard such a rumpus in my life. It was terrible. I got frightened. It sounded almost as though they might be fighting. I didn't want anything like that happening in my hotel so I went to the room to see if I could quieten them a bit.

'When I got into the room they were standing facing each other, one at each end of the table. They were both in a terrible state. Mr Paling had a glass in his hand and he looked as though he was going to throw it at Mr Reardon. As soon as I opened the door things seemed to simmer down a bit. I should think as full-grown men they must have felt a bit ashamed of themselves. Once I got into the room they never said a word. But I'm a business woman, and I don't go round with my eyes shut. I saw Mr Reardon nod his head and Mr Paling nodded back to him. Neither of them said a word.

'Then something very funny happened. This Mr Paling walked over to the window and threw his wine into the garden. Of course, by this time I was flabbergasted. I didn't know whether they'd both gone mad, or what. I thought it was time I said a few words. So I said everybody in the hotel could hear them, and would they mind not making so much noise as it would get my hotel a bad name and what was the trouble about and was there anything wrong with the meal or had something in the hotel upset them.'

The woman paused to pant for breath. Her lungs, working within a massive chassis, could not cope with long, non-stop sentences. The little man's eyes were gleaming, but he made no attempt to speak. She came back with a second wind, paused to lower a little more whisky, and plunged into the narrative with a burst of indignation:

'Mr Reardon's wine slopped over on the cloth when he put the glass back on the table. It was then he told me that the wine was pig swill. Before I could get over the shock of a gentleman saying that, Mr Paling said it wasn't fit for pigs. I told them if they could get better wine in a country hotel I'd like to know where they'd find it, and then they started apologising to me, and saying it must be their palate that was wrong, and they'd only said it on the spur of the moment. Well, I didn't want to say too much because you don't get your hotel full at this time of the year, so I thought I'd let things rest at that.

'Still, I was a bit puzzled about the way they'd stopped rowing as soon as I got into the room, and I didn't like what they'd said about my wine. A bit later that night one of my customers came in and I told him about it. He said perhaps the wine had gone off and I didn't know it. I was so certain that it was all right I told him I'd bring what was left of the bottle and he could try it for himself. I brought the drink and we each had one and there was nothing wrong with it at all. He couldn't understand it any more than I could. He was a bit curious and asked me if I would let him look at the glasses because he said they weren't the kind of men you would expect to make a mistake about wine since they'd be very used to taking it. The table hadn't been cleared and I brought him the glasses.'

She paused again for breath. Petrie was fidgeting with his handkerchief, anxious for the woman to proceed with the story.

'He asked me if I'd lend him the glasses since he was curious about them. You could have knocked me down with a feather when he came into the bar the next morning and said they were right about the wine being bad. At least, he said, one of the men was right. I asked him which one and he said the one who threw his drink into the garden if I'd told him aright which glass belonged to which. I said it was an insult, and he ought to have more sense than to say it, since we both had some of the wine and it was all right. It was then he told me that the wine in one glass had been poisoned!'

She ceased talking and stretched for her whisky. Petrie was frowning, trying to add the latest piece into the jig-saw.

'Who was this customer who showed such an interest in the matter of the wine, madame?'

'Mr Riggs, sir. Mr Harry Riggs.'

Petrie was not very impressed. He took another drink.

'And—eh—what does Mr Harry Riggs do for a living?'

'He is the local chemist.'

Amos replaced his tankard hurriedly and pulled out his flaming handkerchief again. His interest was renewed.

'Would it be possible for me to speak to Mr Harry Riggs?'

'Certainly, sir. It'll be surprising if he isn't in the bar now.'

'I'd be grateful if you would find out for me. If he is, perhaps you'd ask him to step in here for a moment. I'd like to have a word with him before we have another talk.'

The woman edged her bulk out of the room and Petrie played with his tankard. A knock sounded on the door and a small man with a wispy moustache, a slithering gait, and an air of diffidence came into the room. He nodded to Petrie and the little man smiled.

'I've been hearing all about this wine, Mr Riggs. It seemed very odd to me that you should have formed such a startling view about it. Would you mind telling me just what happened?'

'Certainly I will. I drank some of it myself, and I couldn't understand why those gentlemen said it was bad. It seemed to me that men of their station in life should know wine when they tasted it. I was so curious that I asked for the glasses. At the bottom of one of them I saw a sort of sediment that I knew should never have been there. I touched it with my finger and tasted it. That was when I asked the landlady if I could borrow the glasses. When I got back to my shop I started to analyse the stuff as well as I could. I don't reckon to be much of a hand at that game now. It's a long time since I did any of it. But this stuff was easy.'

Petrie bent forward eagerly.

'And what was the sediment, Mr Riggs?'

'Arsenic, sir. No doubt about it. The wine was dosed with arsenic.'

Amos took off his glasses and wiped them. His memory was running back to the discovery in Paling's rooms. But according to the proprietress the poison was in Paling's glass!

'Didn't you think of informing the police when you found that a murder had been attempted, Mr Riggs?'

'I did, sir, but not for long. You see, I knew who Mr Reardon was, and I daren't do anything about it. I thought it might be a pure accident and since the men had been quarrelling it was obvious that they both knew about it. I thought it over and came to the conclusion that it was best to let sleeping dogs lie.'

'I can see your view and I must say that under the circumstances I might have done the same. I would like you, Mr Riggs, to put your statement into writing within the next few minutes, get someone in the bar to witness it, and let me have it before I leave. Will you?'

'Certainly, sir. I'll do that immediately. Shall I tell the landlady that you want to see her again?'

'If you will. I'm greatly indebted to you. Have a drink with me?'

The chemist nodded and vanished. Mr Riggs seemed to be growing more important. He made his exit more proudly than he made his entrance. A minute later the landlady walked in. Petrie ordered some more drinks, including one for the chemist.

'I want to know, madame,' he commenced, 'whether there were any more peculiar happenings while these two gentlemen were here.'

'The very next night, sir. Another most extraordinary thing it was, too. There was some more trouble about the wine. They sent for me, and told me that the burgundy was sour. I didn't say much about it because of what Mr Riggs told me that morning. This time neither of them threw any drink away. They left it in their glasses and told me to get them some champagne. I took out the bottle of burgundy, and their glasses, and sent in the champagne. Mr Riggs was in and we both tasted the wine from their glasses and then poured some out from the bottle. It was all as sweet as a nut. There was nothing at all wrong with any of it. Now what do you think about that, sir?'

'A very queer story indeed, madame. There was absolutely nothing wrong with the very glasses of wine they complained about?'

'Certainly not. At any rate I know burgundy when I taste it and I thought it was good enough for anyone.'

'Most odd. Did anything else happen while they were here?'

'No, sir. It was only the first couple of nights. After that they had friends here to dinner each night and everything seemed to be quite all right. If there was anything wrong I didn't see anything of it and didn't hear anything of it.'

'Did they have any further quarrels, or did they seem to get along amicably?'

'Of course, I didn't see much of them, sir, but from what I did see I'd say they were quite friendly. Mostly they stayed in their room.'

'I take it that you mean this: When they were seen in public they were quite friendly, but as to their conduct when they were alone you know nothing. Is that about right?'

'I'd say you've hit the nail right on the head, sir.'

'You really have been most helpful. By the way, who paid the bill?'

'Mr Paling, sir, paid for both of them.'

'Thank you. I must be getting along now, madame. Would you mind telling my chauffeur that I am ready to return?'

Petrie sank into the back of the car and wrestled with the odd problem throughout the return journey to Brockenhurst. A stream of questions coursed through his brain. If Reardon tried to poison Paling, why on earth did Paling buy the poison? If Paling tried to poison Reardon, why did Reardon join in the effort to cover the attempt? He had the troublesome blackmailer at his mercy, had the poisoned wine on the table, but instead of calling in the police he approved of the wine being thrown out of the window. And why was the alarm raised on the second night—the false alarm? Purely for artistic reasons? And if Paling had a reserve store of strophanthin, why fool about with arsenic? Strophanthin is twenty times stronger. He could have arranged it so that Reardon fell dead after the first sip. And why . . .

Petrie's head was reeling by the time the car pulled up at the hotel entrance. But many things were clarifying themselves. Daylight was showing in many spots where before all had been darkness.

The first person he met as he entered the hall was Ferguson. The Minister scowled as he sighted the little man, advanced to meet him with a far from cordial welcome.

CHAPTER XIX

FERGUSON IS BUNKERED

THE Cabinet Minister was not easy to recognise in the tweeds of a golfer. He looked as though the keen air of the New Forest had blown away some of his worries; it certainly looked as though he did not appreciate being reminded of them.

'What the devil do you want to chase me down here for?' he asked snappily. 'I thought you'd fixed all the business with Curtis. Didn't he tell you all you wanted to know? I don't want you pestering me.'

'He couldn't tell me what is known to you alone,' replied Petrie calmly. 'Where are your friends?'

'They stayed behind with friends of Watson's at Bournemouth.'

Petrie slid out of his overcoat, hooked it on the stand and walked back to Ferguson. The Minister was growing more annoyed.

'I'm not going to talk any more about this wretched affair. If you've come down here to question me you've wasted your time.'

'I don't think I have. We'll find a private room. By the time I've finished I don't think you'd enjoy the conversation in public.'

Ferguson flushed a trifle, seemed startled. He followed Petrie into an empty smoke-room, lit a cigar, slumped into a chair, and regarded his companion as one might regard a diseased animal. By now the Cabinet Minister had again submerged the golfer.

'Well,' he said sharply, 'what is it I know and Curtis doesn't?'

'One of the things he could not tell me was what passed between you and Edgar Reardon when you were alone in his private room.'

Petrie's tone was casual. Yet there was an unmistakable bite in it.

'God bless my soul!' exclaimed Ferguson. 'I believe the man is going to accuse me next.' Apparently he addressed the remark to the ornamented ceiling. There was an element of comedy about his air of astonishment, but it seemed genuine enough.

'If I were accusing you,' said Amos steadily, 'I would have begun by warning you. Also I—'

'Damme, Petrie, you can't be right in the head.'

The little man's eyes gleamed behind his thick glasses and his tone changed with dramatically sudden effect.

'Don't get childishly annoyed, Ferguson,' he said coldly. 'I came down here to get your assistance and if you give it to me I may be able to save you a lot of annoyance.'

'Petrie, I am quite prepared to give the police every assistance provided it is properly asked for. But I must tell you that your present manner is particularly offensive.'

'Forget it!'

Ferguson moved in his chair as though he had been struck.

'You're an annoyance by yourself, Petrie, and I can't for the life of me understand how anything I can tell you would save me from another annoyance.'

'If you don't know, Ferguson, I can tell you. If ever I get as far as making a charge against Paling the case for the Crown will be that he committed his crime when he was alone with Edgar Reardon in that private room at the House of Commons.'

Ferguson pulled at his cigar and waved his hands impatiently.

'These details don't interest me in the slightest, Petrie.'

'No? They ought to. If such a case does not interest you, what Paling's reply to it is should certainly interest you a hell of a lot.' Petrie spoke more slowly: 'He is pointing out that there were others who were alone with Reardon after he left the room. And you, Ferguson, are one of those others.'

'But this is monstrous. I've never heard of such a thing. Quite the most stupid suggestion I've ever heard. Pshaw! Sheer nonsense.'

'I'm not disputing that for the moment. But will it save Paling's skin? That's all he is considering. You've got yourself to think about. I can rather imagine what the trial would be like. Can you stretch your imagination as far as that. Can you visualise the counsel for the defence pointing a forensic finger at you? Can you hear him declaiming about the Cabinet Minister who is *not* in the dock? I can, Ferguson. And without very much effort.'

The questions acted like a cold douche. Ferguson drew a deep breath. When it left his body his manner had completely changed. The air of a Cabinet Minister seeped away. He replied as a golfer:

'It's your hole, Petrie. I thought I was only on the edge of the rough. Now I find I'm bedded in the bunker. Don't be astonished at the next thing I say. I've always been willing to help you. I can see that my manner was all wrong. I want you to get me out of this bunker. Would you mind having a try?'

'My reply to that will depend upon what you tell me.'

'You see, the awkward thing about this business is that I can't say I did this, or I said that, while I was in that private room with Reardon. The truth of the whole matter is that I did not go to that room to do anything.'

'Then why on earth did you go?'

Ferguson hunched his shoulders and paused for a while.

'Oh, I don't know. My turn at questions in the House was over and Reardon had told me that his wife was coming down to the House. I find her a nice, chatty little woman—and, of course, I had nothing particular to do.'

Petrie's lips parted as a smile spread over his face.

'If Mrs Reardon heard you say that I'm sure she'd be most upset. You paid her quite a lot of attention, you know—offering to show her the Budget speech.'

'That offer was only a joke. I told you that before. For the love of everything don't start asking me to explain jokes.'

Amos stared at him curiously.

'Did Mrs Reardon appreciate that it was meant as a joke?'

'She wasn't meant to. To be honest about it I was pulling Reardon's leg about something that happened at Milford.'

'You are referring to the night he was drunk and you took charge of the papers?'

'So you've heard of that? You're precisely right. Now you can see just what I meant. Reardon made a fool of himself that night. He made the chambermaid a speech—all for herself.'

'How was it that you didn't take some action immediately you realised that Reardon was drunk, and you knew that papers of the highest confidence and importance were being exposed to outsiders?'

'I was a fool, Petrie. If I hadn't been a fool I wouldn't be wanting your assistance now. If I had interfered Reardon might have told me to play my own ball. That's not the whole of it, either. You have to remember that I only knew Paling as a most intimate friend of Reardon's. I looked upon him almost as a member of Reardon's family. The man had been invited to sit with us each night at dinner. I assumed that he was a man of honour. I had no reason in the world to assume otherwise. And you know I'm not sure I could have done anything that would have made a real difference. I simply did the best I could do on the spur of the moment when I got the tip from Dick Curtis. I've been thinking the matter over a good deal since, and I'm not at all sure that by going back for those papers I wasn't slogging at the tee after the ball had gone.'

'You mean that Paling would have seen all he wanted to see before you returned and took the papers away?'

'And even long before then. He was with Reardon all day and every day when we were not there. Edgar seemed to be very careless.'

'Carelessness is hardly the word for it, unless Reardon had some reason for thinking that he might be able to control Paling better than he had been doing. Can you think of anything that would justify such a belief, Ferguson?'

'No, I didn't see anything to arouse suspicion either one way or the other throughout the whole time I was with them.'

'But at least you saved Reardon from the possible consequences of that one particular piece of lunacy?'

'Yes, I certainly did that.'

Petrie was staring into the fire when he asked the next question:

'You made no mistake about that? I mean you are quite sure that you took away the whole speech?'

'Of course, I did. Damn it, man, what do you take me for? The speech was in seven sections and I took all of them.'

Amos pursed his mouth and produced his handkerchief. It was the first time that he had heard the sections mentioned. Ferguson noted the little man's concentrated interest. Petrie saw that the change in his expression was observed and immediately swerved away:

'Now I want to ask you something that must have come under your notice as one of Reardon's executors. Have you come across any trace of Paling acting as Reardon's nominee in the speculations on the Budget you've been trying to cover up?'

'No, I believe Reardon used a bank as nominee.'

Petrie straightened in his chair, looked at Ferguson incredulously.

'Are you trying to tell me that a man fitted to be Chancellor of the Exchequer let his bank into the guilty secret? You honestly astound me, Ferguson. I thought the one thing certain about this man was that he wanted to save his reputation. And yet you suggest to me that he gave those big buying orders through the bank?'

Ferguson stroked his bald scalp as though it tickled.

'I'm afraid I hadn't much thought about the machinery involved in the speculation. I know he used his bank. But, of course, you're right in thinking he wouldn't let them know any more than he was forced to. He dare not.'

'Quite. And for another reason he couldn't have given these

big orders to stockbrokers, could he? That would have let them know what his game was, and they would have dived into the market on the ground floor with him.'

'More than one broker would be used, Petrie. Not one individual broker would know all that he was doing. He camouflaged it.'

'But, Ferguson, the man was buying wholesale, and he was doing nothing but buying, and all the securities were of the same class. Do you mean he scattered hints of what he was doing among half a dozen stockbrokers? Surely if that had been the case, prices would have rocketed before the Budget? And there would have been no interruption of buying during the last account. He must have had a nominee. Perhaps more than one. I want their names.'

'Then I'll have to find that out for you.'

'You don't know now?' Amos found the fact hard to credit.

'No, I don't. Will it do if I get the information on Monday?'

'It might be a member of the Cabinet who was acting.'

'Oh, come. I can see you don't like my position at all.'

'Were I in your position I'd be praying that I might never be subjected to cross-examination. But Monday will do.'

'I don't think you see, Petrie, how unimportant the name or names of the nominees can be from my point of view. As executors we will have to use them—because Reardon used them, and because the only way out of the mess is to sell as quietly as possible all that Reardon bought. Still, we haven't got to set up the machinery ourselves. We've only got to use what is ready to our hands and pray hard that we don't get burnt while we're doing it. The very last thing we want is to have more to do with these tools than we can possibly help.'

'From your point of view—splendid. But I haven't your choice.'

'I can see that yours is a different point of view. You may rely on me. I'll have the information for you on Monday. What about the rest of the inquisition, or has it finished?'

'Not quite. We'll get a couple of drinks to sustain us, and then finish the talk. I'll order them.'

Ferguson seemed grateful for the break. It was not until the drinks were served that Amos resumed his questioning:

'Tell me about the Budget Day Cabinet. I don't want to pry into secrets of State. I am more interested in procedure than anything. Did you spend the whole time discussing the Budget?'

'No, we did not. Another rather urgent matter cropped up, and, as a matter of fact, we took that first. That delayed us with the Budget, and made the meeting last longer than any of us anticipated. I remember that because we'd arranged a little luncheon at the House and it had to be put back half an hour.'

'You didn't go to the House with Edgar Reardon?'

'No, he had to rush back to the Treasury as soon as the meeting was over. He was having the notes of his speech typed out for him.'

'You mean the notes he did not take to the Cabinet meeting?'

'Exactly. Forgive me if I forget sometimes that you're a stickler for precision. What I meant was that he wanted to check the typing, and see that everything was in order for the speech.'

'I'm afraid I let you run away from the Cabinet meeting before you told me about the discussion.'

'I didn't mean to evade anything. But there isn't much to tell. Reardon expounded, and we listened, and criticised or approved. For myself I was one of the strong silent men that morning.'

'And may I take it that Reardon had no occasion to part with his notes at any time at that meeting?'

'None of us fingered any of the papers, if that's what you mean.'

'Don't lose patience just when you're beginning to tell me what I consider is useful. It is essential for me to know these details.'

'Perhaps my patience does need stimulating,' said Ferguson, raising his glass and taking another drink. 'Now, fire away!'

'If those papers were not touched at the Cabinet meeting we

go straight from there to Reardon's private room at the House. Is your memory equally clear about the people you met on your walk along the corridors at the House? Be careful before you answer!'

Ferguson accepted the warning and hesitated for a space.

'I don't know that it is,' he said. 'There was nothing to recall.'

'Do you mean by that that the corridors were empty?'

'Of course not. There were plenty of people about, but they were just the ordinary folks.'

'You saw nobody there who had no right there?'

'Not a soul. I would have remembered that, naturally.'

'All right. Let us see if you can help me about something else. How did you find Edgar Reardon? Was he alone?'

'Practically. Watson was with him, of course. He doesn't count. He made himself scarce as soon as he saw me—just as every well-conducted P.P.S. should.'

'And Watson was a model of good behaviour that day?'

'Quite. I begin to wish he hadn't been. That would have helped to keep me out of the bunker, wouldn't it?'

'It might have assisted. What was Watson doing when you called?'

'Nothing in particular. I think he was waving the stump of a cigar in the air and talking. Reardon was doing the same.'

At least, thought Amos, that meant that Reardon had not got Quiller's opinion in his hand. He questioned Ferguson about that document. The Minister had seen no sign of it.

'He might have given it to Watson to put away?' asked Petrie.

'Most certainly. In his position you'd trust him with anything.'

'How far would you carry that trust? Might a Parliamentary Private Secretary see a confidential Cabinet document?'

'He ought not to—except to fetch it, or take it back again.'

'He might see it?'

'Yes, he might. After all, he is not a servant. He's a friend. Quite often a friend who expects you to give him a leg up into office the week after next.'

The questioning lagged. Into his vaguest replies Ferguson imported a suggestion of anxiety to help. There was in his answers an undertone of confidence, quiet, and unexpressed in words, but always suggested. However awkward his position Ferguson created the impression that he was relying upon Petrie to get him out of it. Suddenly the door opened and a servant entered. He spoke to Ferguson:

'Your friends have just returned, sir, and will be dining shortly.'

'Join us at table, Petrie,' said Ferguson rising and heading for the door. He seemed grateful to escape.

'No, thanks,' answered the little man. 'It's most kind of you, but I have one or two odd jobs to do before I can grub and I wouldn't like to keep you waiting. But I'd be glad to join the party with coffee after dinner, if I may.'

'We will be delighted,' said Ferguson, closing the door behind him.

Petrie smiled. Ferguson did not always tell the truth!

CHAPTER XX

GOLDEN KITES WITH SILKEN TAILS

PETRIE dined alone. Mrs Reardon, her father, Watson, and Ferguson were in sight, but out of hearing. Canned music was being injected into the room from a loudspeaker. Amos listened and winced. The party of four seemed jolly enough, though obviously conscious of the little man's presence. The widow had extended a gracious bow as he took his seat. Bút until the meal was over, his desire for solitude was respected.

Then Ferguson strolled over to his table.

'Come and join the mob, Petrie. Coffee for one sounds like the aftermath of a duel.'

'I always thought duels were affairs involving questionable wounds and tremendous honour for both parties. I'll join you with pleasure. The meal, I thought, was good; the music, nerve shattering.'

Petrie ambled across the room at the side of the taller man as though uncomfortable. The surroundings were not arranged for men like Amos. Nor could it be said that his dinner suit had been a work of inspiration. It hung about him as though the tailor cut it with a view to allowing his customer ample scope for growth.

Watson and the widow's father rose with forced smiles on their faces. Mrs Reardon sat with an elbow lolling on the table, handling a cigarette with an expertness that sat oddly upon her. Petrie settled down in a proffered chair at the side of the window. The commencement of the conversation was dramatic and sudden.

'I'm offering you my assistance again,' said Mrs Reardon, almost cheerily. His eyes were brighter, her tone almost sarcastic.

The implied challenge was accepted with a promptitude that made her gasp and caused the men to stare. Amos dived into a pocket and produced a small metal case. He unclipped the lid and with one sweep of his arm scattered part of the contents over the tablecloth in front of her.

'Have you ever seen these before?' he asked.

Mrs Reardon recoiled, pressing back into her seat as though on the brink of a faint. A chill coursed through her body and a shadow of fear flickered in her brown eyes. She seemed fascinated as she stared at the objects on the table. They were of a rich fawn colour, tinged with green and each of them had a tiny tuft of silk attached to it as if by an invisible filament. The widow did not seem able to avert her gaze.

'Are these the things,' she asked huskily, 'that the police have been questioning my servants about?'

'They are. Mr Watson will recognise them. They were left at his flat last Tuesday night. Seen them before?'

Mrs Reardon was slowly recovering her composure. The men were watching her anxiously. So, also, was Petrie.

'Why should you think that I know something about them?'

Amos did not reply for a while. Ferguson pushed a cigar case across the table. The little man shook his head and slid it back again. The atmosphere had become suddenly uncomfortable.

'I thought there was just the chance,' he said at last, 'that your husband might have brought them with him when he returned home from Africa. I've been trying to trace their arrival in this country and many inquiries lead me to think that something of the kind must have happened.'

His manner was reassuring, but it did not reassure. The elbow on the table supported an arm held rigid by conscious effort. There was a tell-tale waver in the smoke that rose from her cigarette. Petrie noticed the quiver on her lips as she shaped her mouth to speak. When the voice did come it was little more than a whisper.

'I'm afraid I can't help you, Mr Petrie.' There was an interruption; one that the widow appreciated. It came from Ferguson:

'What are the golden kites with silken tails, Petrie?'

'That's not a bad description of yours. If it's original you must have remarkably keen eyes.'

Amos was assessing the distance at seven feet. The Minister was not slow to appreciate the implication. But Amos was shaken somewhat by the reply:

'I'd like to claim that it was original. But it's not. That's what Edgar used to call them.'

The widow dug her nails into her palms until the knuckles shone whitely. Watson bent over her almost protectively.

'That's strange, too,' remarked the little man. 'Mrs Reardon has just been telling me that she had never set eyes on them before. When did Reardon apply that description to them and where did you see them?'

'I remember it well. He showed them to me in his room at the House almost immediately after he returned from his African trip.'

'How long would he have been back in England when he showed them to you?'

'About a week; maybe a little less.'

Petrie glanced at Lola Reardon. She had turned her profile to the man she was anxious to assist. The hand holding the cigarette had fallen to her side. Only a sharp rise and fall of her chest betrayed emotion. Amos turned to the Minister again:

'Did Edgar Reardon happen to tell you why he'd brought this very deadly poison back from Africa with him?'

'Not in so many words, Petrie, not in so many words.'

'I don't mind whether he informed you by suggestion, implication, indication, or in any other way. I just want the effect of it.'

'He treated them as a joke. Perhaps it would be more accurate to say that he looked upon them as a curiosity. I'm not defending his taste, but the fact remains that he did joke about them. To be quite honest with you I didn't know that they contained poison at all. I got the impression that they were just the sort of things people do bring back from outlandish places.'

'A most interesting impression. So he looked upon them as a mere curiosity, as something of a joke?'

'Certainly. I never thought of them in any other way.'

The widow turned her head and found Amos staring full into her eyes. She was averting her glance when he smiled and spoke:

'Seems very remarkable that he didn't show these items of such curiosity, these examples of what he considered a joke, to his wife.'

The widow bit her lip and Watson swung round in her defence:

'Can't we have a holiday from this wretched business for a single night? I hear of strophanthus seeds and strophanthin all day and dream about it all night. For the love of everything, lay off.'

Ferguson looked across the table at the widow. She was trembling. The colouring on her cheeks showed up hard and patchily against the white skin.

'Perhaps we might postpone the remainder of this interrogation for the time being,' suggested the Minister. 'After all it can't be very pleasant for Mrs Reardon and I'm available at any time so that you can question me all night if you like.'

'Very kind and considerate of you,' said Lola, 'but I'd rather you didn't make any fuss about it on my behalf. I'm all right. Really, I am. I'm just a little tired and worn out and that's why things affect me that ordinarily I wouldn't notice at all. I think my nerves have been tried up more than they can stand.'

'And not surprisingly, either,' asserted Watson, as though issuing a challenge to the world to contradict him.

She smiled the palest of pale smiles and reached for the water. Petrie sat wondering which move to make. If he antagonised the party he might close their mouths; if he permitted the opening to pass it might never offer itself again. He was still undecided when the matter was entirely removed from his mind. The wireless began to bellow again.

'This is the Second General News Bulletin,' said the announcer in tones so magnified that each syllable was a buffet to the ears. Petrie remained silent. To have spoken would have been like talking in a railway tunnel with the carriage window open.

'Powers . . . B.B.C. . . . against you,' shouted Ferguson, laughing. The little man closed his eyes for an instant and sat back. Then every thought was beaten out of his head by the words of the announcer:

'Detective-Sergeant Mellor, of New Scotland Yard, one of the officers engaged in investigating the death of the late Chancellor of the Exchequer, Mr Edgar Reardon, on Budget Day, collapsed and died while in his office late this afternoon. Detective-Sergeant Mellor . . .'

A wineglass full of water fell from the hand of Mrs Reardon, and crashed on the floor. With a low moan, she fainted. Watson clutched her body as it toppled from the chair. Ferguson sprang forward to assist him. Brandy was poured down her throat, more trickled down her chin. Her father seized her hands and commenced to chafe them. They gave her more brandy. Slowly she opened her eyes, thrust the glass away from her mouth with a shudder and was half carried to a settee in the corner of the dining-room. There she sat moaning, rocking to and fro as though in pain.

Petrie had been left alone. He was not sorry. Fear was flooding his mind. Mellor was handling routine inquiries under Ripple's direction . . . the fatal Budget speech had been left with Ripple . . . Mellor had to report to the Yard every three or four hours . . . The little man shivered, jumped from his seat and ran into the hall, heading for the reception office.

'I want to make a private call to London at once. Which phone can I use?'

'I'll get the number, sir, and put it through to you in that box.'

'Whitehall 1212,' said Petrie and marched nervously up and down the hall until the bell jangled in the box.

'I want Chief Inspector Ripple,' he called, closing the door behind him as he waited. Ripple's agitated voice came over the wire.

'Amos Petrie here. What's happened to Mellor?' The tone was curt.

'He's dead. Went the same way as Reardon.' Ripple's voice trembled.

'How the hell did it happen, man?'

'I told him about the poison just as you told me. Then I had to leave the office for a few minutes. I left the speech on my desk. He was looking at it when I left. I got back to find him on the floor. We did the best we could. It was hopeless. Mellor was dead!'

'You told him all about the way in which Reardon died?'

'Yes, just as you told me.'

'H'm. A tragedy, a very painful tragedy. But poor Mellor seems to have caused it by his own carelessness. There's no blame attaching to you, my lad, so don't upset yourself about it. Lock that speech in the safe immediately, and don't issue any statement to the papers about the cause of death. I'll be back early in the morning.'

Petrie slammed down the receiver wearily and returned to the dining-room. Mrs Reardon was dabbing her eyes with a fragment of cambric. The others still hovered round her.

'I'm afraid I've been making a silly of myself?' she said to Amos.

Ferguson did not wait for any comment from Petrie.

'Go to bed, dear,' he urged. 'What you need now is a long sleep.'

The advice was taken and Watson assisted her out of the room. As they left the Minister turned to Amos and shook his head reprovingly.

'You've been pressing, Petrie, and if you were a golfer you'd know how useless it is.'

'I'm not playing a game,' snapped Amos. He was still thinking of Mellor, picturing the effects of his death on the melancholic Ripple.

'A game!' snorted Ferguson. 'I call it a damned outrage.'

Watson returned. The widow's faint seemed to have shaken him more than it did her. The man was pallid and shivering.

'I'm feeling rough,' he said to Amos. 'If anything you want to say to me will wait until the morning I'll go to bed.'

'That will suit me,' agreed Petrie. Mrs Reardon's father made the same request. It was granted. When they left the room Amos led the Minister into the small smoking-room.

'How often did you see those seeds?' he inquired as soon as he closed the door.

'Only the once.'

'But Edgar Reardon talked of them more than once?'

'Quite a lot. I've told you that he made a joke of it.'

'Never mind the joke. Everybody but you seems to have forgotten it. In any case the joke wasn't very amusing at the finish for Reardon. Tell me where he kept them.'

'I don't know. When I saw them they were in a sort of earthenware jar on his table. I'm afraid I can't tell you more about them than that—except that he seemed to have shoved the jar to one side to make room for something else on the table. It was standing just beyond the edge of that screen he had round his table.'

Petrie tugged at his handkerchief and was silent for a time.

'The screen is news to me,' he said. 'There was no screen in the room when I saw it, and I was definitely told that nothing had been moved. Are you quite certain about this screen?'

'Not the slightest doubt. Whoever told you that nothing had been moved gave you the wrong story. Edgar always had a screen at the back of his desk. It was specially put there to cover his chair, so to speak, and cut off any draughts. Edgar had a few eccentricities. The fear of draughts was one of them. I've never known a man so scared of them—even worse than the King's Bench Division judges, and that's saying something. Why, of course the screen was there. We used to pull his leg about it and ask him how his pneumonia was getting on.'

Petrie sat with his legs crossed, one of the few remaining wisps of hair drooping over his forehead, his hands fastened round his knees, his mouth twisted in a way that might have indicated anything from complete surprise to subdued amusement.

'Was that screen in its usual position when you saw him before the Budget speech?' he asked.

'I'm almost certain it was. But I can't swear to it. I was so used to seeing it there that I might have imagined I saw it, even if it had been moved. Have a drink, Petrie?'

'Beer for me, thanks. Push the bell and sound the alarm for the waiter. While we wait for him tell me some more about this screen. Had Reardon erected that screen as soon as he took over office?'

'I think not. You're carrying my memory back a fair way, but I seem to remember that he'd been Chancellor a few months or so before he complained about the draught and insisted that a screen should be installed. We weren't surprised. A draught to Edgar was about the same as a sick headache to an ordinary man.'

'Some folks are reared that way. I've met them. Now let—'

He ceased speaking as the waiter entered and took the order. Even when the man vanished he continued to stare into the fire. He didn't want the questioning interrupted by the rattle of glasses on a tray.

The waiter arrived. They toasted each other in silence. Petrie laid his tankard on the table and resumed the barrage:

'You say the earthenware pot containing these seeds had been moved. Curious thing to be certain about, Ferguson. Why?'

'I can easily answer that. The jar, when I saw it, was standing at the side of a bundle of documents, about a foot from the inkstand. I told Edgar that when the messenger came to collect the papers he might take a fancy to his golden kites as well. He laughed. But when I came into the room on the afternoon of Budget day I noticed, quite casually, that the jar was standing on the far side of the table. I suppose it would be about a foot beyond the edge of the screen.'

'Where was the Budget speech when you were in the room'?

'Let me think. Eh . . . it was lying on the table at the side of the jar. Yes, I'm sure it was, because that's when I noticed that the jar had been moved. But what the hell is all this talk about?'

'Nothing much. I'm sure you're tired. I know I am. Heading for bed?'

They mounted the stairs together. Petrie sat in his bedroom and amused himself by jotting down the known facts of the case. When he had finished writing and was considering what he had written, a low murmur of voices attracted his attention. The sound came from Watson's room. Listening carefully, Amos thought he detected a note of distress. He rose quietly and walked into the corridor. Without noise or ceremony he opened a door on the far side of the passage and looked inside. Mrs Reardon's hat and coat hung on a peg. The lady herself was absent. Amos went back to his own room as quietly as he had come. But before retiring to bed he added another to the list of facts.

CHAPTER XXI

PALING DECIDES TO TALK

PETRIE left the hotel in the misty haze of early morning, stifling yawns as the car tore towards London, wakening himself by performing mental somersaults. His thoughts strayed from chub to Mellor, from pike to Edgar Reardon, from roach to Watson, from perch to Ferguson, from tench to the widow, and from thence to an odd association of ideas linking coloured water with the screen that had been in the Chancellor's private room. Of one thing he was certain—that, although the solution of the problem seemed a mile away, the intervening barriers might easily fall under a lucky assault.

Big Ben was chiming nine o'clock when the car turned under the arch and pulled up outside the Yard. The little man was surprised to find that Ripple had already begun work. The Inspector looked gaunt and drawn. Blue shadows threw half moons under his eyes, his lips seemed even more bloodless than ever, his hands revealed an unexpected twitch.

'Never expected to see you so soon,' he said listlessly. 'I haven't been to bed all night. This case is breaking me, busting me up.'

'Rubbish, Sunshine. Never say die. Are you letting Mellor's tragedy weigh on your mind? The fault wasn't yours, lad. Anything else keeping you awake?'

'I'm working in the dark. I don't know what you're doing, and I hardly know what I'm doing myself. There are half a dozen reports here for you to look at, but it doesn't seem to me that they take us any further. You'd better look them over. I was working like hell until three this morning after I got the report through from the City police. You'll find their stuff, and mine, among the pile.'

'Did you happen to telephone Paris about the purchase of that arsenic we got from Paling's place?'

'Yes. No doubt about it—Paling bought it.'

'One more question and then I want you to settle down in the corner and sleep for a couple of hours. You've had the servants at Reardon's place questioned and you've seen the stuff that was left at Watson's flat. Did any of your men find a servant who had seen those seeds at 11 Downing Street?'

'Yes. One of the maids said that she had seen them.'

'That explains little Lola's fainting fit,' said Amos.

'Dunno what you're talking about.'

'Doesn't matter, Insomnia. Bed yourself down in the corner. If you are wanted I'll kick you in the stomach. Go to sleep like a good boy. Can I get you anything to eat or drink before you settle down?'

'Nothing, thanks. Wake me when I can arrest the murderer. That'll give me time to sleep for a month. Best of luck.'

Petrie threw off his hat and coat, settled down before the pile of papers. Within ten minutes Amos realised that the news from the City, like everything else connected with the case, was tantalising. Ripple had been supplied with a list of names, detailing all the big operators speculating in the pre-Budget market. The City police identified most of them as eminently respectable businessmen buying in the normal course of business, taking advantage of the market movements they saw around them. Not one of them could, by any possibility, have seen Reardon on the day of his death. There were a few others still to be checked.

Petrie read twice through the list before looking at Ripple's detailed report on each man. He noticed that three names stood out. And all were newcomers to the market. Amos turned with increased interest to read Ripple's reports on the three strangers, the three big speculators of whom the City police knew nothing. The more he read the greater his interest became.

One was Mr J. P. Hermanos, of Rasdon Chambers, Jermyn

Street. Ripple had made a call on the gentleman without success. Still, his comments upon the matter were illuminating. Mr Hermanos had taken a most comfortable suite of rooms two months before the Budget. He had not been seen in them since the day following Reardon's death. According to the description he was of medium size, dark, foreign looking, and seemed a little shy. Amos imagined that the same description might well fit another million men and decided that for the moment Mr Hermanos could be left to seek his own salvation.

The second man on the list was even more mysterious. He was Mr Thomas Price, of Wigan Street, Bloomsbury. It seemed from Ripple's report that Mr Price was a much-travelled man. He stayed away from his rooms for weeks and months at a stretch. The Yard man had missed Mr Price's last stay by about a couple of weeks. Even more singular was the fact that on that occasion Mr Thomas Price had almost rendered the landlady delirious by paying six months' rent in advance. It was only natural that after that the landlady was prepared to take an indulgent view of his eccentricities. It was even possible that the effect of being six months in advance with the rent instead of six months in arrears had disturbed her descriptive faculties at the time when Ripple asked about the appearance of the elusive Price.

She described him—enthusiastically, but vaguely—as a perfect gentleman. Beyond that she did not seem prepared to commit herself. From the tone in which Ripple penned his report Amos gained the impression that a cross-eyed mulatto with a list of convictions long enough to cross the Atlantic, with a partiality for robbery with violence, and a general tendency towards murder, would have affected the wings of an angel, the disposition of a saint, the manners of a complete courtier, and the air of a nobleman if he paid a year's rent in advance.

Ripple had certainly concentrated his attention on the third mysterious buyer. He was Mr William Hepworth, of the Rue du Fossee aux Loups, Brussels. Like the other men of mystery, there were some peculiarities about Hepworth. He had arranged for the opening of his Stock Exchange account by letter. The brokers had never seen him in person. Nor were they anxious to meet him. He had deposited the 'cover' for his transactions in cash. Who were they to question why?

Mr Hepworth had stayed in England during the two or three weeks which covered his active buying. His operations were certainly of a size to justify the visit to London, and he had stayed at a West End hotel which fitted well with the importance of his business. It seemed curious that on inquiry at the hotel, Ripple discovered that William Hepworth had occupied a most modest room there. His conduct, also, had been most unobtrusive. He was seen very little, and the only thing by which he could be recalled with any certainty was the punctuality with which he had paid his bill.

Perhaps the most significant thing about the man was his address at Brussels. Ripple had communicated with the Belgian police. Their inquiries revealed that his name did not appear in any of the Brussels directories, and he was entirely unknown, even as a visitor. Furthermore, his address in the Rue du Fossee aux Loups was tenanted by people who had neither seen nor heard of him. Even more curious was the fact that the Belgian police had telephoned Ripple again, and he had added their message as a postscript to the report. One of the tenants had broken down sufficiently to admit that he had drawn money by handling a desultory correspondence for William Hepworth.

It seemed that the elusive Hepworth did not call for the letters in person. Sometimes he sent telegrams instructing their dispatch to hotels in other towns. Occasionally a messenger arrived—always at weekends—with a letter authorising the tenant to hand over Hepworth's correspondence to bearer. The Bruxellois could only describe the caller as '*un Anglais*.'

Ripple had done his work well. Originals of the telegrams sent to the Fossee aux Loups had been produced for him by the Post Office. But they were typed, even to the signature.

Added to that the typing looked as though it had been done on a brand new machine with a virgin ribbon. It was completely characterless. Mr Hepworth, like Mr Price, had run to earth.

Even the specimen signatures secured by Ripple from the brokers revealed nothing. The signature of Price was large and untidy; that of Hepworth almost Gallic in its neatness. There was a noticeable thickening of the e in Hepworth, indicating the use of a fine, soft nib, and all the other letters were finished with scrupulous care down to the crossing of the t. The writing of Hermanos was different from either. Without being small, it was round and backhanded, and had a squat appearance.

Amos drew from Ripple's drawer a few original notes they had in Edgar Reardon's handwriting. The comparison did not enable him to draw any definite conclusions. He was still poring over them when Ripple rose and stretched himself.

'No good,' he announced. 'I can't go to sleep here. I'll carry on now until I collect a real sleep. What do you think about things?'

'These things are purposely confused, Sunshine. That's painfully obvious. Still, I may be able to persuade these most retiring gents to step out into the open.'

'I wish you'd tell me how you're going to do it. I'm bent, battered and bewildered. Gosh! I feel bad.'

'You ought to sleep, laddie. These men, Dynamite, will come to me fast enough if this confusion and muddling was only arranged to protect Edgar Reardon. In the meantime you'll have to send a man over to watch that address in Brussels. I suppose you've got folks watching the two addresses on this side?'

'A bright lad on the doorstep of each now.'

'Good. Since you don't want to sleep get in touch with the private detective who looks after Ferguson.'

'Collins?'

'Yes. He hasn't been taken down to Brockenhurst. Find out from him what Ferguson was doing last Tuesday. If Collins was told to run away and play that night he'd better say so; then he, or you, can find out what Ferguson did during his absence.

But make it plain to him that I want to know what he was doing, what Ferguson was doing, and how he knows what Ferguson was doing. I don't want guesswork.'

'I'll do that now. It might keep me awake. Anything else?'

'Yes. When you get down below tell them to bring Paling here to me. Have you seen him while I've been away?'

'Yes. You might as well talk to a lump of ferro-concrete.'

Petrie turned again to the reports, and was still reading when a detective knocked, opened the door, and ushered Paling into the room. Petrie looked at him, and was surprised. The man was as spruce as when he had been taken into custody. But the doubts and worries of the intervening time had left their mark on his face. A rim of discoloured flesh showed under each eye, and his movements had an abruptness that advertised jangled nerves. There was a suggestion of dread in the look he fastened on Amos, but his voice was steady:

'How much longer do you intend to detain me from my business?'

'That depends. I'm afraid I can't give you any promises, or even hold out any hopes at present, Paling. Since I last spoke to you I've found out very many things. Sit down, and make yourself as much at home as possible.'

Paling sat down. His escort moved over and stood with his back against the door. The prisoner raised his trousers to preserve the crease, and elevated his eyebrows.

'So you've found out many things, eh? Such as?'

Amos thought the matter over before speaking. Then he gambled:

'I heard, for instance, that while you were staying at Milford an attempt was made to murder Edgar Reardon by poisoning him.'

Paling jumped from his chair and threw his hands aloft.

'I thought that would be the next thing,' he said. 'I could rather see it coming. I've never heard such utter rubbish in my life.'

'There are witnesses,' remarked Amos quietly.

'Witnesses? Of course there are! Witnesses who can prove that an attempted murder was tried by poisoning at Milford. Apart from that they're absolutely and entirely wrong.'

'I don't follow you at all. What do you mean?'

'I didn't try to poison Reardon. He tried to poison me!'

'With arsenic that you had bought. Doesn't sound reasonable to me.'

'But it's true, horribly and damnably true,' shouted Paling. His face whitened. Then words burst from him in a torrent, like water streaming through a suddenly opened sluice. 'I bought the arsenic. Oh, yes. I bought it to oblige Reardon by his special request. That was the devilish, the damnable cunning of the man. And I was such a fool I couldn't see it at the time. My God! I can see it all now. Why, as long ago as the beginning of last January, Edgar Reardon had decided to murder me. And all the time, before then and since, he fawned round me as a friend, making plans with me about the future, getting me to help him in a hundred and one ways. Oh, Edgar Reardon was a fine friend. And I was the sucker, the boob, the fool to fall for the murdering hypocrite.'

Paling's vehemence left him breathless. Amos was amazed at the change in the man. But he was without mercy as he probed deeper in his search for the truth.

'Was it part of Reardon's plan to murder you with poison that was actually in your own possession?'

'No, of course it wasn't. He had the poison right enough. But do you imagine for a minute that I was going to leave it with him when I found that he was using it to murder me? Ask yourself. After that attempt of his at Milford I made him hand it over to me. That's how you came to find it at my place. He had to give it to me. I told him that if he didn't I'd report the attempted murder to the police. I demanded it as the price of my silence.'

'The price seems modest enough. I confess I was surprised to find that the police weren't called in by either of you.'

Paling took a deep breath, and plunged into another sea of words.

'That's what I ought to have done, Petrie. I was a damnation fool to throw away that poisoned wine. It put me right away into a false position. You see why? It gave the cunning swine the chance of working against me again! He just suggested to his friends that whatever the trouble between us was I must have been the cause of it. I was a fool, a complete fool. But . . . oh, I was tied hand and foot.'

Petrie's head began to sway to and fro. With a flurried movement he grabbed for his handkerchief. His glance did not move, though, from Paling's face. The little man decided to take the plunge.

'That's not the version of your association with Reardon that I've heard, Paling. Looks to me as though you'll have to explain.'

'I was his partner,' announced Paling, almost defiantly.

'J. P. Hermanos,' suggested Amos helpfully.

Paling nodded. 'I'm glad you know. It makes things easier for me.'

'Thomas Price was in the same line of business?'

The man frowned for a second and then shook his head.

'No. I've never heard that name before. Don't know him.'

'Know William Hepworth, of the Rue du Fossee aux Loups, Brussels?'

A blank look appeared in Paling's eyes, and again he shook his head.

'Both those men,' said Petrie slowly, 'were engaged, as you were, in speculating on the Budget, and, like you, both used false names.'

Amos could see the blood pulsing through the veins at the sides of the man's forehead. His hands were clenched, the eyes sparkled with concentrated venom.

'Reardon always told me,' he said, 'that he dare not let anyone into the secret. He said that it would mean his irretrievable ruin if he did. That's why it was so essential for him to have someone he could trust. And that's where I come into the picture.'

'And he felt that he could trust you, did he?'

'It wasn't a matter of what he felt. He took jolly good care to see that he could. Edgar Reardon wouldn't trust any man.'

'I must hear more about this. What did he do to ensure your complete fidelity in his interests?'

'I suppose there's nothing for me to gain now by staying dumb. You seem to know plenty. Want the real answer to that question?'

'Of course I do. You'll gain nothing by sitting on the fence.'

'Well, here is your answer. Edgar Reardon could trust me because of the money he made me put in the partnership. Add to that the way in which he worked the business, and you can see that I couldn't play crooked with him if I'd wanted to. God! It was very cunning.'

'You'd better tell me the complete story, Paling. It may help you.'

'All right. Get me a cigarette, and I'll tell you all about it.'

The detective at the door stepped forward and opened his case.

CHAPTER XXII

PALING'S STORY

PALING inhaled some smoke and hesitated like an inexpert diver about to take the plunge. Amos sat back and folded his arms.

'Well,' commenced the man, 'the arrangement was that he should put eight thousand pounds into the business—'

Petrie held up his hand. 'Wait one second. How could he do that if he were to remain in the background?'

'He transferred the money to me in the first place.'

'When?'

'Oh, at various times since the beginning of the year. When I was prepared to put in my money he would put in the equivalent, and then, when the pass-book was in order and I was ready to put in more money, he would do the same.'

'You mean that you also invested eight thousand pounds?'

'Sixteen thousand! He insisted on me paying in double to take a half share of the profits. He kept pointing out that he was the one supplying the information on which the partnership operated, and he was the person taking the risk.'

'But, Paling, that wasn't getting you into his power. It was the other way round. He was putting himself into your power. You could have walked away with the profits, and he would have been powerless—unless he wanted to sacrifice his political position.'

'So he said, Petrie. He told me over and over again that if there was any trouble about the division of the profits I'd only got to sue him, and he'd be compelled to pay up. Believe me, it didn't work out that way. Follow me carefully. Since he insisted that it would work out that way, that all the risk was with him, and that I held all the security, he insisted on me supplying some guarantee. The only condition on which he would enter the deal was that the signature of the firm should be his. I didn't even sign a buying form, except per pro. The bank had authority to honour none but his signature. He signed all the cheques on the Hermanos account.'

'So that you tied up your own money in this venture?'

'Exactly.'

'But you were compensated by very large profits.'

'Which I've never been able to touch, Petrie. I couldn't even get my own money back without a cheque from Edgar Reardon. That's what he put to me at Milford when I found out about the poison. He said that if I made a criminal charge he'd fight me, and if he fought me he'd see me damned before he returned a penny to me. He was going to claim not only the profits, but also the entire capital of Hermanos.'

'But if you acted reasonably?'

'Then he'd play fair, and I'd have my half share as arranged.'

'And what guarantee had you that he would play fair?'

'Almost nothing. I only had the guarantee that had already failed me. I could sue him and still leave him something to save. He forced me to return to that position.'

Paling talked on for ten minutes. By then Amos held a complete explanation for every suggestion that had been made against the man with regard to the incidents at Milford. He gave Petrie the address of the safe deposit in which the Hermanos papers were kept. He even wrote out an authority to withdraw them from the deposit—at the same time expressing doubt as to whether they would accept it. He showed no hesitation in writing Hermanos, Price, Hepworth, or any other word, or collection of words. At Petrie's dictation he wrote fast and he wrote slowly; he wrote with a fine nib, and with a broad one. But his writing had always the same characteristics. Except when it degenerated it was a mere scrawl, slim and stilted, an oddly unpractised hand. He could never have attained to the careless boldness shown in the signatures of either Price or Hermanos.

One other thing interested Amos. That was the appearance and development of the blind spot in Paling's mind. When he had been questioned before he had been quick to seize on points in his own favour. Now he seemed to be incapable of seeing the very obvious pit he was digging for himself. Every detail by which he proved the unlikeliness of any attempt on Reardon's life with arsenic only added to the strength of the motive which Paling had to get rid of his embarrassments—and the man who was causing them. Paling did not seem to scent the danger.

Petrie gave him a rude awakening.

'When did you last see strophanthus seeds?'

'I've never seen strophanthus seeds.'

Petrie made a gesture of impatience, and turned to the man at the door.

'Take him away. The gentleman will no doubt think about my very simple question. I would strongly advise you, Paling, to use the next half-hour putting a very considerable jerk into your memory. So far you have done well. But you've only made a start along a long, long road. Let me know when you've recovered your memory.'

Immediately Paling left the room Ripple walked in.

'Collins won't be in town for another hour, so I came back. There was some stuff I forgot to give you. I wouldn't put it among the other papers, because it seemed risky. I left it in the safe. Here you are—my check on Reardon's banking account.'

Amos looked hurriedly down the list. He made one discovery of real importance. Reardon had prepared for his pre-Budget gamble by transferring money and securities worth £30,000 to Thomas Price, of Bloomsbury. Ripple also was impressed by the amount.

'He certainly didn't do things by half,' said the Yard man.

Petrie made no comment. He was comparing the figure with Ripple's note of the cover put up by Price.

'No,' said the little man, 'but Price apparently did. He only used between eleven and twelve thousand pounds of the money. Get a man to go through Price's banking account, and then we can cross-check. You understand? I want this £30,000 traced. What became of the unused balance? Was it allowed to lie fallow?'

'I'll see to that. I'd like to meet that man Price.'

'Never despair. I'm not so certain that you haven't seen him. Oh, get the bank manager at Bloomsbury to improve on the landlady's description of Price. Another thing that must be checked, and I'd like you to do this yourself. Reardon used to have a screen round the back of his chair in the private room at the House. I was told that nothing had been moved, but when I arrived in that room there was no screen. I want to know when it was moved, by whom it was moved, why it was moved, and where it is now. All clear?'

'I'll see to that immediately. Anything else?'

'One thing. I'm told there was an earthenware jar on his table. I want it. If it isn't there I want to know where it is, who took it, when it was first missed, and whether it was empty. The same person can probably kill both birds for you.'

Ripple had not long been gone when the 'House' telephone rang. Petrie was informed that Sir Norris Wheeler, the Commissioner, wanted to see him. Amos swore profusely, collected a battered hat, and locked away all the loose papers. Then he went to meet Sir Norris. The Commissioner greeted him cheerfully.

'I wanted to know how the investigation is advancing, Petrie.'

'Oh, it's advancing—just advancing. That's about all.'

'Surely you're nearer a solution than you were at the start?'

'I think we've managed to make things a bit more confusing.'

'Doesn't sound as though you want much more than luck,' said the Commissioner nastily.

'Perhaps you're right. We could do with luck, more room in which to work, less interference from those not engaged on the case, better weather, and more regular hours of sleep.'

Sir Norris abandoned the effort, and the little man sauntered along Whitehall in time to discover that his favourite hostelry had just opened. He spent half an hour emptying a pint tankard, and browsing over the pages of the *Fishing Gazette*. When he returned to the Yard he found a report waiting for him. Someone had performed a thoroughly slick piece of work. The detective delegated to the job had already seen the manager of the branch bank at Bloomsbury.

It seemed at first that the material secured was scarcely worth waiting for. To the manager, Mr Price appeared as a prosperous customer from the country with gout in the eye. The manager had been so impressed with the gouty eye, and the patch over it, that he had forgotten to look at the sound eye. He had a hazy idea that Price wore hair on his face somewhere, but he couldn't remember where.

'This Mr Price,' muttered Petrie, 'is like everybody else in this case—as full of tricks as a monkey.'

Amos turned to the man's banking account. Apparently Mr Price's gout had not run true to form. It had not had the usual unfortunate effect on the temper. He had presented a cheque for £20,000 to Mr Hepworth of the Rue du Fossee aux Loups! The little man was seeing daylight more clearly.

'Hepworth,' he told himself, 'is the man who impressed himself on the Brussels accommodation address keeper as "*un vrai Anglais*," and who is such an ordinary Englishman that the proprietors of a West End hotel can't remember him at all. Mr Blank, alias Hepworth, alias Price—but not alias Hermanos.'

Petrie was peering at the fire when Ripple returned. The Yard man looked less tired since he had been out in the air.

'I've got pretty well all you want, I think. I'll start with Collins. I found him ten minutes ago. Ferguson has got a cast-iron alibi for Tuesday night. He brought friends home from the House of Commons, and the last of them stayed until after midnight. After they had departed he called the cook up to the room and gave her some sort of a present. It was her birthday, and she'd been entertaining on her own downstairs. Collins was in her party. That's how he knows.'

'All right. We seem to be touching firm ground at last. I'll ring up Ferguson now and tell him to arrange a meeting for me with the mysterious Mr Price for Monday.'

He found the Minister in the hotel. Rain had ruined the golf. The little man told him what he wanted.

'I'll write to him at Wigan Street and arrange things, Petrie.'

'How do you know that he lives at Wigan Street?'

'Because my memory's good, and I've seen the name in some of Reardon's papers. You'll find him at Wigan Street if you go along.'

'Who is he? Where does he come from? What does he do for a living? All I know about him is that he calls himself Thomas Price.'

'I don't know anymore than that myself.'

Amos muttered softly, and slammed down the receiver.

'Another blind alley, Sunshine,' he said. 'What sort of reports did you get from Mellor before he shuffled off the mortal coil?'

'I had him concentrating on that robbery, or whatever you call it, at Watson's. He checked everybody involved in the case. I'll get the reports for you.'

Mellor's style of composition was not notable for brightness. But Petrie was chuckling before he got to the end of the reports. He rang for a large scale map of London and a pair of dividers. He traced Mellor's inquiries stage by stage, striding where the man went, but missing none of the facts unearthed.

Then he turned to the map of London and the dividers. He was measuring distances and comparing times with those given by Mellor.

CHAPTER XXIII

FURTHER DISCOVERIES

RIPPLE sat down while Amos worked, puffing nervously at an incredibly foul pipe. At last the little man turned to him.

'And what about the screen and the earthenware jar, Angel?'

'The screen was moved shortly after the death to shield the body of Reardon from unnecessary sightseers. They thought it would be quite all right. I told them to put it back as it was. They've done that. The jar is still on the table, and it's empty. Anything else you want to know?'

'Not at the moment. Collect your hat and coat. We're walking round to the House of Commons.' When they reached the door of Reardon's room the little man paused to lecture the attendant on the enormity of his sin in permitting the screen to be moved. The penitent assured him that it had been replaced exactly in the original position. Petrie found that the screen was of the popular three-sectional type. He judged it to be about six feet wide when standing, and rather more than that in height. It stood some four feet behind the chair at the table, and a couple of feet away from a curtained window.

Amos bent down on his hands and knees, pulled a magnifying glass from his pocket with an apologetic air, and commenced to examine the floor inch by inch. He seemed disappointed, and turned his attention to the skirting board. At first glance the result seemed almost negligible. Suddenly he bent lower and altered the range of the glass. There were two deep, and several slighter, indentations on the board at a low level—not more than half an inch from the floor. Apart from them the only other things to be noted were the 'tidemarks' left by a careless floor-washer, and some curved bootmarks on the skirting.

Ripple walked round the room, bending low, staring at the skirting.

'Those marks are only in one corner,' he announced.

Petrie stared at the skirting cheerfully and nodded.

'That's just what I hoped, laddie. I'm glad the meaning of it is obvious to you. Concealment behind this screen may not be absolute unless the person hiding crouches a little.'

He came from behind the screen, walked round to the far side of the table, and then backed away from there towards the door, staring at the screen the whole time. Apparently his impression was confirmed. He returned to the screen with a smile broadening on his face. Even Ripple tried to grin. The effort seemed to trouble him.

'It's a certainty, Sunshine,' said the little man, 'that the screen was used for more purposes than to protect Reardon from draughts.'

'But who on earth could it be? The thing seems ridiculous.'

'Not if we can assume visits to the Chancellor's private room by Mr Hepworth or Mr Price. Wouldn't a cautious statesman wish to keep them dark? You bet your life he would. Suppose the Prime Minister walked in while he was telling Messrs. Hepworth and Price the inside story of the Budget!'

'I don't think they could both hide behind that screen.'

'Nor do I. I think there's only one of 'em!'

'Looks as though we'll have to begin the hunt all over again from the start. Hell! By Christmas we might get a useful lead.'

'Forget it, Depression. You're falling into the dumps again. The man we're looking for couldn't be anybody. He'd have to be someone with Hepworth's very peculiar gift of self-effacement. Otherwise he couldn't get out of the room again without attracting attention. Think, laddie. How would an ordinary man exercise those gifts in the House of Commons? I'm not troubled by that. I want to know when he was last here—and how I'm going to prove it.'

Where design failed, chance helped. Petrie, for the first time, was in luck. He wanted to step out the distance between the

Ferguson residence and Watson's flat. He stopped by Lambeth Bridge to explain why, and as they leaned against the Embankment parapet they watched the river flowing sluggishly over the sleek green bed. Someone touched the Yard man's shoulder. He turned to find a grinning taxi driver by his side.

'Hallo, sir. I've taken you back home many a time from there.' He pointed a thumb towards the Yard. 'Mind giving me a bit of advice?'

'So long as it doesn't take long for me to give it.'

The driver fumbled in his pocket, pulled out a note.

'I had a fare the other night, sir, and he gave me this. It was dark, and I didn't know till he'd gone that the note was foreign. What can I do with it, mister?'

Petrie bent over, spurred by idle curiosity. The driver held in his hand a Belgian hundred-franc note.

'Mean you couldn't tell that from an English note?' he asked.

'It was passed to me in the dark, sir—House of Lords porch in Palace Yard. I turned round to the lamps, but he said, "Ten bob," and I knew he wouldn't try to twist me.'

'You've driven him before then?'

'Often, sir. That's why I didn't look at the note. The man's a gent—a perfect gentleman.'

Ripple commenced to laugh. But Petrie showed no sign of amusement.

'Funny,' said the driver, 'the last time I saw him he was standing just where you are now. Oh, I'll recognise him all right when I see him. I only thought you might tell me what to do with the note.'

'When did this happen?' asked Petrie. 'You'll remember that, eh?'

''Course I do, sir. It was after midnight last Tuesday.'

Amos took his spectacles off, wiped them on his handkerchief.

'You interest me. Mind telling me what you did that night? You said you dropped your fare in Palace Yard. After that I suppose you remained in your cab?'

'I went on to the bridge for a cup of coffee with George,' he replied, pointing his finger towards Westminster Bridge.

'Splendid idea, too. How long were you with George?'

'Best part of an hour. It must have been mostly one o'clock when I left his stall.'

'That's very extraordinary. If you left your fare in Palace Yard, stayed at the stall for an hour, and then saw him again here he must have been walking very slowly.'

'He'd stopped walking altogether.' The driver laughed. 'First he took off his coat, and then I reckon he stopped for a rest.'

'Didn't you offer to pick him up again?'

'I hooted, sir, but he waved me on.'

'I suppose you didn't happen to notice his overcoat?'

'I did when he got out of the cab, sir. It was one of them loose raglan things.'

'You seem to have noticed a lot, seeing that you missed the note.'

'I knew he wouldn't twist me, sir, and I didn't find out about the note until I got home about six.'

'I'd like you to drive us round to Scotland Yard if you will. In the meantime hand me that note. I'll give you three pounds for it. You can take it from me that should be about right.'

The men climbed into the taxi. The driver smiled cheerfully.

'This seems too good to be true,' said Ripple. 'Luck like this never happens to me. There must be a catch in it somewhere.'

Arriving at the Yard, Amos led the driver to Ripple's office, and talked in a whisper to the Yard man.

'All the men involved in this case are well known, Sunshine. There must be photographs of them somewhere about the place. Collect pictures of Ferguson, Watson, Curtis, and tell them I want Paling brought up to me at once.'

Ripple hurried away, and Petrie talked to the driver about most things—except his midnight fare. Paling arrived before the Yard man returned. Petrie questioned the driver:

'Ever seen this man before, cabby?'

'No, sir. That's not the gentleman I drove.'

'Thanks. Sorry to trouble you, Paling. I'll see you in a minute.'

Paling retired, and Ripple arrived with the photographs in his hand. Amos handed one of Watson to the driver: 'Is that the man you drove?'

'No, sir, nothing like him at all.'

'What about this one?' He handed over a picture of Ferguson.

Again the driver shook his head.

Petrie had a singular glint in his eye when he passed the third photograph to the cabby.

'What about that one, eh?'

There was no trace of hesitation. The driver's face broadened.

'That's him, sir. I'd know him anywhere. Couldn't mistake him if I tried to. He's the one who gave me that foreign note.'

Dick Curtis had been identified!

They sent the driver into the waiting-room. Ripple was genuinely horrified. He looked like a bad case of concussion.

'What—what does all this mean? Do I get another waiting-room ready for Curtis? Everybody's gone mad, completely barmy.'

'Sunshine, you do not get another waiting-room ready. You get the best man you've got to see that Curtis doesn't move out of this country between now and Monday. After that you swear out a search warrant. On Monday we'll visit the chambers of Mr Curtis together.'

'You think we're entitled to swear out a warrant?'

'I'll say we are. Ripple, we've both known an industrious man who walked a quarter of a mile, committed a murder and picked up an alibi—all in twenty minutes. What is to stop a beginner doing a comparatively simple housebreaking job in twice that length of time? Get your search warrant, and don't get the jitters.'

'I don't think we ought to leave it until Monday. All sorts of things can happen between now and then. What about doing it now?'

'I'm not going to hurry, Ripple. We're not dealing with an ordinary man. There are a few odds and ends to clear up before we take the jump, and I want to think them out a bit. Curtis isn't only a genius in crime—he's a first-class barrister who knows every loophole in the game. If we make one mistake we're permanently sunk.'

'I don't like doing it, but you'd better have it your own way.'

'Grab Paling for me again. I want to see him before I go home.'

When the man arrived Petrie's questions were brief and succinct.

'Reardon made heavy payments to you early this year. I was told that they were blackmailing payments, that you were extorting money from him in connection with the alleged French wife. Explain.'

'That's all rubbish. The payments he made to me were only made for me to transfer them to the Hermanos account. I never had a penny of it. The only person who was swindled was me.'

'What's all this about the French wife?'

'Quite genuine. Reardon introduced her to me in Paris one night when he was drunk. She told me the whole story. I've been friendly with her ever since. But I never used that information.'

'You tried to get money out of that woman, tried to start her bleeding Mrs Reardon for more. Why?'

'It seemed my only chance of getting some of my own money back.'

'That was your first attempt to use that information?'

'Certainly. Now I've told you everything, can I go home?'

'I'm sorry. You will be released on Monday, Paling.'

'Why on earth can't I go now that I've cleared myself?'

'Because you're a lot safer where you are. I'm holding you in order to protect you. Be grateful for that. See you on Monday.'

CHAPTER XXIV

NEARING THE END

AMOS was busy throughout Monday morning. His interviews with Ferguson, Watson and Mrs Reardon were brief. He emphasised to the Minister that he did not now want the names of the nominees. Petrie visualised Ferguson visiting Dick Curtis for advice! He drew Watson to one side and whispered to him:

'For a man of your age you behave very childishly, Watson. Any trouble you've struck is your own fault. Next time you fall in love don't make a fool of yourself over it. That's all.'

Watson blushed, but offered no retort. He had spent most of the weekend considering his course of conduct. Now he realised that he had done nothing of which he might be proud. As he left them Petrie made a last request:

'I am most anxious that you should all remain in your homes until you hear from me. That's not an order. It's a very urgent request.'

Returning to the Yard, he asked Ripple to collect half a dozen of the best men he could find, men with plenty of brain and with mouths as close as oysters. The Inspector soon found them.

'I want you men to look after the entrances of the House of Commons as closely as you can without attention. You all know Dick Curtis by sight. If he tries to enter the House, don't let him in. Try any sort of an excuse. Tell him, if you like, that I want to see him here. Then dump him in a waiting-room, keep an eye on him and telephone me at his Temple Bar number. Don't make him panicky.'

The two men had lunch. Then, armed with the search warrant, they presented themselves at Curtis's chambers in the Temple. A young man opened the door, informed them that

Mr Curtis was out, and commenced to close the door again. Ripple showed him the warrant.

'I'm his secretary,' said the man, with sagging jaws, gaping mouth. He led the way inside. Curtis used the rooms for a dual purpose. His offices were there, and at the rear was his home. Petrie closed the door and looked on the back of it. There was no overcoat to be seen.

'Was Mr Curtis wearing a raglan overcoat when he left here?'

'No, sir. He didn't take an overcoat with him.'

Amos walked through into the sitting-room, and then turned to Ripple: 'You've got a man downstairs. Tell him to take this young man to the Yard and hold him until he hears from us. We don't want him prowling round here.'

The Inspector disappeared, and Petrie began a close search. The drawers of the desk were locked. Amos produced a bunch of 'twirls,' and opened them. Underneath a pile of legal documents in the bottom drawer he found a small mortar and pestle. Tucked inside a dry cleaner's box on the top of a cupboard was a collection of laboratory apparatus. Ripple returned and joined in the search. The safe in the corner defeated them. He telephoned the Yard, asking the barrister's secretary whether he had a key. The youth informed them that it was always hidden in the bottom of the clock in the office. There Ripple found it. Nearly all the documents in the safe were of a type one would normally expect to discover in a barrister's office. But one small sheet, dotted all over with figures, certainly had nothing to do with the law. Petrie studied it with interest.

'I see,' he said, 'that Mr Price has made out an account of Mr Hepworth's Budget speculations and left it with Mr Curtis. Odd, eh?'

In the meantime Ripple had been experimenting with the typewriter in the office. He raised the sheet of paper with a smile.

'Some hot evidence here. Look at this busted capital H. That's exactly the same as the H on those Hepworth telegrams.'

'Splendid. Neat work. But where the hell is that overcoat?'

'I can't see it. Perhaps it's in the domestic quarters.'

'Very unlikely. We'll walk through and take a look.'

They arrived in the kitchen to surprise a woman working furiously over an ironing board. She dropped the iron and retreated. Ripple commenced to explain who they were, and why they had come. Her fears seemed to grow.

'Don't let us interfere with your ironing,' said Petrie.

She seemed glad to have something to do, slammed the iron on the gas ring with unnecessary force, and threw the holder on to the table. Petrie's eyes turned involuntarily towards the holder. He continued to stare. It was a curious iron-holder—not a thing bought made up, but an improvisation. As it fell on the table so it unfolded. The cloth was dark, rather like a Cheviot in texture, and it was sewn all round the edges. While the Inspector searched round the kitchen Petrie picked up the holder. It looked as if it had originally been a pocket sewn on to some garment.

'Where did you get this?' he asked the woman.

'Off something the master threw out.'

'Off a coat?'

'No. Just an odd piece of cloth.'

Petrie, to the woman's astonishment; picked up the holder, and took it into the other room. There he slipped his fingers into the slight opening between the surrounding seam. He could feel nothing. Moving nearer to the window, he drew a knife from his pocket and scraped round the seam. For a minute or two he found nothing but dust. Then something attracted his attention, and he tipped the dust from the palm of his hand on to a sheet of white paper, spread it out and pulled the magnifying glass from his pocket.

A broad smile creased his face when he stood erect and called to Ripple:

'Come and take a look at this.'

The Yard man looked for a while before he could discern anything. He straightened with a frown on his forehead.

'I can see a few bits of dust and a shred of silk. That's all.'

'It's quite enough. That shred of silk, my lad, is one of the silken tails from the golden kite. A million pounds to a bean that it's the filament from a strophanthus seed!'

'My God! Of course it is.'

'And this iron-holder, Sunshine, is all that's left of Curtis's overcoat. He tried to be too cautious.'

Things moved rapidly in the first few minutes after that. Ripple ordered the charwoman, housekeeper, cook general, or whatever she was, out of the premises, telling her to return at six o'clock. Amos seized the telephone and rang the Yard. Ripple was astonished to hear the little man's voice ringing through the rooms in a way that amazed him. Amos was growing more red in the face each second.

'Stop him!' he shouted. There was a pause. 'He's gone? No, I'm not saying that it is your fault. But don't let him get into the House of Commons, whatever you do. Try Ferguson's place. On the Chelsea Embankment, yes. Damn the warrant! It'll be my funeral. Charge him with the murder of Edgar Reardon. That's all you need worry about. Yes. We'll stay here in case he comes home to change his clothes. Yes, all his clothes are here. Eh? Certainly, telephone me here at his place.'

Petrie laid down the receiver with a loud sigh and spoke to Ripple savagely:

'The man has had the damned nerve to call on Watson. I must have missed him by minutes when I left Watson.'

'Talk about nerve! That fellow's got a brain like an iceberg.'

'I'll say he has—the impudence of the devil. That's what first started me thinking about him. You can't tell to what extremes a man like that will go.'

'What's all the excitement about him not getting back to the House of Commons?'

Petrie laughed and settled down in a chair.

'If he does manage to arrive there you'll know why I was worrying about it. You might even have something to worry about yourself then. And I mean real worry, not the sort of stuff you manufacture.'

'What do we do now? Twiddle our thumbs?'

'We sit tight here until we either see Curtis or hear from the Yard. Here's your chance to take a sleep for a while.'

'Lordy, I can't sleep now. What made you start thinking about Curtis?'

'Light your pipe and I'll tell you. It'll pass the time away.'

While Ripple filled his pipe Amos turned again to the papers he had taken from the safe, running through them casually to pass the time away. The Yard man was searching for his matches when Amos pursed his lips and whistled softly. In his hand he held a sheet of foolscap paper. Ripple puffed out smoke and bent forward.

'What's all the new excitement? Thought we'd had enough for the time being. Have you found a written confession?'

'No, but I've got something almost as damning. I think a smart cross-examiner could put Curtis in a tough corner with about four questions. I told you about the missing opinion from Quiller, and you know what Curtis told me about it. I'd love to see how he faced these four consecutive questions in the witness box. "Reardon left you at the corner of the corridor and went to his room, taking Quiller's opinion with him?" The answer must be "Yes." "You did not enter the deceased's room before he entered the House of Commons?" Obviously, the reply must be, "No." "And you were never alone with him again?" Curtis must reply, "No." "Then will you tell the jury how Quiller's opinion came to be found in the safe at your private office in the Temple?" I'll leave Curtis to work out the answer to that one himself. He'll need all his ingenuity, Sunshine. There can be no argument at all about it.

'This is the opinion given by Quiller, the one that was missing. Curtis must have been given it by Edgar Reardon. Incidentally, Quiller thinks the French marriage was illegal, void in law. But that is neither here nor there. We'll come back to Curtis, and I'll tell you what I thought about the case.'

CHAPTER XXV

AMOS EXPLAINS

'BEFORE you start,' said Ripple, 'I'll be honest with you and say this: I thought it was a neck-and-neck race between Paling, Watson and Ferguson. I even had doubts about the widow.'

'Let's start with the Watson burglary,' commenced Petrie. 'It was obvious from the start that the murderer arranged that. The motive was only too obvious. The intention was to throw suspicion on Watson. I studied him carefully, wondered whether he had enough cold nerve and sufficient brain to stage the fake himself, and so throw a red herring across the trail. I was certain he had neither. From that point I didn't take much interest in Watson as a possible murderer. In any case, he wasn't the type at all—too nervy.

'But we did know that if the burglar came from the outside he must be a man of some address, and familiar with the place. You told me that some unidentified drunk who called at the place upset your inquiries. I rather imagine that was our cunning friend, Curtis. He found his way up the back staircase, walked from the back of the flat to the front, passing the bedrooms, in order to place the glass of seeds in the sitting-room. It was the murderer's most clumsy move. One knew instantly that if Watson murdered Reardon he would not leave strophanthus seeds in full view of everyone's sight.

'I think he did it for two reasons. He wanted to throw suspicion on Watson, and he wanted to play on Watson's nerves. He knew that his victim might crack, talk rubbish, and land himself into a hole. That would act as a smokescreen for the murderer. Watson didn't help me much. I thought then, and think now, that the man is a complete boob. At that time I didn't know much about the murderer. But the means by which he committed the crime later told me a lot. There was a deftness about the substitution of that fraudulent section of the Budget speech, a horrible thoroughness in the way in which he gave his victim something to think about while he was being poisoned. The material in the faked portion of the speech, and the way in which it was arranged, showed intimate knowledge. Obviously the murderer was either connected with the Government, or he was in Reardon's confidence. By the substitution of that fraudulent part of the speech he showed that he was a man capable of swift and decisive action.

'We'd have been in a poor way if he hadn't given us some of these indications of character. You never know, we might have hanged the wrong man. If you follow it carefully, though, you'll find the same tricks of the mind in everything the man did. You most definitely find them in the interview in which he tried to lead me up the garden path. With one exception he never altered the facts. He simply twisted their meaning. Even the exception, when he moved from the facts, I can only prove by inference. He denied entering Reardon's room. Quiller's opinion and the other surrounding facts are all we have to pin on him.

'Curtis was a trifle too cautious. He meant to impress me with his story about the steak. Instead he insisted on it so firmly that I became suspicious, and formed the view that he was making a deliberate attempt to lead me to an alibi that he had already prepared for me. I refused to bite. But that story of the lunch might make trouble for us at the Old Bailey.'

'Good God! You don't think he might get off?'

'I hope not. Still, he'll always have a bare chance. His defence will be that he wasn't in the room, and couldn't have committed the murder. We can use Quiller's opinion as a weapon against that argument, and a few additional oddments. We can prove that he was in possession of the poison at the material time, because I'm positive we can prove that he burgled Watson's flat. We can ask him why he wanted to plant those seeds on Watson at all, how this filament came to be in his overcoat pocket, why he destroyed the overcoat, how he came to have a Belgian hundred-franc note in his possession, and we can get the taxi driver to relate the events of that night. And, of course, as I'll show you in a minute, we'll prove that he had a most definite motive for the murder.

'Before we come back to the framework of the crime, let's take a look at the others. I went to Brockenhurst to eliminate a few of them. I played a trick on Lola Reardon to test her nerve. She crumpled up. She showed she had no more nerve than Watson. People with their mental make-up can't commit murders of this type. Either might have committed suicide, but murder—never!

'Ferguson was much more likely. I'll tell you why. When I told him that he was a suspect he calmly bought me drinks and told me that my job was to get him out of the scrape. I imagined a man like that might well have murdered Reardon. But the time of that burglary at Watson's flat was emphatically in his favour, and he wouldn't offer a poisoned speech to Mrs Reardon even as a joke. Added to that, I couldn't quite see what he was going to gain by it.

'So now we come to Paling. Let us start at the wrong end by taking Milford first. Every word he spoke about the events there was the truth. His other statements were corroborated in all sorts of ways. For instance, I knew before he told me that Reardon had paid him money this year. It was Curtis who twisted the reason for the payments. Reardon undoubtedly tried to murder him at Milford. And a damned clumsy effort it was. Paling got the arsenic back from him, and they decided that it would be best to disarm suspicion in the hotel. That's why they faked the stuff about the wine on the following evening—to show the landlady that they had made a mistake on both occasions. They knew nothing about her chemist customer. In any event—and this is vital—Paling had every reason for wishing

Reardon to live. It doesn't matter which way you look at it, that reply can't be avoided. If he were blackmailing him, he wouldn't murder the goose that laid the golden eggs. And now we know the truth, the reason for Paling not doing it is even more overpowering.

'I don't know now whether he would be committing forgery if he grabs the Hermanos money. That involves a pretty point of law. But I'm sure that at Milford, Reardon told him it would be forgery. And there was something else about his story that impressed me. He was so full of it that he thought it only had to be told to be believed.'

'Then why didn't he tell you all about it at the outset?'

'Because he thought we might not find out about the Hermanos account, and that would have left him with a clear field, since he imagined that the existence of the account was known only to the dead man and himself. He knew that he was innocent of the murder, and never thought for a second that he would be arrested. By talking, by speaking the truth, he had nothing to gain and everything to lose. By Saturday his position had changed. He had spent some time in the cells, and was beginning to be frightened of a murder charge. Then he discovered that I had learnt of the Hermanos account, and after that he had nothing to hide. I am sure that as yet he hasn't touched a penny of the Hermanos money.

'Then we began to hear things about Mr Price and Mr Hepworth. If one fact was clearer than any other it was that Paling was not all three. So I looked into the technique of Messrs. Price and Hepworth. It was instructive. Like the murderer, they both worked by creating simple impressions on the mind. When we go round with the photos I don't suppose we'll have the slightest difficulty in getting them identified.

'So, in many different ways, I was driven back to consider the case of Dick Curtis. On Saturday I asked you how Price or Hepworth could exercise their gifts for self-effacement in the House of Commons. Curtis could, being an M.P. The position of Price and Hepworth is vital on the question of motive. I take it that Curtis brought that Belgian note back after making a visit to Brussels as Hepworth. The typewriter here adds to that proof. Just turn this over in your mind—I never had the slightest doubt about the advantage it would be to Price and Hepworth if either, or he, happened to be one of the two executors to the murdered man's estate.

'You see, the executors had decided to cover up Reardon's pre-Budget gambles. Ferguson knew practically nothing about them. He only knew enough to warn the Prime Minister that Reardon had been speculating. The executors wanted to cut the whole thing adrift by turning the estate into cash. What a chance for Curtis—who knew the whole inside workings—to step in and help himself! Ferguson could never tell me what I wanted to know. Therefore I knew that Curtis was the active spirit in the business. All he had to do was cook the accounts for both Price and Hepworth, and also abstract suitable rewards.

'Now what did I know about Price or Hepworth? Several things. The pecuniary relations between the two would undoubtedly help if Price were prepared to act the part of fraudulent executor. I don't know that Reardon ever heard of Hepworth. I do know that he trusted Price with thirty thousand pounds. Price was transparently the trusted friend, or agent. Don't worry for the moment about how he got his instructions, or where they met. We'll come to that. Just consider what I knew about the appearance of the man.

'Price had, or pretended to have, gout. Therefore he is a man approaching fifty, or one who could be mistaken for that age. But he was not peevish or obviously in pain. He has to talk about the gout to create the impression he wants. The bank manager thinks of him as prosperous, and from the country. A florid complexion is suggested. His manner might have been sardonic, whimsical, or hearty. It would be unsafe to speculate. But there are all sorts of indications, negative indications, about his height and girth. He is not described as tall, short, fat, or thin. "A fine figure of a man, and a perfect gentleman," and "not much to look at, but a perfect gentleman," are phrases we hear. He was prosperous, and in a prosperous man of that age we may expect a well-covered frame, with some thickening at the waist, and some thinning of the hair—'

'You're describing Dick Curtis,' interrupted Ripple.

'Right. So we can turn away from that and look at something else. When Curtis told me that he advised Reardon about his matrimonial affairs he made the point insistently that there was a need for discretion in arranging the interviews. It was a bad move on his part. I thought of it instantly when Ferguson told me about that screen. Can you doubt that when finance, wholesale trickery, abuse of office is added to law as a subject for discussion the need for discretion becomes intensified? Once I got on to that line I found it very fruitful.

'All through this business Curtis has made one bad mistake. He's given us too many cross-checks on him. He's had his fingers in too many pies. He's been too promiscuous in spattering other people with suspicion. In spite of his horrible ingenuity and his uncanny gift for making other people think and do as he wants, there was something lacking in his mind—and that's balance. I expect he thought he'd better give us something to think about while he decided exactly what he would do with the money. That's precisely what he waited for in the case of Reardon. He wanted the man to have something to think about while he substituted his poisoned section in that speech. And that is what happened.'

'When that Treasury messenger left Reardon's room?'

'I thought you might guess it. That's my view, too. Reardon and Curtis had been in that room talking—probably about the opinion received from Quiller. It was time for Curtis to leave. When that messenger arrived Curtis knew precisely what Reardon would do. It wasn't done for the first time by many a score. Of that I'm positive. He knew that Reardon would have to see that the coast was clear before Curtis left the room. And, of course, Reardon had only one object in taking that messenger to the door. He wanted to see whether the corridor was empty, whether Curtis could leave as quietly as he had come. Curtis had been behind the screen, waiting, tensed, ready to move, for that space of seconds when Reardon was on the other side of the door. The speech, we know, was on the table. Curtis had the poisoned section in his hand. He knew exactly where to place it. To remove the original sheets—all clipped together—and slip in the fatal chapter would not take more than three or four seconds. By the time Reardon returned to tell Curtis that the coast was clear, that it was safe for him to leave, everything had been arranged, and the original section was in Curtis's pocket.

'That was typical of the coolness with which Curtis worked all the way through. Let me tell you one small thing to show you how coldly calculating the swine was. In the House of Commons he caused a burst of merriment by sitting on Tranter's hat. Why did he do that? So that if any finger of suspicion came his way he could point to the episode and ask whether that was the act of a man who was waiting to see his victim die! Curtis had an abnormal brain.'

'They ought to do things to that devil before they swing him.'

'Don't get venomous about it, little one.'

'He turns my stomach sour.'

'He certainly gave us a good run. Just to wind up, Sunshine, I'll tell you how I see the whole thing in broad outline. Reardon was not being, and never had been, blackmailed. He was naturally avaricious, and had no scruples, no public or political conscience. He knew that he would not last for ever as Chancellor of the Exchequer, so he decided to make hay while the sun shone. If he speculated on his exclusive knowledge of the Budget he would be betting on a certainty. The only difficulty was to secure the services of intermediaries he could trust. He dare not take chances. He had known Paling in Paris, and when he proposed the scheme to him he gained a supporter with money.

'When the plan got under way—using the name of Hermanos—he tied Paling up in such a way that the man dare not squeal, dare not take any action. Every penny he had invested was at stake. Reardon did not have to trust him. He had fastened the man hand and foot. But Edgar Reardon was both avaricious and cautious. He wanted to gamble on a large scale, but he didn't want to trust one man too far. He thought his commitments with Paling were heavy enough, and he looked round for another ally. He found one in Dick Curtis.

'Curtis assumed the name of Price, and Reardon paid £30,000 into that account. He trusted Curtis much more than he did Paling. Curtis was a personal friend, his executor, and a Member of Parliament. So he also had much to lose if the plot happened to be discovered. He didn't know that Curtis was a bigger twister, a more thorough-paced rogue than he was himself. You can see what happened. Curtis took one long look at the money banked, and later invested, in the name of Price, and decided that there wasn't going to be a lion's share for Reardon and a morsel for himself. So he settled down to consider ways and means. He apparently knew about the Hermanos account; he knew that feeling was running high between Reardon and Paling. At last he made his plans, and transferred money from the Price account to the Hepworth account. I don't suppose for a second that Reardon knew anything about that.

'The moment he had waited for arrived. While Reardon was thinking of murdering Paling, and Paling was wondering how he could twist Reardon, our friend Curtis stepped in between them and murdered Reardon. After that, satisfied that as executor he could collect the whole of the Hepworth money and a portion of the Price money, he played the part of a grieved friend of the deceased's, and waited to see what would happen. The only person who might have known enough to make things awkward for him was Paling. And that, my dear Ripple, is why I wouldn't risk Paling's life by releasing him until Curtis has been arrested.

'It only remains to add one thing about Reardon's attempt at murdering Paling. Since Paling had bought the arsenic, Reardon would have sworn that the man committed suicide before he could stop him.'

A heavy step sounded on the staircase and halted on the landing. There was a double knock on the door. It was a queer knock—not peremptory, like a policeman's, not timid like a poor relative's. In some indefinable way it suggested that the knocker was not thinking of what he did.

The Yard man looked towards Amos. The little man nodded his head and rose to his feet. Ripple straightened his shoulders and moved swiftly to the door.

CHAPTER XXVI

THE END OF IT ALL

OUTSIDE stood Sir John Ferguson. He raised a finger nervously and bit his nail when he saw Ripple standing in the room. Both seemed too astonished to speak. The Yard man, torn between disappointment and excitement, lost his head and promptly forgot that he was barking at the President of the Board of Trade:

'You! What the hell are you doing here?'

Ferguson moved his feet restlessly, too amazed to be annoyed.

'About the same as yourself,' he said. 'Any reason why I shouldn't be here? You might know, since I arrived, that I've called to see Curtis. It seems to me that everybody connected with this case is going mad. What other reason could I have for coming here?'

'That's no answer to my question, and you know it.'

Ferguson elevated his hands and blew violently.

'Don't talk to me like that,' he snapped when he had recovered his breath. 'I'm really here on your business. I wanted to know what Curtis was doing about Price.'

'Don't let the doorman frighten you,' shouted Petrie. 'He's really very harmless when you get to know him. I think he's only peeved to find that you're not Curtis. Still, I don't think you wanted to meet him quite as urgently as we do. Believe me, we really are going to give him a reception. If I hadn't known that he wouldn't knock for admission to his own room I'd have come to the door myself to extend a welcome. Please come in. By staying outside you might spoil things for us all—and that would be just too bad. Come away in.'

The President of the Board of Trade was beyond surprise, and he ambled into the room like a man sleep-walking. But his astonishment returned when he saw the disarray caused by the search, and his brows rose upwards as though to meet his scanty hair. For a second he gazed at the oddments collected on the dining-room table.

'Has this place been looted?' he asked. 'Or is Curtis removing?'

Petrie wiped his hands on his handkerchief and smiled towards Ripple. There was an awkward silence.

'You heard me,' said Ferguson.

'I did,' replied Amos. 'Mr Curtis is certainly removing, absolutely and definitely removing.'

'Where on earth is he going to?'

'To the condemned cell in due course.'

Ferguson was utterly routed. His lips flickered like those of a landed fish, and he slumped into a chair. Then he gaped towards Petrie.

'That is quite serious, and since you are here—'

Amos stopped talking suddenly. The telephone bell rang. Ripple waved his hand towards it, and Petrie moved the receiver. The call came from Scotland Yard. Petrie listened for a few seconds only, swore, and slammed down the receiver viciously. It was Ripple's turn to register astonishment. Only a couple of times before had he seen Amos annoyed.

'So that wasn't Curtis on the line?' he asked.

'Was it hell as like!'

'Then why all the fluster and temper?'

'I wish to heaven I'd never dabbled with this case. Everything is arranged perfectly, nothing could be better—and now all I've done, all the scheming I've arranged, has gone up in air.'

'How? Why? What? When? Where?' Ripple drew a finger round his collar.

'I've just been saying that he was going to the condemned cell. I had made the arrangement. At this moment our little friend Curtis is ensconced in his seat in the House of Commons! The devil alone knows why he was allowed to get back there, but whoever is to blame ought to be taken into Whitehall and publicly pole-axed.'

Ripple adopted an expression intended to portray grief. He looked as though a faint was imminent. He placed an elbow on the mantelpiece.

'Give me that warrant,' snapped Amos, 'and we'll go.'

'Just a moment,' interrupted Ferguson. 'Surely you daren't try to execute that warrant in the House of Commons? Why, such a thing has not been done since Lord Cochrane!'

'Or Bellingham,' said Amos primly.

'No, no,' remarked Ferguson. 'Bellingham's case bears absolutely no resemblance to this, except that it was one of murder. I know something about these things. Bellingham was seized by the servants of the House, and committed for trial by one of its committees.'

Petrie nodded his head and smiled.

'I know that. If all else fails I must ask you to persuade the House to follow the Bellingham precedent. Let's hope that matters can be arranged differently.'

Ferguson was alarmed by the prospect.

'Please, please, Mr Petrie,' he said, 'do let me remind you that there is another way in which your end can be achieved. I believe there was an occasion when the police wanted a member, and they waited until the House had risen. Then they took care to see that a detective was driving the taxicab. Couldn't something be done in that way? You may be sure that the House would be grateful to you if you can avoid any interference with its liberties. And you would still be able to execute the warrant.'

Petrie took off his thick-lensed glasses and wiped them. He shook his head with emphasis.

'I had thought of that. I don't usually act impetuously. But the difficulty about your plan is twofold. Firstly, Curtis never takes a taxi when the House rises. He always walks. Secondly, the House, I am informed, will sit through the night.'

'Lord!' exclaimed Ferguson. 'I'd forgotten that they're on Budget resolutions. That's funny.'

Petrie laughed softly. The coincidence was appealing to his sense of humour.

'This Budget will certainly take its place in history,' he said. 'I want you to come along to the House with me. We're in an awkward fix, but there might be some exit from it.'

The taxi was travelling along the Embankment when Amos spoke:

'I'm going to the Yard first. I want Watson to write a note to Curtis begging him to go round and see him. That might do it.'

There were difficulties in the way. In the first place Lola Reardon fainted with such effect that it seemed she had passed away for ever. In the second place, Watson proved sulky. Both were removed to a private office, and the transfer produced a better spirit. At the end of twenty minutes Watson unwillingly consented to pen the note. The persuasive power at his elbow was Lola.

Ripple was delegated to take the note to the House, and while he was away Petrie explained to Lola and Watson exactly how they had become involved in suspicion, and why they had been treated somewhat callously. Then Petrie left them in order to make the necessary arrangements for meeting Curtis in Westminster Palace Yard.

'Look here,' said Ferguson, somewhat timidly, 'I don't want to meet Curtis after all that has happened.'

'Nor do we,' announced Watson.

Petrie had just returned to the room. He grinned.

'All right,' he said. 'I hope that my enthusiasm will atone for you.'

The telephone bell jangled. Petrie spoke for a moment. When he replaced the receiver he was no longer smiling.

'Don't worry about meeting him yet,' he said. 'Instead of walking out into the arms of the police, he smelt a rat, took alarm and doubled back into the House of Commons.'

The news had the effect of dispersing those in the office. But they were immediately called back by Petrie. He took Ferguson by the arm.

'Isn't it time we talked to the Cabinet about Bellingham's case?'

'Come on, then,' said Ferguson. For a moment he had feared that something more drastic was being planned by the little man. Ferguson had no idea what would happen.

There was only one man in London who might have guessed. And he was in his seat in the House of Commons, like a badger in his earth, unable to move because of watchful terriers, but hearing the sound of spades as hunters dug down to him. Apart from Curtis there were only a dozen members in the House, waiting for an opportunity to air their views in the dull hour that follows dinner.

The Chairman of Committees occupied his seat at the Clerk's table.

Quite suddenly—too suddenly for the weary nerves of bored members, the swing doors were flung back with a crash. Excited voices were heard in the lobby outside. Members swarmed into the room like sheep trooping through a gate before a barking dog.

'Order, order!' called members awaiting their chance to speak.

'I must ask members to enter more quietly,' roared the Chairman.

One of the newcomers shrieked with piercing loudness:

'It's the police!'

'There are no police in this House,' shouted the Chairman.

'There soon will be,' bellowed another arrival. He was right. As the last straggler rushed through the swing doors the blue coats of following constabulary could be seen through the glass. Then helmet-shaded eyes searched the chamber.

'I can see more in the lobby behind the Speaker's chair,' called Tranter. He waved his hand in that direction.

Their eyes had barely had time to follow the line of his gesture when another member raised his voice in a stentorian bellow:

'They're in the Noe Lobby as well.'

The House was blockaded!

The Chairman issued a message ordering the police to

remove immediately. The command was ignored. Members were huddled in groups.

'Lock all the doors,' shouted the Chairman.

Disturbed while in conference, Mr Speaker rushed back into the House at the urgent, almost hysterical summons of his deputy. He was followed by Joe Manning and all the leaders of the Opposition and the Treasury Bench in a body.

Amos Petrie slipped into the Civil Servants' pew under the gallery. As he did so Dick Curtis nodded grimly to him. The man had not before given the slightest sign that he was aware of his surroundings, that he was troubled by fears, or that the tumult had any interest for him.

Willie Ingram, the Prime Minister, stepped to the table. It seemed to surprise members that Ingram should want to speak instead of listening. Most of them had lost mental balance. Still, even under those circumstances Ingram's manner defeated them. The Prime Minister stood for some moments with his face twitching and his lips trembling. But no words arrived.

The silence was palpable.

At last he told them. There was a warrant out for murder. The police had entered the chamber to execute it. He expressed a pathetic certainty that the person named in the warrant would be the first to want to answer that charge—in the proper place. For the guidance of that person, and for no other reason, he would give the name:

'Richard Curtis!'

As the name was pronounced, as a sighing gasp soared through the chamber, Curtis half rose and bowed towards the Premier.

'Unlock the doors!' called Mr Speaker.

They were swung back. But though the way was open, Curtis made no attempt to move. He smiled serenely in the direction of Amos Petrie and dabbed a pinch of snuff to his nose. All eyes were concentrated on him, everyone waiting for the expected move.

It became obvious that he did not mean to leave the chamber.

Instead, he settled down more firmly in his seat. Those nearest to him commenced to move restlessly. Many of them edged away until they huddled together on other benches, or crowded the gangways.

A policeman's head appeared once more at the glass of the door leading into the lobby.

Joe Manning abruptly drew attention to himself.

'If the member in question has not the decency to withdraw, I move that he be expelled.'

The Speaker moved uneasily in his chair. A dozen members shouted their support. Still Curtis made no move.

The Speaker rose with stiff dignity, gathering his robes round him.

'As the House is about to discuss this motion,' he said, turning to face Curtis, 'I must ask the honourable member to say what he has to say in self-justification, and then to withdraw in accordance with the rules.'

The man he addressed made no attempt to speak. He sat with one shoulder turned away from the Speaker, his chin on his shoulder, as though ashamed but immovable.

Patience was exhausted. The Speaker ordered his removal. Rising from his pew, the Sergeant-at-Arms rose briskly to obey the order. At the Bar he bowed before entering upon the ground reserved for Members. With one hand on the hilt of his dress sword, he strode up the floor of the House. Twice more he halted to bow. Another few steps, and members saw a shirt cuff shoot out as the black-coated arm outstretched to touch the obstinate shoulders; the little dress sword jutted out behind black tail coats as the Sergeant bent to whisper in the too deaf ear. The Sergeant-at-Arms drew back his hand as though stung. He looked into the averted face and recoiled.

The man he bent over had gone to join Edgar Reardon! In his hand he held a snuff-box. It contained strophanthin!

THE END